The Three Towers of Afranor

A Novel

Scott R. Larson

www.ScottLarsonBooks.com

To

Miss Kiefer
for indulging me when assigning
a story to write in her high school Spanish class

J.R.R. Tolkien, Stan Lee, and Dan Curtis
for firing my youthful imagination

and

Maggie
for providing the opportunity to retell my story
night after night during countless bedtimes

This book would not read nearly so well absent
the time and thought generously put into it by my
great friend Dayle Moss. Not only did she hold me
to a higher standard than to which I held myself
but, to my embarrassment, she frequently
approached the story more seriously than I.
Likewise invaluable were the insights,
suggestions, fixes—not to mention
much-needed validation—provided by
my *viejo amigo* and ageless fellow
fantasy fanboy Michael Morrow.

Contents

1
Afranor

THE MOUNTAINTOP was surrounded by clouds, like a tall island amidst a sea of swirling mist. The three men on horseback emerged from the fog and looked up at the sunlight.

The tallest and eldest of the trio had curly black hair. His name was Adryan. He closed his eyes and, in spite of the icy breeze, enjoyed what little warmth the light brought to his face.

"It is good to see the sun again," he said.

The other two nodded in sincere but unenthusiastic agreement. One had brown hair, a shaggy beard and an ugly scar on his left cheek. He looked at the road ahead of them that wound down back into the mist.

"The fog is even thicker in front of us than it is behind," he said. "I still insist that returning home by land was a bad idea. And I fear that I will soon be proved right."

Adryan replied, "Your complaining will bring us no luck, Benet. I do not like this journey any more than you do, but there was no other choice."

"Well," said Benet, weighing his words carefully, "if you had not quarreled with your woman, we would be returning to our home the same way we left it—by sea. No one from our country has crossed through Afranor in generations. Have you ever heard of anyone going there and returning? Has our father ever spoken of anybody ever doing so? We should have avoided Afranor at all costs."

Adryan had little patience for this talk.

"I did not quarrel with Valloniah. She quarreled with me. And, in any event, our quarrel was no reason to put me—us—off her ship. Did we not fight faithfully at her side against the southern corsairs? And this is how she repays me!"

"Well, clearly," said Benet, "she did not become known as the Pirate Queen because of her sweet temper."

The slender youth with the dirty blond hair, following behind, finally spoke. His face was scruffy with a miserably failed attempt at a beard, but

1

his most notable feature was that one of his eyes was brown and the other was blue.

"Is it too late to avoid going through Afranor?"

"Going around this country would have added weeks to our journey," said Adryan, losing his patience. "To turn back now and go around would add more than a month."

"Better to lose a month," said the youth quietly, his voice trailing off, "than to lose our lives."

As soon as he said it, the callow lad hoped that his brothers had not heard him, but they had.

"Do not forget who you are, Chrysteffor," said Adryan sternly. "You are the son of a king, the same as Benet and myself. I know that you are young still and that this life of traveling dangerous roads does not exactly suit you. At least not yet. But your words could be taken as cowardice, and they do not reflect on you alone. Everything you say and do reflects on our entire family. Even things you say among only the three of us."

Chrysteffor bit his lip and said nothing. His face was burning.

Benet added, "Never forget. We are known far beyond the borders of our own country. Even in places where we have never journeyed, people speak in awe of the fighting princes of Alinvayl."

"We have no choice," said Adryan. "We must keep going. The faster we travel down this road, the sooner we will be home. Let us go."

Adryan continued along the road, down the other side of the mountain. As Benet and Chrysteffor watched him and his horse disappear into the dark mists, they shuddered involuntarily. Neither looked forward to leaving the sunlight and returning to the cold clamminess of the vapors swirling below. Reluctantly, they commanded their horses to follow.

The fog had been thick enough coming up the mountain, but it was much denser and darker as they descended on the northern side. They knew the sun was shining not far above them, but the air around them had so quickly become thick and black, they could easily have believed that it was now the middle of a moonless night. The suffocating quiet, broken only by the clopping of the horses' hoofs, was eerie and more than a little unnerving.

As they rode, Adryan felt as though he should be talking to the others, keeping up their spirits, but he could not think of anything worth saying. Besides, the quiet felt as though it did not want to be disturbed. And the younger two certainly were not contributing any chat either.

The three of them rode the stony path down the mountain in silence. As they came to the bottom of the mountain, the trees grew thick around them, making the air seem darker than it had been before.

Benet broke the silence.

"I do not mind saying that I do not like this one single bit. It is not natural. We know that it is daytime, and yet it is as dark as the middle of the night. I have never seen anything like this in my entire life. I can barely see the hand in front of my face."

"It is, I admit, strange," said Adryan. "I too have never seen anything like this, but it can only be a matter of time until the fog lifts and things around us become clearer."

"How do we know we are following the right road," asked Chrysteffor, "if we cannot see anything? How do we know we are really heading in the direction of home and not becoming lost?"

"There is no chance of getting lost," replied Adryan testily. "We have only to make for the sea and then follow the coast. As long as we ride with the sea to our left, we cannot end up anywhere but home. And your nervous questions will not get us there any faster."

The lad bit his lip again and fell silent. Benet pulled up alongside his older brother. As they continued to ride, he spoke to him quietly, hoping that the lad would not hear.

"You are very hard on him, Adryan. I think you forget how young he is still."

"I know well his age, but we will do him no favors by protecting him. You know as well as I how harsh and unforgiving the world is."

"I agree, but I also see that he is not the same as you and I. He does not have a warrior's temperament. He was not born to fight. Our father has two warrior sons. Does he really need to have a third?"

"To be honest, I have begun to think the same thing myself lately. Though I hate to say it, it is only a matter of time until the boy is injured or killed in one of our exploits. I do not want that on my conscience. When we arrive home, I will propose to our father that Chrys be given new duties in the castle and that he need no longer accompany us on our forays."

"Yes, I think that is for the best," said Benet.

"In the end," said Adryan, "I suppose we do not all have to be the same. We do not all have to be cut from the same cloth. There is room in this world for the likes of him. After all, he will never have to worry about one day bearing the burden of the crown, as I will. Why not let him live his life as he pleases?"

The pair fell silent. Benet was pleased to hear that Adryan had at last softened his views regarding their youngest brother, and he knew that Chrysteffor would be pleased as well. As for Chrysteffor, while he had not been able to make out their words, he had his own idea of what they were discussing. He expected he would be getting another unwelcome speech from Adryan. He hated the fact that he never measured up to his brothers' expectations.

The three continued their progress, as they trusted the horses to follow the road. Each of the brothers found himself repeatedly sniffing the air, hoping to detect the salty smell of the sea that would assure them they were indeed headed in the right direction. In the end, all they could smell was a faint odor reminiscent of sulfur hanging heavy in the dampness of the fog.

Adryan suddenly stopped his horse. The other two did the same, and they all listened quietly.

"What was that?" asked Adryan softly.

The three brothers remained motionless as they continued to listen. Benet and Chrysteffor wondered what Adryan had heard, but then they all heard it. At first it was distant and hard to make out, but gradually it became louder. It was the noise of heavy footsteps in the forest. It seemed to be a large group of men—big and heavy men from the sound of them. And they were getting closer all the time. The three princes stayed still as statues, waiting to see what would happen next.

Then they saw them.

They could just make out the shapes emerging from the shadowy mists. Maybe it was a trick their eyes were playing on them, but these did not look like any men they had ever seen before. Their clothes were in tatters. They wore armor, but none of them appeared to have a full suit—only odd, rusty pieces that did not completely cover their bodies.

What mainly drew the three men's attention—and struck fear in their hearts—were the faces. The creatures' skin barely clung to their skulls, and there were black holes where their eyes should have been. Were there truly no eyes in their sockets or was it an illusion conjured by the darkness? The princes had little time to wonder. The creatures were making straight for them with wooden clubs raised. There was no question but that this was an attack.

Adryan raised his sword and shouted, "Defend yourselves, princes of Alinvayl!"

Chrysteffor too raised his sword, although not as enthusiastically as Adryan. Benet's preferred weapon was a heavy spiky metal mace. He began swinging it around by its chain and knocking it against the heads of several of the creatures. When it hit them, it threw them off balance, but they invariably got back to their feet and continued the attack.

The other two brothers were having no better luck. Adryan thrust his blade into the chests of several of them, but that only slowed them down.

It did not stop them. And each time Adryan withdrew his blade, he was unnerved to see that, for all the soggy bits of flesh that clung to it, there was no blood. The worst thing was the smell of the creatures. They stank of rotting meat. It was all the princes could do not to be made sick by the stench.

"By all that is holy," muttered Adryan under his breath, "what manner of creatures are these?"

The horses carrying the three princes reared up in absolute panic. In the animals' sheer terror, they tried frantically to throw off their riders. It did not help that the creatures were battering the steeds with their clubs. The brothers clung to the backs of their mounts as long as they could, but it was only a matter of time before each, in turn, was thrown to the ground. The horses fled into the darkness, leaving in their wake only the echoes of their terrified screaming.

The trio rose quickly to their feet and continued the fight as best they could, but they were completely surrounded and their opponents' numbers seemed endless. Adryan threw himself into the fight with new vigor, swinging his sword ever more fiercely. Benet gamely followed suit with his mace.

To no one's surprise, Chrysteffor was faring less well than his brothers. He frantically struck at one creature and then another, but his efforts were not even slowing them down, let alone stopping them. He desperately wished he had put more effort into convincing his brothers to take the longer way home.

Adryan was determined not to give in to despair. Even if he could not kill these enemies, he could keep them off balance and at bay. The problem was that there were so many of them. They were everywhere. In a fit of anger, he swung his blade as forcefully as he could against the neck of one of them. He watched with satisfaction as he managed to sever its head from its body and the head rolled along the ground. He half-feared that the headless body would continue fighting anyway, but to his relief it crumpled to the ground and lay still.

"The only way to stop them," he yelled to the others, "is to cut off their heads! Nothing else seems to kill them!"

The problem, as Adryan was all too aware, was that a well-aimed and forceful motion was required to sever a head. With so many creatures swarming around him all at once, it was difficult to get a clear shot at any of them. Benet was having better luck with his mace. Yelling at the top of his lungs as he swung it around in a circle, he managed to strike several of the warriors directly in the skull and send their heads flying.

Chrysteffor, meanwhile, was having no luck and getting no good swipes at the necks of his adversaries. When all else failed, he resorted to stabbing them in the chest but, as Adryan had found, that barely slowed them down.

Benet tried to watch his younger brother out of the corner of his eye, but unfortunately all of his attention was required for his own defense and for his own attempts to behead as many of the creatures as possible. He worried for Chrysteffor. While the lad had been in a fair number of battles for someone of his young age, he had never encountered anything like this. None of them had.

It was only a matter of time until Benet's worst fear was realized. As Chrysteffor was swinging his blade as furiously as he could, one of the creatures rose up from behind him and delivered a solid blow to the back of his head with a rough wooden club. The young prince collapsed immediately in a heap on the ground. A small pool of blood formed on the ground beneath his head. Benet had little doubt that the blow was fatal, and he was ruefully grateful that the boy's death had been so swift.

There was no time to dwell on Chrysteffor. There would be time for mourning and regrets later. That is, if he and Adryan survived the battle. And that was by no means certain. The two remaining princes continued the battle with all the strength they could muster. The pair were persistent fighters and, by this point in their lives, were well tested in the heat of combat, but the sheer numbers were against them. They both knew it was only a matter of time until the hordes wore them down. Still the brothers refused to give up.

In the midst of the grunts and the roars and the sounds of clubs and swords and the mace striking flesh, the princes heard another sound. It was the unmistakable sound of a horse's hoofs, and it was steadily growing louder. The brothers' hearts sank at the thought of yet another enemy coming to join the fight against them, especially one on horseback.

It seemed no time at all until the rider appeared through the darkness. He did not look like the creatures they were fighting. He was wearing proper armor and, though it was difficult to tell, he seemed to be a normal man and not one of the unearthly creatures. He was not particularly large, but he brandished a gleaming sword over his head with clear skill and determination. And, to Adryan's and Benet's relief, this newcomer was using his weapon not against them but to lop off heads of the creatures.

They now had a much needed ally, and a formidable one at that. They marveled at his horse and how it had not been made mad with terror by the creatures, as their mounts had been. The horse gave the rider a major advantage in that he could attack the creatures from above while it was difficult for them to land a serious blow on him. Adryan and Benet continued fighting while watching in awe as the rider decapitated his opponents with frightening efficiency. That inspired them to fight all the harder.

After what seemed like an hour or perhaps two, corpses of the creatures were piled on the ground. The ones that were still alive grudgingly melted back into the darkness. They seemed to know instinctively that their numbers were not sufficient to prevail against their three opponents.

Adryan and Benet sighed with relief and exhaustion. They were anxious to speak with the mysterious warrior who had saved their lives and to learn what they could about the creatures they had been fighting so frantically. Adryan turned to address him and to thank him but, as he did, Benet sensed something moving behind them. At the same time, the rider indicated alarm. Benet swung around to see one of the creatures, who had been lying on the ground, raise himself up and lift his large wooden club.

With horror, Benet watched as the creature swung the club around with all his might and struck Adryan on the back of the head with such force that his head separated from his body. Benet's scream echoed through the forest's darkness but then was stifled by the fog. Without a moment's hesitation, he whirled himself in a circle to work up maximum momentum for a strike with his mace. He struck the creature's head squarely and saw it fly into the darkness for what seemed like an entire league.

Benet dropped to his knees and screamed again, this time toward the heavens. He looked on his brother's headless corpse with disbelief. For the moment he was frozen with grief and rage. He screamed one more time. He detected movement nearby. He still was not rid of the infernal beings. Three of them, smaller than most of the others, came scampering over a pile of corpses. They did not seem interested in Benet or the rider on horseback. One grabbed Adryan's head off the ground, while the other two dragged his body away.

More enraged than before, Benet jumped to his feet and swung his mace as he chased after them. They were surprisingly agile and much faster than the ones which had been fighting. He quickly lost track of them in the darkness. Seeing his brother killed in such a brutal fashion was terrible enough. Not being able to give him the proper burial he deserved tortured his soul even more. His voice released one more cry, this one more full of sorrow than rage. His heart was completely broken.

Suddenly, he remembered Chrysteffor, and he wondered if they had dragged his body away as well. He began searching frantically among the corpses to see if he could locate the remains of his other brother, but the search was not easy. These creatures, as impossible as it may have seemed, stank more dead than they did alive. The smell made him sick to his stomach, but he kept up his frantic search, hoping he could give at least one of his brothers a proper burial.

"This one is still alive."

The voice was so unexpected and so unlikely in that terrible place that he thought he had imagined it. It was strange and foreign to him, but at the same time it was an extremely pleasing voice. He marveled at its beauty, but the words it spoke alerted him to expect more danger. He looked in its direction and saw the mysterious rider, who had dismounted and was kneeling by a body on the ground. Benet clutched his mace in case there was one more creature to fight.

He approached cautiously. As he drew closer, he saw that the rider—with the helmet now removed—was attending Chrysteffor. Benet was less amazed at the possibility that his younger brother might somehow have survived the terrible blow he had received than at the realization that the valiant rider who had come to their aid and who had slaughtered so many of the fierce creatures was a young woman.

"Ye gods!" he exclaimed. "I have never seen anyone fight as you did. Yet you are so small, so young. How is this possible?"

She paid Benet no heed. She was intent on inspecting the wound on the back of the blond youth's head. She rubbed something into the wound. Whether it came from her saddle bag or was some plant she had found nearby, Benet could not tell. He was just grateful that she seemed as skilled at healing as she was as at fighting.

"Can you tell," Benet asked, "will he live?"

"I honestly do not know how he is alive even now," she said. "But if he opens his eyes soon, I reckon he will be right enough. He is fierce lucky. I would not mind at all having his luck, but I definitely would not want the headache he is going to suffer when he wakes."

"My lady, I am in your debt. I am Benet, son of Allard, king of Alinvayl. May I ask the name of the one who has so valiantly saved the lives of my brother and myself?"

She did not take her eyes off Chrysteffor as she replied. "I am Eilís, daughter of Reicheart, high king of Afranor."

Her language was strange to Benet. He had not heard anything exactly like it before, but it was similar enough to the tongue of the nearer Eastern Lands, which he knew well. He could make out what she was saying with little problem.

He still could not believe how slight she was. Her hair was coal black, as were her large, round eyes. Her skin was pale and as smooth as a child's. He would have thought her quite pretty if not for the grime and sweat on her face and the long, thin scar that ran along the edge of her eye and down her cheek. However impressed she might be with Chrysteffor's luck, he thought, she herself was extremely lucky that she still had both her eyes.

Chrysteffor slowly awoke and looked up into Eilís's face. Benet tried to imagine what must be going through his head at that moment. *Surely*, he thought, *must Chrysteffor believe he is looking at an angel.*

The blond prince tried to speak. Eilís put her fingers to her lips and whispered, "Shhh… Do not try to talk. You were injured, but you will be all right now. Just lie quietly for a few minutes." He was more than willing to do as she said.

Eilís quickly got to her feet and said to Benet, "I must go. I was on a journey of some urgency when I happened on your battle. I must not delay any longer."

Benet was loath to see her go. He had so many questions for her.

"What are those things anyway? They are not like any men or animals I have ever seen in my life."

"Most people think it is unlucky to refer to them by any name and so do not, but some of the less superstitious call them the Eidola. That was the word for such beings in the old language. Others call them what they are—the legions of the Black Sorcerer."

"The Black Sorcerer? Do you mean to tell me that someone actually made those things?"

"It is obvious that you are a foreigner in this land. There is much history you do not know. Too much for me to recount for you today. You already know what is most important to know about them. They are dangerous and to be avoided at all costs. Where are you headed?"

"We are from Alinvayl, to the north. We are trying to get home. We planned to follow the coast home."

With a smooth motion, Eilís leapt onto her horse.

"I do not think I would have advised this journey. My best advice for you now is to follow this road. It will bring you to a high cliff overlooking the sea. At the highest point is a castle. It is called Aill Stoirm. When you get there, tell them I have sent you. You will be safe there. My father will give you refuge until you can decide what you are going to do."

"Thank you, my lady. Can you not accompany us? It might be safer for us all."

9

"I cannot. Your best hope is to keep to the road and travel without delay. Did you have horses?"

"We did indeed, my lady, but who knows where they are by now."

"If I come across them, I will do my best to bring them to you or to the castle. For now, though, you will have to walk the road and as quickly as you can. With any luck your brother will be fit for it."

With that, she disappeared quickly into the black fog. Her final words were nearly swallowed by the murk. "Be wary. There are bandits in these woods. Try not to draw their attention."

Chrysteffor had been listening silently to the conversation as he lay on the ground. As the sound of the horse's hoofs quickly died away, he struggled to his feet. He was unsteady, but he did not fall or faint.

"Can you walk?" asked Benet.

Chrysteffor nodded.

"That is good. Because we have a long walk ahead of us through this cursed wood, and our horses are gone."

The younger prince leaned on his brother for support as they set out, but before long he found that he could walk without help. With time he could even keep up a fairly good pace.

"Where is Adryan?" asked Chrysteffor.

Benet looked straight ahead into the darkness.

"Adryan is dead."

2
The Castle Road

BENET WAS impressed by how fast Chrysteffor was able to walk. The head blow he had received did not seem to be slowing him down too much.

What Benet did not realize was that Chrysteffor's head was exploding with pain. He was not feeling nearly so steady on his feet as he was pretending. He was determined to keep walking as fast as he could and not delay their progress toward Castle Aill Stoirm—no matter what.

Neither man spoke as they trudged through the foggy darkness, but Chrysteffor was certain he knew what was going through Benet's mind— that it was Chrysteffor who should be dead, not Adryan. *If I had been a better fighter*, thought the young prince, *perhaps Adryan would still be alive. Surely Benet has to be thinking that his chances of survival would be much better if it were Adryan walking beside him through the woods instead of me.* In that moment Chrysteffor agreed wholeheartedly with his brother's supposed opinion. He truly wished that he *had* been the one who had died instead of Adryan.

Wish as he might, though, he could not change what had happened. All he could do now was try his best not to be a burden to Benet as they tried to get home. As far away as home seemed at that moment and in spite of how much he wanted to get back there, he dreaded the eventual reunion with his father and seeing the old man's face when he learned that his firstborn son was no more.

After they had walked for a couple of hours without speaking, Chrysteffor found the silence oppressive.

"She was really amazing, wasn't she?"

"Eh?"

"That Ae-leesh, or whatever her name was. She was amazing."

"She was that all right," said Benet, neither turning his head nor slowing his pace.

"I wish she could have helped us find the horses before she left. The longer this journey takes, the more I worry that those… things will attack us again."

"Well, there is no point in worrying. The only thing we can do is to reach that castle as soon as possible. Thinking about anything else will not help."

"Tell me. Did... did Adryan die quickly?"

"It was bloody fast. He never knew it happened."

"Was it through the heart?"

Benet did not reply for a full minute or two.

"They took off his head."

Benet could feel the anguish coursing through his brother's heart.

"But like I said, it was bloody fast. He did not feel a thing. He never knew it happened. We should all be so lucky to die such a death. And to die so bravely."

Chrysteffor felt sick to his stomach, but he refused to show it in front of Benet.

"Well, that is something to be grateful for," he said, trying to keep his voice from breaking. "I am glad he did not suffer."

"No, he did not suffer. And he died the way he would have wanted— in the heat of battle and at the side of his brothers. He may not have survived, but he did take a good many of the enemy with him. Our job now is to get home and tell the story of his bravery. There will be many good songs about him in the years to come."

"Valloniah will be sad when she learns the news."

"Aye, I expect she will have many regrets over the fact that, the last time she was with him, they quarreled. But that cannot be helped now."

"I will write my own song about him. It will be the best one I have ever composed."

The talking was beginning to make Chrysteffor short of breath.

Benet said, "We should save the talk for later, brother, and concentrate on keeping up our pace so we can get to that castle."

They went back to walking in silence, but before long they came to two large trees that had been felled so that they lay across the road.

"I do not like the look of this," said Benet with alarm. "Let us not linger in this place."

They began scrambling over the horizontal trunks but, before they could get over them, they heard the unmistakable sound of an arrow flying through the air close to their heads. It buried itself in the ground on the other side of the felled trees.

"Hurry!" hissed Benet. "Bandits have laid a trap for us!"

Before he had finished his sentence, an arrow had buried itself deep in his thigh.

"Damn!" he cried, as he rolled over the trunks and landed on the other side.

Chrysteffor followed quickly. Benet gritted his teeth and pulled the arrow out of his leg and threw it to the ground. It was dripping blood.

"We'd better run for it, Chrys. Are you fit for it?"

Not waiting for a response, Benet leapt to his feet and sprinted down the road. His brother followed. Despite Benet's leg being injured, Chrysteffor found it difficult to keep up with him. Two more arrows flew past their heads.

The blond prince fell farther behind his brother. All the walking he had done, after the earlier fighting, had tired him, and he was still not fully recovered from the head blow he had taken earlier in the day. He groaned in frustration as he watched Benet disappear completely from view into the mist ahead of him.

The fear of being alone in the darkness panicked him and gave him an unexpected burst of energy that made him run a bit faster. Somewhere ahead of him, he heard the sound of another arrow cutting through the misty air and then stopping with a thud. Then came a man's cry. Chrysteffor knew it was Benet's voice, and the young prince stopped dead in his tracks.

His heart was racing. He realized there were bandits ahead of him as well as behind him. Taking no time to think, he did the only thing that might save him. He left the road and ran into the woods. When he came across a tree that he could climb, he crawled up its trunk and lifted himself onto its lowest branches. He climbed as high as he could and then huddled, shivering on a branch with his back resting against the trunk.

He did his best to control his breathing, which had become an endless series of deep loud gasps. It was so loud in his ears that he was sure it could be heard miles away. Not only did he not want the bandits to hear him, but he wanted to be able to hear any noises that might tell him what was happening down on the road. The darkness was so thick that he could not see anything beyond the branch he was sitting on—and certainly not anything on the ground far below him. As he managed to calm himself, his breathing quieted. All that his ears could pick up, though, was the eerie muffled silence of wisps of fog in the darkness.

Then, suddenly, he heard a voice. It was not a voice he had ever heard before. It was a man's voice, and it used the same strange speech that Eilís had spoken. Chrysteffor had traveled the Eastern Lands with his brothers and, like Benet, he could make out the words being spoken. The prince quickly realized the shouting was meant for him. Did the shouter know that he was up a tree? Did he know which one? Or was he simply calling out wherever he thought Chrysteffor might hear them?

"We have your friend. You can have him for a price. We will even give you a choice of two prices. Alive costs more than dead though. Do you want him?"

Chrysteffor's heart began racing again. He had no doubt that, were their places exchanged, Benet would by now have dropped to the ground and charged the bandits in a rescue attempt. But Chrysteffor was not Benet. He was afraid.

Fear was not the only thing that kept the young prince from moving. He was trying to reason out the situation. Knowing his brother as he did, he was sure that, if at all possible, Benet would have called out to him, told him not to give in to their demand for ransom. But there was nothing from Benet. That made Chrysteffor think that they had gagged him or that he was unconscious or dead.

"He has no gold or coins on him," called the bandit. "So he cannot buy his own freedom. You will have to do that for him. And, if you have nothing of value, then you will need to send word to his family to buy him back."

The young prince remained still and quiet on his branch, frozen like a statue. He wished he were as brave as Benet or Adryan and could leap down and take on the bandits single-handed, but he knew, in his case, it would mean his own certain death. If only he could hear Benet call out to him, he might attempt it anyway. But the more time that went on without him hearing Benet's voice, the more he was convinced that his brother was dead or seriously injured. Several minutes passed before the bandit spoke again.

"Well, I guess you do not want him. Too bad for him. We will be cutting his throat then."

Chrysteffor thought he heard something fall on the ground, but he could not be sure. The fog played tricks on his ears. He was certain, though, that he could hear quiet talking among men down on the road.

"Well, he's dead now. I hope it was worth holding onto your coins. I would like to think that *my* friends would not be as stingy as you."

Chrysteffor was not bothered by the bandit's taunts. Instead, it was his own lack of courage that gnawed at him. He prayed that the bandit was lying and that they had not killed Benet. Perhaps Benet had escaped and they were bluffing—hoping to capture Chrysteffor instead. The bandit called to him once more.

"It is too late to buy your friend, but you can still buy your own safe passage. Bring us something nice and we will let you pass through the woods. What do you say? You will not get out of here alive otherwise, so your gold and coins are no good to you anyway."

I do have a few coins, thought Chrysteffor, *but probably not enough to satisfy the bandits. And if I do hand over the coins, the bandits would almost certainly kill me anyway. Unless they think they can get a ransom. I am, after all, the son of a king. But there was no way that they would send to my own country for a ransom. And there is no one in this wretched country who would pay a ransom for me. No, there really is no choice. Dealing with the bandits will only end in death. There is nothing to do but sit in this tree for as long as possible and wait them out.*

"This is your last chance, friend," called the bandit. "If you pay us willingly you can go free. If you do not, we will find you anyway and take your coins after you are dead. The choice is yours."

The prince remained silent and listened for the bandits tramping through the woods, looking for him, but he heard nothing. Perhaps they were afraid to leave the road. Maybe they were afraid of other bandits or, more likely, of those creatures that had attacked him and his brothers. The foremost question in Chrysteffor's mind was, how long to wait until he could be certain they had gone. Would they wait indefinitely, knowing he would have to come back to the road sooner or later?

Chrysteffor resolved to wait hours or days if need be. He was actually quite comfortable on his branch, and he was exhausted. He thought he might nap in the tree. His main worry was that, if he fell asleep, he might roll off the branch and fall to the ground.

He tried to stay awake, but over time he caught himself starting to doze. Every so often he would jerk awake, become alert for a while, and then begin to doze again.

He had no idea how many cat naps he had had when he was awakened by yelling down on the road.

"You! Turn around and there will be no trouble! I am warning you!"

It was the same bandit's voice. Chrysteffor heard scuffling.

"You were warned! You have only yourself to blame!"

Yelling and the sounds of fighting followed. Chrysteffor strained to hear everything he could. He prayed that it was Benet who had somehow freed himself and was attacking the bandits. As the sounds of fighting grew louder, the young prince decided that he could no longer sit and do nothing.

Chrysteffor lowered himself down the tree trunk and dropped to the ground. He unsheathed his sword and advanced cautiously toward the road.

As he stepped on the edge of the path, he saw three men lying face down on the road. After another step, he saw two men attacking a third man, whom Chrysteffor assumed to be Benet. One of the two attackers was aiming a crossbow at their adversary. The other was lunging at him with a broadsword.

Benet certainly has these outlaws well in hand, thought Chrysteffor with relief. *I was right to bide my time in that tree.*

The young prince saw his opportunity to lend his brother a hand. None of the three combatants had noticed him yet. He crept up behind the brigand with the crossbow and pressed the point of his sword against his back.

"Drop your weapon or I will run you through," ordered Chrysteffor, happy to be doing some good at last.

The bandit dropped his crossbow while the other two men stared at Chrysteffor in surprise. It was then that the young prince saw that the man he thought was Benet was not his brother. He was a young man with curly black hair, only a few years older than himself.

With a sick feeling in his stomach, Chrysteffor realized that he had not wandered into a fight between his brother and two bandits but into a battle among three bandits.

They must have fallen to arguing among themselves, thought the prince, and now here he was, one against three. Still he had his blade stuck in the back of one of them.

"Drop your weapons," shouted Chrysteffor, "or I will run this man through!"

The young black-haired man laughed, while the bandit with the sword swung around and lunged at Chrysteffor. The bandit directly in front of Chrysteffor quickly slipped out from in front of his sword and picked up his crossbow.

Whatever quarrel these three had, thought the young prince with a sinking heart, *they all have a common aim now. And that is to finish me off. I have blundered badly this time.*

He knew his only chance of survival lay in acting as quickly as possible. He screamed and charged at the man fumbling with the crossbow. The prince managed to stab him in the thigh before spinning around to face the one with a sword, who was coming at him from behind. Fearing for his life, Chrysteffor swung his sword as hard as he could and succeeded in knocking his adversary's weapon from his hand. He lunged again and was able to put his blade in the brigand's upper leg. Having unexpectedly gained an advantage over those two, the prince prepared to strike once more. The two, both bleeding from their wounds, only yelled curses at him and ran—limped was more like it—into the darkness.

That just left the black-haired man. He raised his sword as he saw Chrysteffor running toward him. The prince hoped he would be as lucky wounding him as he was with the other two, but this man seemed faster than the others and much more skilled at fighting. With one quick motion of his sword, he knocked Chrysteffor's weapon from his hand. Chrysteffor was so determined that he did not stop running and, before his adversary could do anything else, the prince had tackled him to the ground.

I have a chance, thought Chrysteffor, as he saw the other man's sword fall from his hand. *It is just the two of us now, with no weapons.*

Chrysteffor struggled to climb on top of him, but the stranger was amazingly strong. In the blink of an eye he had managed to roll over and put Chrysteffor underneath him. His face was so close the prince could feel the warmth of his breath as he pinned Chrysteffor's arms to the ground.

"You are not even from here," he panted into Chrysteffor's face. "Have things gotten so bad in Afranor that a foreigner like you wanders the country, raising more mayhem than there was before?"

Chrysteffor strained with all his might to free himself. He exerted so much effort trying to break free that he seriously feared his heart would burst, but he did not care. He knew he was likely to be dead within moments in any case.

"What am I going to do with you?" grunted the black-haired man.

"Well, you won't hold me for ransom!" shouted Chrysteffor, as he made a final push to get his foe off him.

The man on top of him seemed puzzled—whether by the prince's refusal to stop struggling or by his words, Chrysteffor could not tell. His puzzlement lasted only a moment. He released one of Chrysteffor's arms long enough to use his own arm to knock him in the head. The prince felt himself losing consciousness and struggled not to pass out.

"I will probably regret this," said the black-haired man as he got to his feet.

He momentarily studied the lad prone on the ground and then strode to a nearby tree.

"If I had any sense at all, I would end your wretched life here and now while I have the chance. But I have had enough of killing for one day. You may or may not wish to thank me—depending on how the rest of your day goes."

A horse was waiting for him at the edge of the darkness. In a quick fluid movement, the young man mounted the horse and, without a look back, rode off into the mist.

Exhausted and dizzy, Chrysteffor could only lie on the ground for several minutes. He sat up and put his head between his knees, waiting for everything to stop spinning. He did not understand why he was not dead, but he was grateful in any case.

He did know one thing for certain. Though the black-haired man had spared his life and Chrysteffor knew he had been incredibly lucky not to die, the prince was not one bit grateful to his opponent. He did not like him. In fact, he hated him. From the first moment he had looked at his face and into his eyes, he had hated him. He did not know why he had had such a violent reaction to him. Something in the man awoke a strong emotion in him. And he promised himself that, if he ever met that man again, he would kill him—without hesitation.

The prince half-expected to be attacked by more bandits at any moment, but he was too exhausted to worry about that possibility. He sat on the ground until his head began to feel right again. After a while, he got to his feet, picked up his sword, sheathed it, then looked around to see if there were anything else nearby that could be of use to him.

If only there were another horse, he thought.

He had a look at the bodies lying on the road. Three of them were obviously bandits, and they were stone dead from various wounds. Did Benet do that, he wondered, or had they done that to each other? He walked back toward where the tree trunks blocked the road. After a few steps, he saw another body in the middle of the road. As he drew closer, a sick feeling welled up in his stomach. The clothes were all too familiar.

He drew closer, praying that he was wrong. He looked at the lifeless face and gave out a cry. It was indeed Benet. There were three arrows in his chest.

He was dead even before that cursed bandit tried to ransom him, thought Chrysteffor bitterly. *He never had a chance.*

Tears pooled in the heartsick prince's eyes.

Those villains never even knew who he was. They did not know he was a son of King Allard, that he was one of the famous fighting princes of Alinvayl. To them he was only a means to steal a few coins, a bit of gold. Is any creature lower than those villains? I take bitter satisfaction that their evil deeds have cost most of them their lives.

Chrysteffor collapsed to the ground and began to sob. He wept without shame. The more he thought about his two dead brothers, the louder his cries became, until he was wailing. Who would have thought that it would come to this? That the fighting princes of Alinvayl would end in this dark place, so far from friends and family?

He knew the longer he stayed there, the more dangerous it was for him, but he did not care. Nothing mattered anymore. He would nearly welcome it if that black-haired villain returned and ended his life right there and then. After all, it made no sense that Adryan and Benet should be dead while he was still alive. He had never been apart from his two brothers, and he should not be apart from them now.

He lost track of the number of hours he sat sobbing and wailing. Eventually, it occurred to him that he had a duty. He got up and wiped the tears from his filthy face, and then he found a flat rock with a sharp edge. He found a spot a ways off the road and began scooping away dirt to make a hole. He was there all night—if one could even speak of night in the continuous darkness of Afranor—digging a grave for his fallen brother.

When the task was done, he placed Benet's body in the hole and covered it. He piled a few stones on top to mark the place.

"You deserve a proper monument, brother," he said softly. "I promise you that I will come back here one day and build it for you. It is not right that your final resting place be in this cursed land so far from our father and everyone we know."

Chrysteffor stood silently a while longer. Memories of his childhood flooded his mind. All the games and pranks that he and his brothers had played as children seemed very far away now.

The prince found Benet's mace lying nearby and hung it on his belt. He said one last silent farewell to his brothers and began walking down the road through the foggy darkness. All he knew to do now was to follow the advice of Lady Eilís and to keep walking down the road to Castle Aill Stoirm.

He did not expect to get there. He was completely alone now, and he knew all too well the dangers that lay in the darkness around him. It was only a matter of time until the hordes of the Black Sorcerer would attack again and behead him as they did Adryan. Or until bandits ambushed him and killed him with arrows, as they did Benet.

He did not care. He fully expected to die. It was only a matter of when and where, and at this point neither of those things mattered to him. Sooner was probably better than later, and here was probably just as good as somewhere else.

After all, he thought, *once you have accepted that your death is certain and imminent, there is really no point in trying to postpone it.*

He walked along the road with no attempt to conceal himself or to be on guard. It was like a weight lifted from his shoulders to have accepted his fate. There was one thing, however. He would not mind if he actually did make it as far as Castle Aill Stoirm. He would like to see what it looked like. And he would not mind at all seeing Lady Eilís one more time.

3
Castle Aill Stoirm

IT WAS scarcely an hour before Chrysteffor saw Castle Aill Stoirm looming suddenly in the mist above him. He marveled that he and Benet had been so near to it when they were ambushed by the bandits.

"We were so close," the prince agonized, "What a cruel world where we should be so near safety yet the valiant Benet should lose his life in such a meaningless way."

The castle stood atop a hill. Chrysteffor could hear the sound of the sea, the waves crashing loudly on the rocks, and knew the water must lie only a short distance beyond the stone fortress in front of him.

He approached the castle's entrance. The two guards became alert and changed their stance upon seeing him. Chrysteffor's mind was numb as he drew near and announced himself.

"I am Chrysteffor, prince of…"

He choked on his words. His own words sounded strange to him, as if they were being spoken by someone else in a foreign tongue. It only now occurred to him that the way he would henceforth announce himself had forever changed.

"I am Chrysteffor, *crown prince* of Alinvayl, son of King Allard. The Lady Eilís told me I could find refuge here."

The guards looked at each other and had a quiet chat as they eyed him suspiciously. One of them went inside the castle and soon returned with an extremely old woman, who was badly hunched over. Her hair was the color of white and gray ash and was matted haphazardly like carelessly stacked straw. Chrysteffor was disappointed. He had hoped that it would be Eilís who would have appeared.

One of the old woman's eyes was glassy, and Chrysteffor supposed it had lost its sight many years before. She shifted her head so that her good eye could study the stranger carefully. She spoke with a raspy voice.

"I am Aigneis, sister of the high king of Afranor," she said. "What business do you have with us?"

The prince repeated his words, this time with more authority.

21

"I am Chrysteffor, crown prince of Alinvayl, son of King Allard. The Lady Eilís told me I could find refuge here."

She continued to stare at him intently. Suddenly, something she had spotted about him gave her a start.

"Your eyes!" she exclaimed.

"Yes, I know," he said wearily. "One of them is brown, and the other is blue. They have been like that since I was born."

Chrysteffor had long since tired of people drawing attention to his eyes. *Frankly,* he thought, *she is the last person who should be drawing attention to other people's eyes.*

Aigneis continued to stare, her mouth agape.

"I am sorry, young prince. I do not mean to be rude. It's just that… there's an old legend in this country about a man with eyes of different colors. At my advanced age I have not thought about it for a very long time."

"Yes, well, it has nothing to do with me. As you can undoubtedly tell, I am not from this country. I am a long way from home. I was traveling with my two brothers. Now they are dead, and I am here alone. The Lady Eilís was good enough to help us when we were beset by horrible creatures in the forest. She told me I could seek refuge here."

Aigneis did not seem as suspicious as he thought she might be, given that she had never met him before in her life. She beckoned him to enter the castle.

"Yes, yes. By all means, come in. If Eilís sent you, then you are indeed welcome. Come inside, out of the damp air."

She led him into the interior of the castle. Chrysteffor found that, in many ways, it was not unlike the castle in which he had grown up. The stones in the walls, however, were larger and more irregularly shaped than he had ever seen before, and there were a good few more hunting trophies on the walls than in his own home. Moreover, the interior shadows were longer and darker, the corridors were quieter, and there was none of the lively activity of his father's fortress. At least in the main room there was a roaring fire in a great fireplace. The warmth from the fire felt good.

"You must be hungry, young prince," said Aigneis. "Please eat."

There was meat on a spit over a dying fire in a smaller fireplace. She picked up a large knife from a table and carved a few slices for him. Chrysteffor had given no thought to food since arriving in Afranor, but now he was realizing that he was ravenous. His rumbling stomach tortured him as he watched the old woman seemingly take forever to serve him.

There was bread on the large wooden table in the center of the room. She poured red wine into a stone goblet, and the prince downed it in a single mouthful. She refilled the cup and watched with great interest as he chewed the meat she had served him.

Even the meat tastes different in this country, thought Chrysteffor, although he was not about to complain.

"You say you have come from Alinvayl?"

"Yes, my lady," said the prince, as he gulped more wine. "My brothers and I were trying to get back there when we decided to pass through your country."

"I cannot remember the last time we had visitors from another country."

It is no wonder, thought the prince, but he reasoned it was better to say nothing out loud.

"May I ask, is Lady Eilís here?"

"No. We have not seen her for two days, but we expect her home this night."

"My lady, if you pardon me…?"

"Yes?"

"It is just that, well, how does one speak of night in this country? As far as I can tell, it is *always* night."

"Yes, it has been night for many years now."

"And does that not seem strange to you? Is there never any sunlight? At all?"

"We think of sunlight all the time, but we have no choice but to live without it."

"So… never a sunrise? Or a sunset? Never a shaft of light breaking through the clouds?"

"I certainly remember such things from the days when I was a younger woman but, sadly, children here have no memories of blue skies and green land."

"And is this the doing of the Black Sorcerer?"

"Where did you hear that name?"

"Lady Eilís mentioned it. She said that the vile creatures that attacked us in the forest were the legions of the Black Sorcerer."

"To answer your question, yes, the perpetual darkness in this land is the doing of the Black Sorcerer. As are all the other evils that we have had to endure."

"And why does no one do anything about him? Why does the king's army not hunt him down and kill him and put an end to all this?"

A slight, bitter smile crossed the old woman's wrinkled face.

"There are those who have tried, but the Black Sorcerer is terribly powerful. The king's own son died trying to stop him. It happened just outside this very castle."

"How?"

"It was a terrible day. The sorcerer came to the castle to make his demands. He stood outside and demanded to be let in. One brave soul attempted to approach him and was immediately struck dead by a lightning bolt."

"And no one else tried to stop him? The king's men did not immediately descend on him en masse and strike him dead where he stood?"

"You have to understand, young prince. They were all afraid. They had seen what he could do. They knew he could strike a man dead with a mere gesture of his hand. No one dared to be the first to move against him."

"Not even one man had the courage?"

"Yes, three did, but only three and no more. Two of them were my brothers, Lúcás and Néall. The other was my nephew Feidhlim, who was then about the age you are now. He could not understand why no one would stand up to the sorcerer. He had not seen all of what the older men had seen. Perhaps that is why he had the courage. Or perhaps that only means that he was foolish. Sadly, it does not matter now."

"What happened?"

"Feidhlim approached the sorcerer alone, with sword drawn, and demanded that he leave. The sorcerer only laughed and caused the sword to fly out of his hand with a mere wave of his arm. Another youth would have been paralyzed with fear at seeing such potent sorcery, but Feidhlim did not hesitate, even for a moment. He charged the sorcerer and tackled him to the ground. The magician had not expected that. Taken unawares, he was forced to struggle with the lad like any other man."

As Aigneis spoke, she led Chrysteffor to another room, one with a high, narrow window between the castle's stones.

"The two of them wrestled on the ground for a good long time. Finally Lúcás and Néall could no longer stand by and watch without doing something. I suppose they were shamed by that beautiful young lad, who had the bravery to fight while everyone else held back in fear. They joined the fight. Still, even with three against one, the struggle went on and on. The rest of us watched in horror, but the longer it continued, the more we began to have hope that the sorcerer might actually be defeated. In our hearts, though, we knew better.

"Néall was the first to fall. When the sorcerer managed to get one of his arms free, he pointed his hand toward my brother and a terrible light flowed suddenly from his fingers. Néall burst into flame and was soon no more than a pile of cinders. Feidhlim and Lúcás continued the struggle. Then, after a few minutes, it was Lúcás who fell. While Feidhlim was wrestling with the villain, the sorcerer put one of his hands on Lúcás's chest. My poor brother began to shake violently. Within mere seconds his body began to smoke as if a fire were burning inside. In no time he was a charred corpse lying on the ground. That left only Feidhlim and the sorcerer struggling. In the end, the two combatants found themselves near the edge of the cliff there."

She pointed out the window. Chrysteffor stepped up to the window's ledge and peered out. He was surprised to see just how close the castle was built to the edge of the high cliff. Directly below him was nothing but mist swirling in the dark. The sound of crashing waves rose up from the depths below. He judged from the muffled nature of the sound that the sea was very far below.

"I watched from this window," said Aigneis darkly. "I saw the sorcerer give poor Feidhlim one final kick and send him hurtling over the edge to the rocks below. I have never felt so utterly without hope—neither before nor since. He was a beautiful young man and, in time, would have made a fine king. It was a terrible injustice that his life should have been cut so short. We were not even able to give him a proper burial. His body washed out to sea and was never found."

Tears came to the old woman's eyes, and Chrysteffor felt sorry for her.

"My lady, I too have lost someone close to me—and not once but twice and on this very day. Sorry, no, it was yesterday. Or was it? I am so confused about time in this country. I have no idea how long it has been since I have slept. How does one know when it is time to sleep in your land?"

"Forgive me, young prince. Of course, you would be very tired. I will show you where you may sleep awhile."

She led him to a small room with a bit of straw and a blanket on the ground. "This may not be as lavish as what you are accustomed to," she said, "but you are welcome to it."

"My lady, I could not ask for anything more than this. I thank you from the bottom of my heart."

The prince collapsed onto the makeshift bed and promptly fell into a deep sleep.

When Chrysteffor awoke, he had no idea how long he had slept. The castle was every bit as dark as when he had arrived. It took him a moment or two to remember where he was and everything that had happened.

Someone was watching him. He rubbed his eyes to be able to see better in the dim light. He was delighted to see that it was Eilís.

"I see that you arrived after all. Where is your brother?"

Chrysteffor scrambled to his feet. He absent-mindedly ran a hand through his hair, as if his appearance should somehow matter.

"He is dead, my lady. Killed by bandits."

"I am sorry for your trouble. He seemed a good man."

"That he was, my lady."

The princess eyed him intently.

"Pardon me for asking, but just how old are you anyway?"

"This is my nineteenth summer—although the word summer seems an odd word to use in this strange land of yours."

"Nineteen," she murmured. "I would have thought you younger. I was born only two years before you, and yet I feel so much older."

Chrysteffor could not stop himself from speaking, though at this moment silence might have been the wiser course.

"I think you are amazing, my lady. You are braver and more skilled than anyone I have ever known before. And you are beautiful. I should like to compose a song about you."

"A song?"

"When I am at home," said Chrysteffor self-consciously, "I sometimes write verses and compose melodies. But I have never before had a subject as inspiring as you."

Eilís laughed. "It has been many years since there have been melodies or poetry in our country. Those sorts of things seem frivolous, given the state of things."

"Even in dark times, people need music and poetry. That is what I believe anyway. And not everyone can be a fierce warrior."

"You really are just a boy, aren't you? Yet I can already see so clearly the man you will someday soon become. Sadly, in times like these, who knows whether you will ever get the chance."

Chrysteffor's cheeks blushed. Her words stung him, but then her face softened.

"Still, you are pleasing to me. And your words are very pretty."

She looked him up and down appreciatively as she continued. "And you yourself are pretty. In a different time and place, in a time when not every day was a question of life or death, I would have been happy to have had a lad like you—even if only for a summer's brief frolic."

26

She leaned over and kissed him. It was the most wonderful thing that had ever happened to Chrysteffor. He had kissed girls before, but it had never been anything like this. He knew instantly in that moment that he was in love with Eilís and would be in love with her for the rest of his life.

Eilís, on the other hand, was unimpressed.

"You are not much of a kisser, are you? Do you even like girls?"

By now Chrysteffor's cheeks were burning red hot.

"I am sorry, my lady. I… I was taken by surprise."

"Yes, well, I suppose boys who wait until girls decide to kiss them are always taken by surprise."

This was too much for Chrysteffor to bear. Could she not see the love in his eyes? Could she not sense the passion welling in his breast? How could she be so close to him and not know what he was feeling? Clearly, it was time for action.

He took her in his arms and kissed her forcefully, with all the fervor in his soul. He kissed her until he thought his heart would burst with joy and pain. He kissed her as though it were the last thing he would ever do, as if they would both die when he stopped. He worried he might actually injure her from holding too tightly, but she was holding him every bit as tightly. He wanted this moment never to stop. Finally, she pulled away from him.

"Well," she said, catching her breath, "it seems there is far more to you, Prince Chrysteffor, than is at first apparent."

There was so much he wanted to say to her. He wanted to tell her that, from this moment on, the thought of not being close to her would always be a torture. He wanted to say that the mere sight of her made him want to weep with joy. He wanted her to know that he could not imagine living without her.

In the end, he quietly said only this: "I love you, Eilís. With all my heart."

Her eyes flashed, as if she did not know whether to laugh or to cry.

"Oh, my pretty Chrysteffor. If only we could have known each other in a different world than this one."

And then she silently walked away.

Chrysteffor was sure he had made a fool of himself. He was angry with himself for pouring his heart out to a woman he barely knew and not keeping his feelings to himself. He was angry that all he could think of was this woman instead of the two brothers he had so recently lost. He needed to walk.

He left the castle under the watchful gaze of the guards. He walked as if to go around the castle, but he soon came to the cliff. The edge of the bluff appeared with little warning. It would have been easy enough for someone as distracted as himself to tumble over.

He stood with the wind battering his face and blowing his hair in several directions at once. Its howls sounded like wild animals screaming in pain. Far below him the sea's waves crashed against the rocks. He thought about Aigneis's nephew and how painful his death must have been. As distressed as the wind and the waves sounded that dark night, their seeming anguish was nothing compared to the torment in his soul. How tortuous it was to have found horror, death and love all in such a brief span of time. He screamed into the wind, only to have the sound of his voice swallowed up in the gales.

4
The Sorcerer's Curse

CHRYSTEFFOR SPENT many hours walking along the edge of the cliff. When he tired of the cliff, he walked up and down the sides of the hill. When he tired of that, he tramped around a wider area surrounding the castle. Occasionally, he would pass where the castle guards could see him. He was aware that they were eyeing him with curiosity and amusement. They must have thought him mad. And perhaps they were right. Maybe, he thought in his confusion, just maybe he really had gone mad. Mad with grief over his brothers and mad with love for the warrior princess he had only recently met.

He completely lost track of time. When there was continuous night and no sunrise, time did not seem to exist. Finally, though, he decided that it would be prudent to go back inside the castle. He was determined to talk to Eilís. He was determined to convince her that he really was in love with her, that it was not just some impetuous infatuation, that his feelings were true and deep and sincere. But then what? What was to happen after that?

In truth, the thought of marriage frightened him. At his young age, so much of life was still ahead of him. There would be more journeys to undertake, more adventures to experience, more memories to make. And all of that might involve other women to know and perhaps to love. His brothers had always advised him not to be too quick to marry—advice they themselves had followed to a fault. Moreover, there was the question of politics. His father would need to be consulted—especially if it involved wedding a foreigner. A prince's marriage could never be a simple love match, as told in children's tales. Marrying a princess would constitute a de facto political and military alliance. His father would definitely have something to say about that—as would the father of Eilís, a man he had yet to meet.

Most importantly, though, what would Eilís think about a marriage proposal? She would likely laugh in his face. After all, it was obvious that she regarded him as little more than a callow youth. Yes, he was a prince, but not one who was particularly skilled at battle. She herself was twice the warrior he was, and that was being generous to himself. How could she consider spending the rest of her life with someone like him? She would doubtless prefer someone like either of his brothers—older, larger, stronger, braver. The very idea of someone like him proposing marriage to Eilís was absurd.

After he had reasoned all that out, he knew there was only one rational way to proceed. He needed to forget about Eilís and instead concentrate on finding the best course of action that would bring him back to his own home. Once he had done that, he would take up his duties as the new crown prince and do his best to belatedly overcome his lack of fighting skill—the same lack of fighting skill that had been responsible for him not being able to save his more worthy brothers. And then he would live out the rest of his days being an exemplary prince of Alinvayl. Yes, that was the only rational way to proceed.

Having finally managed to reason all this out and to see things clearly at last, he proceeded to make his way back to the castle as quickly as possible in order to propose marriage to Eilís before the rational part of his mind could find a way to stop him.

He climbed the hill back up to the castle entrance. The guards, who by now knew him well, let him pass without incident. He made his way down the corridors in search of Eilís. He could not wait to see her, to look on her face again. In his mind it was as though the two of them were already married and should never spend another day apart. Yes, it was madness, but he had now given up fighting it. He had completely given himself over to the fact that he was in love with her and no longer cared how irrational his behavior was.

The first person he met was Lady Aigneis. She was upset. When she saw him, she exclaimed, "Prince Chrysteffor, where on earth have you been? We thought you had surely been abducted by the Eidola."

"I apologize, my lady. I had some serious thinking to do. Important decisions to make. It required my being alone outside the castle for a few hours. And now it is very important that I speak with…"

She cut him off abruptly. "Something terrible has happened."

"Something terrible? What do you mean?"

He was perturbed. Nothing was more important than for him to speak with Eilís and declare his undying love. This old woman and her problems were causing him delay.

"It is… Eilís," she said, on the verge of tears.

"Eilís? What about her? What has happened?"

"She… she…"

Chrysteffor got a horrible feeling in the pit of his stomach.

"What? Has something happened to Eilís? What has happened? Tell me! Tell me, old woman!"

Aigneis attempted to explain but the words seemed too difficult for her. Finally, she said, "It will be easier to show you."

She led him down a corridor to a chamber at the other end of the castle. When he entered the room, the prince saw Eilís lying peacefully on a bed. She seemed to be sleeping. And she was as beautiful to him as ever. Sitting on the floor next to her was a distraught and wizened old man. Chrysteffor's first thought was that he was a servant. Perhaps a longtime faithful family attendant nearing the end of his days but still devoted to the princess's well-being.

Chrysteffor was confused. He could see nothing wrong.

"Lady Aigneis, you had me frightened for no reason," he said. "She seems to be fine. She is only sleeping. Why were you so concerned?"

"You do not understand," said Aigneis. "We have been trying to wake her for hours. She lay down for only a brief nap, but when I went to rouse her, as she had requested, she could not be wakened. That was hours ago."

"Surely, she is simply over-tired. Many are the mornings when I myself cannot be wakened, no matter the efforts of my family."

The old woman looked at him with impatience. "This is no mere case of laziness or drunkenness," she said, eyeing him sternly. "For hours we have been making every effort to rouse her. She is in a deep slumber that is not normal or natural. And there appears to be no way to end it."

The prince was certain that the old lady was imagining a problem where none existed. He walked over to the bed, took hold of the sleeping princess's shoulders, and shook her gently. Her eyes did not flutter and the passive expression on her face did not change. He shook her more forcefully. Even as he did this, he was aware that, by touching the princess so, he was taking improper liberties. He fully expected that Aigneis would insist that he stop, but the old woman said nothing. She was quite willing to give him the chance to try rousing her but, no matter how strongly he shook the princess, she showed no signs of her deep sleep being disturbed.

"Princess, wake up!" he shouted to no avail. "Eilís, I beg you! Wake! Please, Eilís, wake up! I beg you!" Still nothing.

In his stubbornness he lost track of all time, and the more time passed, the greater the feeling of dread in his heart. Panic overtook him. On a sudden and powerful impulse, he leaned over her and kissed her. Her lips felt warm but not alive. He pressed his lips harder against hers and kissed her with more passion. He kissed her the way he wished he had kissed her before—when she had mocked him. It made no difference.

By now Aigneis's indulgence of his efforts was at an end.

"Prince Chrysteffor!" she shouted. "You forget yourself. You are taking advantage of her condition. I must insist you step away at once!"

The prince's cheeks glowed bright red with embarrassment as he stepped back from the bed.

"Forgive me, lady. It's just that… that… it's as though she is under some magic spell, and I remembered something I once heard in a story when I was a child. About a princess being released from a spell when a prince kissed her. I know it sounds like lunacy, but I felt I had to try. Please forgive me."

"I am not the one to whom you should apologize," said Aigneis. "You should make your apology to the king."

Chrysteffor was mortified. "Does the king really need to know about this? After all, there was really no harm done, was there?"

Now Aigneis was looking equally uncomfortable.

"Young prince, you are in the presence of the king," she said drily.

Her eyes motioned to the old man sitting on the floor.

"This is the king?" asked Chrysteffor incredulously.

"I am sorry not to have introduced you properly. In my concern for the princess, I forgot my manners. Your highness King Reicheart, I present to you Prince Chrysteffor of Alinvayl, of whom I spoke to you previously."

The pitiful old man struggled to stand. He showed no sign of indignation or anger. He exhibited nothing but deep sorrow.

"I am sorry not to have welcomed you properly, Prince Chrysteffor. As you have no doubt realized by now, you should not have come to Afranor. If you can possibly find your way back to your own land, I would strongly advise you to do so at the earliest opportunity."

Chrysteffor stared at the old man. He could not believe this was the king of Afranor and the father of Eilís. The king looked ancient, certainly much older than his true years. And he seemed unbearably sad, as if he had the entire weight of the world on his hunched shoulders. Most of all he simply looked tired, as if he had not slept in days or weeks. He was not at all what the prince had expected. He had imagined that the father of the beautiful and strong and courageous Princess Eilís would be someone more impressive. Someone more like his own father.

"Your highness," said the prince, "I apologize sincerely for having overstepped, but I assure you that my only motivation was to wake the princess. It was an act of desperation on my part. You see, I have become, ah, quite fond of her since my brother Benet and I first met her in the forest. I cannot impress upon you enough how important her well-being has become to me."

King Reicheart appeared to have already lost interest in speaking with Chrysteffor. He sat again on the floor and stared forlornly at his sleeping daughter. The prince turned to the king's sister.

"Lady Aigneis, do you have any idea how this has happened to her?"

"You said it yourself, young prince. It is a spell."

"My lady, do you really believe in such things?"

"You have seen the Eidola. You have seen the eternal night that envelops this land. Do you not think that he would also be capable of an enchantment such as this?"

"So it is the Black Sorcerer who has done this? Who is he? And where does his terrible power come from?"

"I am afraid it is quite a long story. And I am not sure that taking the time to tell it to you now will do any of us any good."

"If I am going to defeat him, I will need to know everything there is to know about him."

Aigneis half-laughed as she looked at the young prince.

"Do you really imagine that you could challenge someone with such powers? I do not mean any offense, young prince, but better men than you have attempted it and have quickly died—including two of my brothers and my poor brave nephew Feidhlim."

"I can and I will," said Chrysteffor firmly.

Because the young prince during his long walk had already reconciled himself to the idea of dying, the only things left in his mind to be determined were exactly when and how he should die. He concluded, if he were going to die inevitably, he might as well have a good death—one that would make his father and Eilís proud of him. So he had decided to be courageous. Of course, he knew in his heart that he was not *really* courageous. He also knew, given that he was bound to die in any event, it would not make him any more dead if he *pretended* that he was courageous. At least his death would then have some meaning. If Eilís did someday awaken and she were to hear the story of how he bravely went off to confront the evil sorcerer, then at least she would remember him kindly— and maybe even affectionately. Maybe with love. Because, after all was said and done, he knew he loved her and he felt in his heart that she actually did love him too—even if she had not yet realized it.

"What exactly are you saying, Prince Chrysteffor?" asked the dumbstruck Aigneis.

"I am saying that I will hunt down this sorcerer and I will force him to release Lady Eilís from this evil spell before I end his life once and for all. That is what I am saying."

The old woman looked upon the young prince with a newfound respect. Tears formed in her eyes.

"I have waited many years to hear someone say those words. Honestly, when first I met you, I did not expect that it would be you, but I see it now in your eyes. You are the one. You are the one who will save Afranor. The prophecy will come true."

"Prophecy?"

"Yes. There was a prophecy long ago, about a man with one brown eye and one blue eye, who would save Afranor. I cannot say I ever truly believed it until now."

The prince had no doubt that it was nothing more than an odd coincidence, but he decided not to argue with her. The old wives' tale was convenient enough since it would only enhance the stories he hoped would be told about the courageous death he hoped and expected to have.

"Yes, well, now that we have established that I am the one to hunt down and kill the sorcerer, I think it might be time for you to tell me everything there is to know about him. After all, I need to know where to begin searching for him."

She drew closer to Chrysteffor and spoke quietly.

"Yes, yes, I will tell you everything I know. Let us leave the king and the princess and go to a more secluded place, so that I may tell you the history of the Black Sorcerer."

Just at that moment, the princess suddenly screamed.

"No! No!" she cried. "Keep away! Keep away!"

"She's waking!" exclaimed Chrysteffor with relief. "She's waking up. The spell is broken."

For a few moments he thought that he might not have to undertake his terrible quest after all. He thought that she might wake up and he could marry her and live the rest of his days in Afranor. But the princess's eyes did not open. She continued screaming as if she were being threatened by some invisible menace.

"She is dreaming," said the king sadly. "She is having a terrible dream. Please, my precious girl. Please, wake up. You are with those who love you."

Nothing the three of them could say or do made the princess wake up. Her previously calm sleep was now roiled with cries of alarm, and nothing they did could make them stop.

34

Aigneis said, "Let us go, Chrysteffor. I will answer all your questions. I will help you in every way I can to prepare you for your quest to save our dear Eilís and to release her from this torment."

Reluctantly, Chrysteffor followed the old woman to the chamber with the fireplace, the same one where she had first brought him after he had arrived at the castle. She sat down with him, poured two goblets of wine, and began to speak.

"As you know, King Reicheart is my brother and I had two other brothers, Lúcás and Néall, who are now dead. What you further need to know is that the Black Sorcerer's birth name is Leannain and he too is my brother."

"What?" exclaimed Chrysteffor. "You mean to tell me that all this evil has been unleashed on this land by the king's own brother? How is this possible?"

"It is a terrible story and not one we like to tell, but I will tell it to you now. Of all of us, Leannain was the youngest. He was also the brashest and the most headstrong. And, I have to concede, he was the cleverest of all of us—and that was something about which he himself never had any doubt. He always considered himself too smart to be taught by anyone else or for any other man to be his master—not even his father or his brothers.

"From a young age it was clear he felt none of us had anything to teach him and we should be listening to him. The older he grew, the more he felt it was his role to be the master of us all. He spoke openly against the tradition of heredity, insisting he should be the one to succeed our father as king, rather than our oldest brother, Reicheart.

"We came to fear there would be a violent struggle upon the death of our father. What we did not anticipate was how soon our father would die and how it would come to pass. One terrible night we all woke to a scream that echoed throughout the darkness. We rushed to the king's room whence the horrific cry had come. Imagine our horror upon seeing Leannain holding a dagger dripping with blood as he stood over our father's body sprawled across his own bed. It was like something out of my worst nightmare.

"Néall screamed at Leannain and demanded to know if he had gone completely mad.

"But Leannain showed not the slightest remorse for his traitorous act. He looked at us with nothing but contempt and uttered the words, 'Bow down before your king. I am the one who deserves to sit on the throne, and you have always known this. Now I have saved us all the trouble of a

35

pointless debate. I now claim the crown, as is right and fitting. Bow down to your new king.'

"It was such a terrible shock that, for a few moments, we were all dumbstruck. We could not believe our own brother had committed such a barbarous act. Finally, though, my other three brothers charged the usurper. He could not fend off all of them, and they had him quickly subdued. He was made a prisoner and, after a few days, in a solemn and mournful ceremony Reicheart became the new king.

"We then had to decide what was to become of Leannain. I regret now to say that, despite the atrocity he had committed, Reicheart and I took pity on him. We were the two oldest of the family and we had always indulged him. We had always seen a weakness of character in him, and that weakness had always prompted sympathy in us rather than disdain. Now that he had committed this terrible crime, we knew that he was irredeemably mad and we thus believed he was not truly responsible for his actions. Though we could not forgive him, we did not feel he deserved to die—as Lúcás and Néall urged.

"The four of us had endless arguments over this, but in the end it was up to the new king to decide what to do with him. Over the protests of his brothers, Reicheart decreed that he should be exiled. Leannain was told that he could never again set foot in Afranor. Even on the day he was brought to the border, Leannain was unrepentant. He continued to swear that he would one day return and have his revenge on us all and that he would take his rightful place as king.

"We never expected to hear from him again. We presumed he would live out his days as a recluse or hermit somewhere in the outlands. Every so often travelers would pass through Afranor and bring some bit of news about him. They said he had been seen on the road toward the Eastern Lands. Sometime later we heard he had passed through the Eastern Lands and was seen heading toward the far east, where no one from Afranor was ever known to have ventured. For many years after that, we heard nothing about him at all. We assumed that he had met his end in some uncivilized corner of the world and that we would never know what exactly had befallen him.

"As the years passed, we thought of him less and less and the memory of him receded into the past. It was many years later that, without warning, he returned. Before we actually saw him, though, we had a portent—in the form of the weather. Ominous black clouds rolled in from the east. It was unusual weather, but at first no one saw it as anything other than natural. The clouds grew thicker and thicker until everything became as dark as night. We waited for the rain to fall, but it never did. The darkness endured for hours. Then, later in the day, Leannain appeared at the door of the castle. He looked taller and much older than he had before. He wore a black robe and carried a large wooden staff. He held the staff aloft and the castle doors flew open all by themselves. All the men rushed to the entrance to see what was happening. The king and the princes could not believe their eyes when they saw their long-banished brother in front of them.

" 'Leannain!' cried the king. 'Were you not exiled from Afranor for your heinous crime? Did I not, out of respect for the fact that we both came from the same mother and father, show you mercy? Is this how you repay my munificence? I will not make the mistake of showing mercy again. By coming back here now, you have sealed your fate once and for all. The penalty for your return is death.'

"The king drew his sword to dispense the fatal punishment with his own hand but, with a motion of his staff, Leannain caused the sword to fly out of Reicheart's hand. Lúcás and Néall rushed to fulfill the king's will, but their luck was no better.

" 'I am different now,' proclaimed Leannain. 'I have learned many things and gained new powers in my eastern travels. I have mastered the secrets of the ancient magicians of the orient, and I have gained the ability to bend nature to my will. There is no way you can stop me. I was born to be the ruler of Afranor, and now at last my destiny will be realized.'

"It was as though the nightmare of all those years before, the time of our father's death, had returned—but now many times worse. We did not know how we could possibly fight Leannain with the new supernatural powers he had acquired. I looked to Reicheart to see what he would do. Would he willingly hand over his crown to Leannain or would he put up a fight that looked to be futile? I was not surprised to see him determined to fight.

"You must understand, Chrysteffor, my brother Reicheart was a very different man in those days, very different from the way you see him now. He was not one to act in haste or purely out of hot-blooded passion, but he never backed away from a fight. And I could see that he was not going to back away from this one. He took the sword from the man nearest him, raised it and shouted, 'There will be a reward for the first man to give me this villain's head!'

"Encouraged by their king, all the men charged Leannain, even as that sword too flew from Reicheart's hand. The first few who approached him were thrown back by his mysterious power. The sorcerer raised his staff and their bodies were blown about, like leaves in a wind, but the men did not stop. One after another charged the villain, and when one was

37

repelled another took his place. The wizard was powerful, but he could not contend with so many adversaries at once. The exercise of his power was clearly taking a toll on him. He grew visibly tired. As he faltered, Reicheart saw his chance. He picked up one of the swords that had been forced from his hand and charged toward Leannain. He was no longer sentimental about his youngest brother. Without the slightest hesitation he pushed past the crush of men and drove his sword into the sorcerer's chest. He let go of the sword, leaving it in the breast of his brother, and stepped back.

"At that moment everyone froze. The other men stopped their attack and stared. The ones still on the ground who had not yet managed to get back on their feet looked up to see what would happen next. Aside from staggering a step or two, Leannain just stood there—looking as if he could not believe what had happened. I confess that, yes, I almost felt sorry for him. After all he had done and after all the years in which he had never found any remorse in his heart for his evil deeds, I pitied him as he stood there in disbelief. You see, I was sure that he was dead and that we were witnessing his final moments of life, but I was wrong. He did not die. To be sure, he was in pain and he was suffering, but he was not collapsing. He looked down at the sword in his chest with a mixture of shock and annoyance. He reached for the hilt, pulled the sword from his chest, and let it drop to the ground with a clang.

"We all kept staring. The men seemed unsure of what to do next. After all, if the villain could not be killed, was there any point in continuing the fight? After what seemed hours, Leannain threw back his head and let out a terrible howl.

" 'Is this how you treat your new king?' he cried. 'You have sorely disappointed me. You do not deserve me as your sovereign. For your punishment, I condemn this land to oblivion. I swear here and now that, for as long as I live, none of you will ever see the sun again. You are condemned to spend the rest of your days in darkness, and your children will spend all of their days in darkness. Remember, you have brought this upon yourselves!'

"He walked out of the castle and into the fog that had blanketed the land. And to this day we have continued to live in darkness, just as he swore. Both Reicheart's children, Feidhlim and Eilís, were born into this darkness and never knew anything else for all their lives. People have lived in fear ever since. Reicheart's spirit was broken. With time he retreated more and more into himself until he became the man you see today.

"As the years passed, the Eidola began to roam the land. They sowed even more fear among the people than there was before. It was impossible for them to live normal lives or to maintain order in the kingdom. Roaming brigands took advantage of the constant darkness to rob whoever was so foolhardy as to travel the roads. People cowered in their homes and only the bravest or the most wanton of criminals dared to venture abroad.

"We have seen little of Leannain since that day. Every few years after that, without warning, he would arrive here at the castle to taunt us, to laugh at how his handiwork had destroyed the very soul of Afranor. It was on one such visit just a few years ago that, as I have already recounted to you, Feidhlim challenged him and began a fight that cost him and two of my brothers their lives."

Aigneis's story left Chrysteffor stunned. Doing his best to keep his hand from shaking, he drained the last of the wine from his goblet and pondered the situation in which he now found himself.

5
The Tower Road

"MY LADY," said Chrysteffor, "that is a story of which I have never before heard the like and the like of which I never expect or hope to hear again. Truly this land has suffered a terrible fate."

"Yes it has, Prince Chrysteffor. And now that you have heard the entire story, do you still wish to undertake such a perilous mission as seeking out and destroying the Black Sorcerer?"

The young prince reached for the bottle of wine on the table and refilled the two goblets. He took another sip as he thought hard. In the end, none of the terrible things he had heard really affected his calculation. If anything, they only reaffirmed what he had already concluded—that his death was inevitable and that he might as well make it a good death. He steadied his nerves so that he could effectively feign the kind of bravery he had never before had in his life and certainly did not have now.

"I will be honest with you, my lady. I know this is not the time or the place to say this but, given the circumstances, I will say it to you and to you alone. I am in love with Princess Eilís. I know that I have known her only a brief amount of time, but I have never been so sure of anything in my whole life. And so there is nothing that will stop me from hunting down and killing the villain who has placed this curse on her. So, yes, I still have every intention of undertaking this mission and destroying the Black Sorcerer. Now I need you to tell me where to find him and if you have any suggestions as to how he might be killed."

Aigneis's respect for the young prince continued to grow.

"Yes, I do believe you are the one to fulfill the old prophecy. If you can complete this task, you will truly be worthy of my niece and, while I cannot speak for her or what may lie in her heart, I know that at the very least you will earn her eternal gratitude."

Chrysteffor was quite happy to earn Eilís's gratitude, but he would be crushed if that was all she had for him at the end of his quest. On the other hand, he almost certainly would not be alive to see Eilís awake

40

again, so the question of whether she would have mere gratitude for him or perhaps something more was really moot. He listened as Aigneis continued.

"As you know from my story, it does not appear that Leannain can be killed. At least no one to this day has any idea of how that might be accomplished, but I can tell you the rest of the prophecy. It may contain the answer to our salvation. Along the coast of Afranor, on three separate bluffs overlooking the sea, stand three ancient towers. No one alive today remembers who built them or why. They have always been there, always enduring. The old stories have warned generations not to go near them, and no one has—at least in my lifetime, but the old prophecy did say that Afranor would one day be saved by a man with one blue eye and one brown eye—after he had entered each of the three towers. My understanding has always been that each tower would hold some kind of a test or challenge for the savior."

"Test? What kind of test? This is your hope for saving your kingdom and for the princess? That I go visit these three old towers? Begging your pardon, my lady, but does this not all seem, well, completely daft?"

"I know it must seem so to you, Prince Chrysteffor, but you have to understand that this is a story that has been told to all of Afranor's children from time immemorial. We have to have faith that these stories were passed down to us for a reason."

Chrysteffor decided not to argue about the rationality of what he was being told. In the end, he would be dead, after all, and so what did it matter how crazy was the story that led him to his death? The fact that his fate would be tied forever to such a hoary and revered legend would only endear him all the more to the people who heard it. Perhaps someday Eilís or his father in Alinvayl might hear it and be impressed by it.

"Very well then, Lady Aigneis, tell me where I shall find the first of these towers?"

"That is easy enough. Simply follow the cliffs, keeping the sea always to your left. The first tower is only a few leagues away. I suggest that you get some sleep now. By the time you wake, I will have a hearty breakfast prepared and a horse ready for you."

And so Chrysteffor went to his room and did his best to sleep, but he did not sleep well if, indeed, he slept at all. The hours dragged by. He had the sense that he never closed his eyes, yet every so often he would start and remember fragments of some dream. When it finally came to a point where he could no longer endure lying there, he decided to rise and begin his quest.

Lady Aigneis was as good as her word. There was an abundance of food waiting for him. He helped himself to loaves of thick brown bread and smoked fish fillets, and he washed them down with goblets of watered-down wine. He enjoyed the food and the warmth of the hearth so much that he wished he were not leaving immediately on a cold damp journey to what would inevitably be a terrible death.

When he had had his fill, he took a look at his rucksack. There was precious little to bring along on such a hopeless quest. He wondered if he should empty it of its content in order to bring more food along, but in the end he decided not to. All he had was an extra shirt, a length of rope, a flint stone, and Benet's mace. He had no intention of using the mace, but it gave him a bit of comfort to have it with him. After all, it was all he had left of either of his brothers.

As he put what was left of the breakfast in his rucksack, the prince became aware of a pair of eyes staring at him. He looked up to see a freckled boy, with deep brown eyes and shaggy hair the color of dark rust, standing in the doorway. Chrysteffor judged him to be about 15 years old.

"Are you Prince Chrysteffor?" asked the lad.

"I am indeed. And who might you be?"

"I am Ruaraidh. Is it true that you are going to the three towers?"

"It is indeed true, Ruaraidh. In fact, I am making ready to leave this very moment."

"I am coming with you."

"You are?"

"Yes, I am."

"Did someone tell you that you must go with me?"

"No, they did not have to. You're going to kill the Black Sorcerer, aren't you?"

"That is my plan all right, but it will be a difficult and dangerous task. It would not suit me to be minding children on the journey."

"I am not a child. I am Ruaraidh, son of Prince Lúcás and third in line to the throne of Afranor. It is my duty to accompany you and avenge the death of my father."

Chrysteffor regretted having spoken to the lad so dismissively. He felt a pang of sadness for this boy who had lost his father under such tragic circumstances. He also remembered how he himself had felt at that age when his elders treated him like a child.

"I apologize, Prince Ruaraidh, I did not realize who you were. I have heard the story of your father and your uncle Néall and your cousin Feidhlim and how they died so bravely. You should be proud of all of them. I would like very much to have your help on my quest today, but

42

the truth is that there is a far more important job I need you to do for me."

"More important? What is it?"

"You are aware that your cousin Eilís has fallen under an evil spell?"

"Yes, I know. It is the work of the Black Sorcerer. The same villain who killed my father. That is all the more reason I need to help you destroy him."

"Yes, he must be destroyed but, as I say, there is another, more important task that must be done at the same time. I cannot do both, and so I must ask you to do one of them for me."

"Yes, yes, tell me. I'll do anything."

"Princess Eilís is lying on her bed defenseless. And I am going to tell you a secret. It is a secret just between us two men. I am in love with Princess Eilís and, after I have destroyed the Black Sorcerer, I am going to return and marry her. And so I need to know that she is protected, that someone reliable is standing watch over her. Can you do that, Ruaraidh?"

"Yes, yes, of course, I can. I will never leave her side. I swear it. I will be there day and night. Until you return. You may rely on me."

With that Ruaraidh vanished from the doorway. Chrysteffor was touched by the boy's sincerity. He had no doubt that he would indeed stand watch over the princess faithfully and not desert his post. He could imagine him maturing and ageing over the years as he stood in that place waiting in vain for Chrysteffor to return. The important thing right now, though, was that the lad not be tempted to follow Chrysteffor on his mission. The last thing he wanted was to have that young lad's life on his conscience.

Chrysteffor finished packing his rucksack and then headed to the princess's room to have one last look at her before he departed. When he entered the room, Ruaraidh was standing there, ramrod straight, next to the bed. Chrysteffor took the sleeping woman's hand and kissed it softly. He was nearly moved to tears to see how beautiful she was as she lay there. And he was further moved as he looked at young Ruaraidh, drawing himself as tall as he could and fairly bursting with pride as he stood solemnly. He had a sword at his side and his right hand rested on its hilt. He looked at Chrysteffor with determination and admiration.

"Godspeed, Prince Chrysteffor. I will not desert my post. I will remain here by Eilís's side until your return. When you come back, I will be proud to attend your wedding and to call you my cousin."

"Well done, Ruaraidh son of Lúcás. I too will be proud to call you cousin. And I pray that we will see one another again soon and in happier circumstances."

Chrysteffor feared he might actually shed tears and so quickly left the room. The sight of the young lad standing so faithfully by Eilís's side with his optimism and confidence in Chrysteffor's mission had filled his heart with poignancy. It was one thing for Chrysteffor to head off to certain death in hopes of leaving behind a reputation of courage and adventure, but he had not really thought about what it would be like for the people of Afranor—including young people like Ruaraidh—who would be left behind to live with the consequences of his inevitable failure.

He met Aigneis, who brought him outside to the stables and handed him the reigns to a horse that he recognized. It was Eilís's horse, the one she had been riding when he first met her. It nuzzled his arm, giving every appearance of being quite comfortable with him.

"I wish I had more advice or help to offer you, Prince Chrysteffor," said Aigneis, "but there is nothing more I can tell you or give you. We will all be praying for the success of your mission."

The prince leaned over and kissed the old woman on her wrinkled cheek.

"I promise you, Lady Aigneis, I will destroy the Black Sorcerer and release this country and the princess from his thrall…" The prince took a quick breath. "Or I will die trying. I swear it on the souls of my two brothers."

And with that the prince mounted the horse and left the castle behind him without so much as a look back.

As the horse followed the path along the sea cliffs, Chrysteffor kept a wary eye in all directions. The fog was oppressive. He could not shake the feeling that something dangerous and evil lurked just beyond the distance where he could see. He still had not become accustomed to the constant darkness, and he was all too aware of the possibility of bandits like the ones who had killed Benet or, worse, the chance of encountering the same evil creatures that had killed Adryan. He strained to listen for the sound of anything that might not be his own horse's hoofs.

He found himself now wishing that he had allowed Ruaraidh to accompany him. He knew it was cowardly, but he would have liked to have had the boy's company—someone to talk to and another pair of eyes to peer through the gloom and watch for danger. If he could, he would have brought the boy to him at that very instant—in spite of the danger to the lad. Chrysteffor would not even have minded that the boy would inevitably be witnessing the fact that the prince was nowhere near as brave as he had pretended to be back at the castle.

The only sound that Chrysteffor could hear for certain—aside from the sound of the horse's hoofs on the ground and the accelerated breathing in his own chest—was the muffled crashing of waves on the rocks far below him. He thought of Eilís's brother Feidhlim and how painful his death must have been when he landed on those rocks after plunging from such a dizzying height. Chrysteffor hoped that the horse knew the path well enough not to wander over the edge in the dark.

For the life of him he could not stop his heart from racing. And this surprised him. He had expected to face this journey with nothing but calm resolve since he had accepted from the outset that he would not survive it. To his way of thinking, it was the hope of survival that was responsible for making an experience difficult to bear. Logically, the utter lack of all hope should eliminate that tension. After all, if he had already accepted his fate as a given, what was there to be anxious about? But what he had not counted on was the tension of not knowing the precise moment and manner of his death. Accepting one's fate, he was now realizing, did not alleviate the stress of wondering if this very moment—or perhaps the next—was the one in which he would die.

Moreover, there was the additional anxiety of wondering whether his death would be protracted or painful. He had hoped that his death, when it came, would be sudden and his dying would be over before he was aware of it. The more he thought of all the ways he might die, the faster his heart raced. In spite of having meant to accept his fate, he now found himself wishing that he had stayed back at the castle at the side of the sleeping princess. After all, as long as she was asleep, it did not really matter whether she thought him brave or cowardly.

As he continued his journey, the prince could not shake the persistent feeling that there were creatures lurking in the fog and watching him. He felt as though he could almost make out their shapes, but only out of the corner of his eye. If he turned to look directly, all he saw was swirling mist. No matter how hard he tried to train himself to pay no attention to these apparitions, he could not stop himself from quickly turning his head, first in one direction, then in the other, in an endless series of vain attempts to spot the phantoms.

He wondered, were they ghosts? Or spirits? Or simply products of a mind that was inexorably losing its grip on reality? All he knew was, the longer this went on, the sooner he feared he would descend into madness.

Eventually, he was able to make his mind go numb. He kept riding and convinced himself that this was all happening to someone else and not him. He stopped worrying about what dangers might be lurking in the dark fog. He lost track of time. He was certain he had been riding for hours, but for all he knew it might be days. Time had lost all meaning for him. At one point it suddenly dawned on him that he was hungry. He pulled a bit of bread from his rucksack and slowly chewed it. He was aware that he would need to take care not to use up his provisions too quickly.

After hours of tedium, he was suddenly startled to see a stone structure emerge from the swirling mists in front of him. He frankly had not expected to get this far, so it was actually a pleasant kind of surprise to find himself finally in a place he had hoped but never expected to reach. It also meant more uncertainty—about what was to come.

The horse stood motionless while Chrysteffor looked at the structure. It was definitely a tower. He judged that it was very tall, although the upper portion of it was well concealed in the fog. It was a round tower, not square like the ones they had in Alinvayl. The stonework was rough-hewn, and he could see no door or windows or any opening whatsoever. He wondered if it had been designed for a man to enter and, if so, how.

He got down from the horse, and secured its reins by tying them to a low branch on a tree. He did not want to take any chance of his mount wandering off and leaving him entirely on his own. Warily, he approached the tower on foot and studied it intently. It occurred to him that the prophecy Lady Aigneis had recounted was maddeningly vague. As he recalled, he was meant to be tested in each of the towers. Presumably, that meant he had to find a way inside. Or perhaps the test was merely to arrive at the tower. Maybe he had already passed the first test simply by standing there. Perhaps he should consider this a success and proceed on to the next tower.

In truth, Chrysteffor did not believe in the prophecy. Why should he? He himself did not grow up hearing the story. To him it was like a fable or something made up to amuse small children, but he was no small child and he was not a man of Afranor. The old story meant nothing to him. It made absolutely no sense that there should be any truth in it. And it certainly did not seem like a good reason to die needlessly.

If he had any sense, he thought to himself, he should consider his first "test" a success and simply ride on to the second and then the third tower. After that he should make his way back to Castle Aill Stoirm and proclaim his victory. If his visits to the towers did not result in the lifting of the curse of darkness or the spell over the princess, well, that would not be his fault. After all, he would have fulfilled what had been asked of him. The test of the three towers, after all, had not been his idea.

He was ready to remount his horse and continue his journey when it occurred to him that he should probably find something he could take away with him, something that would serve as proof that he had actually been there. After all, he had come all this way and risked so much, he did not want to waste it by having someone back at the castle accusing him of deception and of being responsible for the curse not being lifted. He looked around for some object that would provide incontrovertible evidence that he had been in this specific place.

The problem was there was really nothing but ground and stones. And the ground and stones looked like any other ground and stones in that country. Nothing really seemed unique to that particular spot.

He studied the tower. He could possibly chip off a bit of stone from the tower itself, but would that chip be any different than any other stone chip? He walked around the tower, looking for anything at all that might provide the proof he needed. He carefully examined its exterior from the ground to the upper reaches that melted into the mists above.

And finally he saw something. It was difficult to make out exactly what it was, but it was unusual enough that it just might serve as the proof he needed. It looked like two small pieces of wrought iron in curled shapes. One was bolted to the side of the tower several yards above his head. The other was entwined in the first, dangling in the slight breeze that kept stirring the mists. He judged that the dangling piece might be easy enough to pull free. He would just have to climb up to it. He was hopeful that, if he could bring that piece of iron with him, it would allay the doubt in anyone's mind he had been at the first of the three towers.

The stonework in the tower was uneven enough that he could climb up the side as far as he needed. The protruding bits of stone would provide enough places to get a foothold here and there as he climbed. He glanced around one last time to make sure the horse was still there and that none of those shapes, which he was still certain he had seen, had materialized. He began his ascent.

The side of the tower was damp and slick. Moss had accumulated in some of the more sheltered crevices. Chrysteffor had to be careful to keep from slipping as he made his way up. Fortunately, the stone was rough enough that it generally provided enough traction to keep his hands and boots from sliding off. He progressed slowly and deliberately, keeping his eye constantly on the prize above—not on the ground below. The smell of the damp stone filled his nose. It was not exactly pleasing. He could actually see the warmth of his breath turn to vapor as it touched the wetness. His sword, which hung from his waist and twisted and turned along his ascent, was a nuisance. He wondered if he should have left it below, but in the end he felt safer having it ready to hand.

Finally, the pieces of iron were within reach—if only just barely. He studied them to see how difficult it would be to separate the dangling piece from the bolted one. It could not be simply lifted out but, with a bit of turning and tugging he thought, it might well come loose. He made certain that he had a firm grasp on the side of the tower with his left hand and then reached with his right hand to grasp the piece of iron.

He took the dangling piece in his free hand. It was so unexpectedly cold that it gave him a shock. His fingers quickly began to go numb. He moved the piece in every direction he could, hoping it would slip out of the grasp of the other, like some simple puzzle. No matter how many different ways he moved it, though, it did not want to let go of its mate. Finally he aligned the dangling piece at a right angle to the fixed one, positioning the largest gap in the one against the narrowest part of the other.

Bracing himself as best he could against the side of the tower, Chrysteffor jerked the dangling piece of iron with all the strength he could manage. As he did so, one foot slipped, causing both feet to go flying into the air. He held on to the piece of iron with all his might and quickly brought his other hand over to grab hold of it as well. As he dangled there, he looked down and saw several yards of empty air between his feet and the mist swirling over the ground. He feared the piece he was hanging from would break free, causing him to fall. That would be one way to get his prize, he thought, but possibly at the cost of a broken arm or leg. The two pieces held together, however, and the prince continued dangling there. He did his best not to lose his grip as he tried to regain a foothold on the side of the tower. Try as he might, he could not get his foot to a place where it did not immediately slip off again.

As the strain on his arms began to wear him down, he wondered if he could drop down and land without seriously injuring himself. He knew there were stones below him, though he could not see them. If he landed on one of them, he could be hurt badly. The longer he hung there, the more it became clear he had no choice.

The pieces of iron he was hanging from began to give way. He presumed at first that the fixed piece was coming loose from the side of the tower, that his weight had put more strain on it than the bolts could take. But that was not the case. He could see that the iron piece was not bolted at all but was deeply embedded in the side of the tower. It was not coming loose but sliding down a groove in the tower's side. He could see that the groove in which the piece of iron was embedded had become so filled with dirt that it had ceased to be a groove at all. Now his weight was forcing the piece of iron down the groove, clearing the obstruction.

Chrysteffor could hear stone grinding against stone. At first he thought the tower was collapsing, but as he was slowly lowered toward the ground, he could see a portion of the tower wall shift simultaneously with his descent. He let go of the iron, took hold of the repositioned wall, and scrambled back down to the ground.

For a few moments he stood and pondered the situation. It had been the weight of his body that had forced the iron piece to move and cause a section of the tower wall to shift. It was as though the tower were some sort of machine that could be opened by pulling a handle. *How clever those ancient people of Afranor were*, he thought, *to have devised something as elaborate and amazing as this*. But why was the handle so high and difficult to get to, he wondered? It occurred to him that there had probably been a rope hanging from it which the tower's occupants could pull when they wanted to open the door. Apparently the rope had long since been removed or, more likely, disintegrated with the passing of many years.

He wondered how the door was meant to be closed but quickly decided not to waste time with that question. He had no interest in closing the door—only in opening it wide enough so he could pass through. Chrysteffor was so happy with himself for working out the puzzle, he had completely forgotten that a few moments before he had actually had no intention of entering the tower.

He remembered the rope he had left in his rucksack and was glad he had decided not to leave it behind. He threw the coiled rope over his shoulder and climbed back up the tower wall. He then tied one end of it to the dangling piece of iron and let the other end drop. Back on the ground, he tied loose end to the horse's saddle and led the horse away from the tower. The strength of the horse, together with his own weight guiding the rope toward the ground, forced the lever downward. To the prince's delight, he saw the wall shift further, creating an opening. As soon as he could see that the gap was wide enough for him to pass through, he stopped the horse and retrieved his rope.

With the horse again secured, Chrysteffor approached the tower's opening warily. Up until now he had been pleased with his discovery and the fact that he had made an entrance for himself. Now he had to decide if he would actually go inside the tower. It had suited him when it appeared that there was no way of entering it. Now that it was possible, there were new questions to contend with.

He had nothing to show people back at the castle that would prove he had been to the tower. He could, however, describe to them how he had solved the riddle of the tower to create an entrance. If anyone doubted him, they could journey to this spot and see for themselves that the entrance had indeed been made.

Something unexpected then happened in the young prince's mind. Having come this far and having had this much success, he found that he was emboldened. Moreover, he found that he was curious. He was in fact quite keen to learn what was inside the tower. Maybe there was nothing at all. Maybe it was dark and empty and contained nothing more than musty smells. In his heart, this is what he believed and expected, but he wanted to know for sure. He wanted to see it for himself. On the other hand, what if there were some terrible danger inside? As unlikely as that seemed—after all the tower had clearly been closed up for ages—he did feel afraid. It would be dark in there. And who knew if something had managed to live and survive inside for all this time?

In the end, the prince settled the debate that he was having with himself by remembering his original reason for undertaking the quest— that he was probably going to die anyway. His luck so far had lured him into thinking of ways to survive, but that kind thinking was a mistake. Moreover, something was different now. He was curious. What was inside the tower? If he was going to die, he might as well die satisfying his curiosity. He was also starting to wonder if there was something to the old prophecy. Could Lady Eilís's salvation really lie inside that stone structure? He had come this far. He might as well find out.

Chrysteffor peered through the gap in the side of the tower. It was not merely dark inside. It was blacker than pitch black. It was as though light had never once intruded inside the structure—and never would. It was as though the space inside was not part of the world. It was not just an absence of light. It was more the absence of existence. It made the young prince shudder but, now that he had made up his mind, he would not be deterred.

He searched the stony ground around the tower until he found what he was looking for—a piece of a fallen tree branch. He retrieved the flint stone from his rucksack and made a spark to set the piece of wood aflame. Not wanting to waste any of the burning branch's light and not wanting to think too much about his decision, he quickly slipped through the opening and entered the tower.

6
The Dead Tower

EVEN WITH the light from his crude torch, Chrysteffor could see little or nothing inside the tower. By the time he had taken two steps inside, he could not make out the opening he had just passed through. He wondered how he would find his way back out, but he decided not worry about that for the time being. He just wanted to explore the inside of the tower as thoroughly but as quickly as he could and then leave again. He just wanted to know in his heart that he had done everything that had been asked of him.

He crept cautiously next to the inside wall, using one hand to feel his way along the stony surface. Since he could see nothing, he reckoned that circling the periphery of the room was the best he could do.

It was not long, though, before the utter lack of light began to have a disorienting effect on him. He felt as though he had left the world altogether, that there was no up or down or any other direction. In addition to not being able to see anything, he could not hear anything—except for his own breathing, which seemed to be echoing on the inside of his ears. His footsteps made no sound, and that seemed strange to him. In the pervasive gloom, he could not be sure there was even a floor beneath him. The result was that he felt a constant need to lean against the wall to ward off a persistent sensation of dizziness.

The prince proceeded along the wall for what seemed to him to be an unreasonably long time. After all, the tower was not exceedingly large. It should not have required so much time for him to circle its interior. He could come up with no explanation for why it was taking so long. Furthermore, the lack of vision or sound was beginning to play tricks on his mind. At one panicky moment, he convinced himself that he had been inside the tower for hours or maybe even days and that the tower's interior did not obey the same laws of nature that existed in the outside world. In the tower, his alarmed mind told him, it appeared to be possible to follow the wall endlessly—without ever coming back to the point where he had started.

He became convinced that the opening through which he had come had somehow sealed itself up and that there was no way out. In his fear, he had the impulse to leave the wall altogether and to run straight in the direction where he thought the exit might be. Yet he knew that, if he did that, he would become yet more disoriented, without the wall next to him to give him some bearing. He swallowed hard and kept proceeding in the same direction—trusting that he would eventually come back to the gap in the wall.

Suddenly it struck him that there was a noise—and not one caused by him. He stood motionless to listen. He heard nothing and presumed that he had imagined it. When he took another step, though, he heard it again. It was like a scraping sound—like someone's heavy boot being dragged along the stone floor. He froze again, and again everything went quiet. His heart sped up. Was he imagining things or was he not alone?

He took his hand away from the wall and put it on his sword's hilt, as he continued to listen. There was still no sound, apart from his own breathing. The thought that there could be a man or a creature standing in the dark, just outside his limited vision, preyed on his mind. He held the torch out, as far as his arm would extend, toward the interior of the tower. He nervously studied the darkness, trying to make out any shape that might be lurking there.

And then he saw it. Or at least he thought he did. He thought he had caught the nearly imperceptible shift of a shadow in the darkness. He took a step away from the wall and toward the interior, and he strained to stretch his arm farther in front of him. He stood completely still and studied the emptiness.

This time he saw the motion without question. There was definitely something there—something at least as large as himself. For a moment, he wondered if the horse had somehow followed him inside, but he quickly dismissed that idea. The horse's reins were well secured and, in any event, there is no way it could have fit through the gap. Chrysteffor had opened it only wide enough for himself to pass through. Moreover, the horse would undoubtedly have too much sense to venture inside such a forbidding place. No, whatever was in front of him had actually been waiting for him—perhaps for a very long time.

Chrysteffor saw no other course than to confront whatever was standing there. He drew his sword and took another step toward the interior, peering ahead. He took another step. That is when he saw it. It was a man, but not a normal man. The shock of what he saw made him drop what little remained of his torch. The ebbing light it gave from below illuminated the figure's legs and lower torso. Chrysteffor could not believe what he thought he had seen, but the clothes that the figure wore were all too familiar to the prince.

He took another step forward and, with a trembling voice, called weakly, "Adryan?"

The sound of his voice seemed to evaporate immediately into the dark. It died in the oppressive gloom and made him feel as if he had made no sound at all.

The figure did not move or answer. Chrysteffor kicked the barely burning torch closer to the figure, throwing a tiny bit more light on him. The clothes and body were definitely his brother's, but the head was not right. As the prince looked in horror, he realized that he was indeed looking into Adryan's face, but it was not the face of a living man. It was the face of a corpse, and it rested at a strange angle on top of his shoulders—as if it had been hastily stitched onto his body.

Suddenly the thing that had been Adryan shifted a foot clumsily toward Chrysteffor. The prince searched the face for some glint of recognition, but it did not seem to be looking at him at all. Instead it stared blankly and uncomprehendingly at some distant point in the darkness. There was no sign that any vestige of Adryan's mind or spirit was present in the battered body.

In his shock Chrysteffor lost his balance and stumbled to the floor. He had left Castle Aill Stoirm fully expecting to die. He had thought that acceptance would ward off all fear because, if one accepts death, what is possibly left to fear? Now he knew that were things worse than mere death. He looked upon the thing that had been his brother, and his soul ached thinking of the hell in which his brother's soul now dwelt. The terrors in this cursed country had transcended death. There was no eluding it, and not even death itself was an escape. His head now felt as if it had become weightless, and he knew he was on the verge of passing out. He drew on all the will he could muster to stay conscious. He took slow, deliberate and deep breaths, and then he struggled back to his feet. A few tears seeped from his eyes, and then he staunched them with anger. Rage, he realized, was the only alternative to surrender and helplessness.

"Ye gods!" screamed Chrysteffor. "Adryan, what have they done to you?"

Distraught, Chrysteffor answered his own question.

"They have made you one of those... those things," he wailed. "One of what Lady Eilís called the Eidola. How could they do this to you? How could they not let you rest in peace?"

Countless memories of his brother's life flowed through his mind in an instant. They made him angrier still, but now the time had come to act.

The thing that had once been his brother was wielding a sword, and it was now raising it for an attack. With surprising speed the thing delivered a blunt blow with its blade. Chrysteffor barely managed to avoid being split in two by the brutish force of the blow.

Despite his natural hesitation to fight back, the prince accepted that his own life was at stake and he resolved to do whatever he had to in order to survive. The problem was that he had no idea how to fight something that was not even alive. As he pondered his dilemma, the thing raised its sword for another lunge. This time the flat of the blade struck Chrysteffor's back as he tried to avoid the blow as best he could, and he was knocked to the ground. He looked up to see the thing that had been his brother preparing to deliver a death blow and immediately rolled out of the way as fast as he possibly could. He put all thoughts of hesitation out of his mind and accepted that this was not his brother but an evil creature that desired nothing in this moment but his imminent death. He put all of his memories of his beloved Adryan out of his mind and leapt to his feet with his sword drawn.

"You always wanted me to be a warrior!" he yelled at the uncomprehending monster. "The same as you and Benet. You always told me I was wasting my time on music and verse, that they would be of no use when my life was at stake. Well, for what it is worth, I have now learned the lesson you wanted to teach me. You and I shall see whether an unwilling student's lifetime of training can defeat what you have now become. What an irony that making you die a second time might be the thing that at last would have made you proud of me!"

He began aggressively lunging at his adversary while constantly moving out of the way of its counter-attack. His advantage, or so he believed, was that the enemy was slow and lumbering. Surely, he thought, he would have no trouble avoiding its clumsy thrusts. But the prince was alarmed to note that, the longer the fight went on, the faster the creature seemed to move. It was if, the more energy Chrysteffor expended in battle, the more his foe absorbed for its own use. Wasting no time, the prince lunged frantically over and over. Though he succeeded in piercing the thing's body more than once with his blade, the wounds did not slow the creature's movements in the slightest. It gave no sign that it felt any pain or, for that matter, annoyance at being pierced.

How can I have any hope against an enemy that cannot be wounded or killed? despaired the prince.

He could see no choice but to keep fighting and to keep wounding the creature—even if the effort seemed pointless. After all, to do anything else would be tantamount to accepting a quick death. He could attempt to flee, but he had no idea where to search for the gap in the wall. And if he moved beyond the illumination of the torch he would be wandering blindly. He would not be able to see the thing as it attacked him.

Since its eyes gave no sign of having or using vision, he had to assume that it did not need to see and could operate as equally well in the dark as in the light. The prince could see little hope for his situation, but he could see less hope in fleeing into the dark. The problem was that it was only a matter of time until he began to tire and his movements would gradually slow. And the more slowly he moved, the sooner and more likely that the creature would succeed in injuring him and then killing him. But he could not think about that. He could only deal with the precise instant in time in which he was living, and that meant fighting on—without taking the time to think ahead.

Chrysteffor was surprised to feel a sudden gust of ice-cold wind. He could not think where it could have come from. As far as he had been able to tell, the tower was completely sealed, with no windows or doors. The only possible place where wind could have come from was the gap he had made, and that was so narrow that he could not imagine such a major gust blowing in. Stranger still was the effect that the wind had on the torch. It fanned the flame on the branch and made it burn larger and glow a hundred times brighter. Suddenly he could see much more of the tower's interior—not that it did him much good. There was nothing to see but more of the stone floor and gloomy empty space.

Chrysteffor continued the battle. The creature grew ever more agile—as if it were somehow drawing Chrysteffor's youth and liveliness away from him. A lucky swipe with the thing's sword ripped a hole in the arm of the prince's garment. Another well-placed thrust actually drew blood from his thigh.

This is not going well at all, thought Chrysteffor, as he did his best to keep his spirit up and not lose heart.

As the prince continued his dance to avoid any further injuries, he noted that the sword his dead brother was wielding was not his customary one. He wondered if this was of some significance. Where did Adryan's own sword go, and where had he gotten this one? The blade was extremely well polished. At least it seemed so, since it reflected the torch's light brightly. It was almost as if the sword were glowing.

Another close call had Chrysteffor jumping out of the glowing sword's way and, in his exhaustion, he tripped. He looked up in a panic as the thing came for him. He felt more terror still when he noticed that there was someone else standing behind the creature.

As quick as he could, he leapt back to his feet while avoiding another thrust from the glowing sword. He had no time yet to worry about the other figure he saw—only a scant moment to wonder if it was yet another adversary or, hope against all hope, someone who might help him. He would know soon enough.

He continued his game of dancing back and forth and occasionally inflicting an incision into a creature that paid no attention to such injuries. As he moved around, he caught sight of the second figure, and his heart nearly leapt out of his chest. He had to maneuver around for a second glance to be sure of what he saw, but there was no doubt.

It was Benet.

His first thought was that this was good news. He thought that it must mean that Benet was alive, that Chrysteffor had been mistaken and, in his hysteria, had buried him alive. There would be much teasing in the years to come over how the panicky young Chrysteffor thought his brother was dead and dug him a grave and left him there—only to learn later that he had never died at all and that he had to dig his way out of the ground and come looking for him and together they defeated that creature that had been their brother Adryan.

"Benet!" called Chrysteffor. "Thank the gods you are here. I do not know how you found me, but I am grateful that you did. Help me fight this creature. It may look like our brother, but it is not. It is an abomination created by the Black Sorcerer. I have so much to tell you. I have learned so many things in this strange country."

Chrysteffor wondered why Benet did not answer him, but in his heart he knew the reason. Every glance he stole while in he heat of the battle only confirmed what he feared. Benet had the same dead stare as Adryan. Benet was indeed dead. And, like Adryan, he had been reanimated and made into one of the creatures. Chrysteffor was barely holding his own against one foe, and now he had a second one with which to contend. His battle for survival was now all but over.

Like Adryan before, Benet was lumbering slowly, but Chrysteffor had no doubt that he would gradually be picking up speed, just as Adryan had. Preoccupied as he had been with the battle, the prince had been able to avoid dwelling on the hopelessness of his situation, but now he could avoid it no longer. There was absolutely no hope for him. This is where it ended. And his death would come at the hands of two creatures that had once been his own brothers.

He could not think of a reason why he should not simply drop his sword and stand still and allow the end to come quickly—rather than drawing it out. Yet for some reason he could not bring himself to cease his efforts. Just as the thought of dropping his sword had flashed through his mind, the thing that had been Adryan knocked his sword from his hand with a swing of the glowing blade.

Sorely missing his sword, Chrysteffor jumped and twisted to avoid the thrusts and blows of the creatures, while trying to get to where his weapon had fallen so he could attempt to retrieve it. To his frustration, the creatures had positioned themselves on top of it so that he could not get close without being cut down. Benet's mace hung from his belt but, as he had precious little experience with that weapon, he dearly preferred to have his sword once again in hand.

It's just a matter time, moments really, thought the prince, *until it is over. I am fast running out of strategies to try.*

Unexpectedly, though, he found that having two adversaries could actually be something of an advantage—at least for a while. Despite his growing fatigue, he discovered that he could jump quickly enough to put one of the creatures in the way of the other when they tried to assault him. He knew, however, that this would not last. He had no doubt that they would inevitably learn to work together against him—just as they had seemed to learn to move faster by fighting him. His only hope, as far as he could see, was to somehow retrieve his sword.

As he did his strange dance of trying to avoid the attacks of the creatures—Adryan with his glowing sword and Benet with a roughhewn club—he hoped desperately for an opportunity to grab his own weapon. Before that could happen, though, Benet surprised him with a glancing blow against his forearm. His arm throbbing with pain, Chrysteffor swung around and resisted the advance the only way he could—with a quick kick to the knee. He missed and nearly fell in the attempt. As he swung back around, he spotted Adryan bringing his arm around for a blow. Quickly, the prince gave another kick, this time in the other direction, and to his surprise his foot knocked the sword from Adryan's hand. Seizing his chance, he scrambled forward and put his hand on it. Perhaps there was a bit of hope after all.

He had but a moment to admire the strange weapon he had unexpectedly acquired. It felt surprisingly light and warm to the touch. Its strange ghostly glow would have entranced him—if he had had time for admiring it. Instead, he went back to his previous strategy of thrusting at his opponents with his blade. Unfortunately, Adryan had become extremely agile by this point. He could move nearly as fast as the smaller and younger Chrysteffor, but the prince kept it up and, finally, managed to stick the blade into the thing's thigh. To the prince's amazement and delight, the thing staggered, as though it were feeling pain or, at any rate, had been injured.

Chrysteffor stole a quick glance at his blade. It seemed to be glowing brighter than before. He had little time to work out what was happening, but he sensed that there was some sort of enchantment in the blade. It was actually capable of hurting the creatures, whereas his own ordinary sword had not been. Encouraged by this lucky turn of events, he threw himself into the fight with greater energy.

Now his strategy was to stab and puncture the two creatures at each and every opportunity that presented itself. And this yielded results, as the creatures were prone to stumble and wander every time that his blade found a mark on their bodies. For the first time the young prince felt as though he were in a true fight and not merely staving off his own inevitable defeat. Still, he had to wonder whether being able to injure his opponents really did him any good if they were able to continue fighting in spite of everything he could do. Was there no way to stop them or—and this thought seemed strangely meaningless, given that his opponents were already dead—kill them?

When the opportunity at last presented itself, Chrysteffor plunged the glowing sword into Benet's breast. It was a wound that would have killed any man and, indeed, it did cause the creature that had been Benet to stop and stagger as if he were seriously injured. Too soon, though, he recovered and was quickly back in the fight. Then, a few moments later, the opportunity presented itself for Chrysteffor to bring his blade down on Adryan's wrist. The force of the blow severed the creature's hand from his arm. The young prince half-expected to see blood come pouring out of the wound, but none appeared. And Adryan barely slowed in his battle against the man who had once been his brother.

Nothing he was doing was having any effect—certainly not as it would have had on a mortal man. There was nothing left to try but the one thing that Chrysteffor had hoped he would not have to do. And the prince was by no means sure that he could manage it or whether it would make any difference, even if he could. But he knew he would have to at least try.

He kept up his dance and got in a jab when and where he could—all the time waiting for the opportunity for a serious attack. Finally, he saw that he had a clear shot at Adryan. He grasped his sword firmly with both hands and swung around in a circle with as much force as he could. As he spun around, he aimed the blade squarely at the thing's neck. He felt the force of his weapon strike and then tear through the sinews of the creature's throat. The collision made his hand ache. The sight of the blade tearing into his brother's neck made his heart ache. The sword did not sever the neck entirely, but it left the creature's head dangling precariously in front of its collarbone.

Still the monster continued the fight. Though it was not defeated, the thing did seem disoriented. In fact it was at a distinct disadvantage. Wasting no time, Chrysteffor spun around again for another strike at the creature's neck, but he was tripped by Benet, who had taken advantage of the young prince's focus on Adryan. Quickly, Chrysteffor scrambled back to his feet and out of the way of Benet's attack.

Luck was with him in that he was able to give Benet a kick to the side and send him sprawling. That gave Chrysteffor the time he needed to spin around and deliver a conclusive blow to the other creature. With a sickening impact of his sword against what remained of its neck, he managed to send the thing's head flying. It tumbled through the air and into the darkness, where he could hear a dull thud once it had landed. The prince paused for a moment to see what would happen next.

The headless body stood motionless in front of him—as if in shock. The next few seconds seemed to last an eternity. He half-expected the creature to keep fighting—even without a head. He was relieved to see it topple over and fall in a heap on the ground.

Chrysteffor could not believe that this part of the battle was over. He had actually succeeded in stopping one of the creatures. He had scant time to enjoy his victory before the thing that had been Benet lumbered back to its feet and was resuming its attack with seemingly fresh energy. Fortunately, Chrysteffor had renewed energy as well. His triumph over at least one of his adversaries had given him encouragement and hope.

The two rejoined their battle. Chrysteffor hoped that he would be able to dispatch Benet with no more trouble than he had Adryan. (As much as he tried not to, he found himself continuing to identify the creatures as his brothers.) After all, he had only one opponent to fight now. That should have made things simpler, but Benet was showing much more vigor than Adryan had. It was as if whatever force had been animating Adryan had now been transferred from his useless body and into Benet's, doubling his energy. The creature was moving surprisingly quickly and seeming to anticipate the young prince's every move. Chrysteffor knew that, if the creature managed to land his club against his skull, he would be killed instantly.

After a few near misses, the creature succeeded in grazing Chrysteffor's crown with a glancing swing of its weapon. The prince tumbled to the floor and nearly blacked out. He fought to stay conscious, knowing full well that he would never wake up if he closed his eyes, even for a moment. A voice in his head wondered whether it would not be easier if he did close his eyes and let it all come to an end. Yet his defeat of the creature that had been Adryan had given him something he had not had since arriving in Afranor. It had given him hope. He wanted to live, and he was now determined not to give up without fighting to the last. At least now he had an enemy in front of him with which to do battle. No more waiting for something to surprise him by leaping out of the darkness. He was in the midst of battle now, and all he had to do from this point on was to not give up.

Chrysteffor threw himself back into the fight against the thing that looked like his brother but which reeked of everything that was unholy. There was absolutely no hesitation now. He knew that the creature he was fighting was not his brother, and he was determined to kill it or—given that it was not properly alive in any meaningful sense—do whatever he had to to stop it from fighting him.

As the creature swung the club at him again, he reached out with one hand and caught it in mid-air. The pain from absorbing the force of its momentum against his palm was excruciating, but his mind was no longer focused on any pain he was feeling. With stubborn determination he grabbed the club and pulled it out of the creature's hand. Now his opponent was unarmed and Chrysteffor had his opportunity. He flung the club to the ground and swung around with all his strength to bring the sword's blade against the thing's neck.

The creature fell to the ground, its head barely attached to its body. It sickened Chrysteffor to see the corpse that was, to all appearances, his brother's lying there in that defiled state. Its arm made a motion to pull itself up. Without hesitation, the prince lifted his sword and brought it down swiftly to finish the job of severing the head. He stabbed the thing's torso—just for good measure.

Panting loudly, he stood there, waiting and watching to see if the thing moved again. After a few minutes he was satisfied it was at last truly finished and he allowed himself to relax. He tried to catch his breath as he thought of the fight he had been through and which seemed to have begun hours before. He had no true sense of time or how long he had been in the tower.

All the emotions he had suppressed during the fight came rushing into his head and into his heart. He mourned for his brothers all over again. He ached over the grief his father would have when he learned of the many terrible things that had happened. The enormity of it all overwhelmed the prince. He threw himself on the floor of the tower and sobbed uncontrollably and inconsolably.

7
The Nightmare Tower

CHRYSTEFFOR HAD no idea how long he had lain weeping in the dark. He was only glad that there was no one to witness his weakness.

Now he accepted the fact that, the sooner he was out of that cursed place, the better it would be for him. He stumbled to his feet and picked up the sword. Even covered as it was with the remnants of his now vanquished opponents, the light from the blade shone and illuminated a bit of the darkness around him.

He wanted another look at the corpses on the ground, to be sure that they were truly without life, but he could not see them. The remnants of his torch that had been dropped to the floor had long since burnt away, so he was all but blind in the darkness. He could not be certain whether he had stepped away from where his adversaries had fallen and had thus simply lost sight of them in the gloom—or whether they had actually vanished, as if by some magic. He knew he would be curious about it later and might come to regret that he had not taken more time to investigate, but for now he wanted only to escape the evil and foul place in which he found himself.

He held up the sword and let its dim light shine on the space around him. He then walked in the direction that felt to him as though it should lead him back to the point where he had entered. In a surprisingly brief amount of time he was back at the gap in the wall where he had first come through. It seemed as though the tower had somehow grown in size while he was wandering along the wall but had shrunk back to its normal size now that the battle was over.

He slipped through the gap and felt the cold fresh air of the outdoors on his face. He took a deep breath. As dark as it was outside, it was a relief to be away from the more intense darkness inside the tower and, most of all, away from its sickening air.

He was relieved to see that the horse was where he had left it. He had had a fear of it being gone and of him being left stranded and alone on foot. Luckily enough and to all appearances, he had not attracted the attention of anyone—or anything—during his journey from Aill Stoirm to the first tower—in spite of his nagging feeling of constantly being watched.

Tempted as he was to rest awhile before continuing on to the second tower, he decided that it was probably best not to delay. His success—or at least survival—in the first tower encouraged him to proceed with no delay to the next one in the hope that his luck would hold out. He mounted the horse and then let it find its way northward on the path along the sea cliff.

The fears that had dogged him during his journey to the first tower were still there. He continued to be plagued with the sense that he was being watched and that something or someone lurked just outside his field of vision. He was more resigned to it now, but he continued to be wary. At the same time he was determined not to let his fears overwhelm him. To that end, as he rode along, he concentrated his mind on what had happened in the first tower.

He wondered how those things that had been his brothers had come to be in the tower, waiting for him. Was it by pure chance? Did they just happen to wander across the countryside and arrive at that spot by nothing more than pure coincidence? That seemed unlikely. Moreover, how had they found their way inside the tower? There was no way to go in or out until Chrysteffor had arrived and found the mechanism for making the wall part. Or was there perhaps some other hidden way to go in?

No, there was clearly some sort of design behind the fact that he and the animated corpses of his brothers had all come to be in the same place at the same time. He wondered if there might not, after all, be something to Lady Aigneis's talk of a prophecy. He had to admit that it was exceedingly strange that the prophecy would mention someone with eyes of different colors. He had never in his entire life met or heard of someone else with eyes like his, and that caused him to consider that there might actually be something larger at work here—something that he did not fully comprehend.

Lady Aigneis had spoken of the towers as a series of tests. If so, who or what was being tested? Was fighting his brothers some sort of test for him? Had he passed the test? And what would be the next test? He shuddered to think of how he could be tested more than he had already been, but he was curious. He actually wanted to know what was to be found at the second tower. He wanted answers to his questions. And that meant riding forward. He no longer had any thoughts about turning back. If the prophecy was real and the tests were real, then the rest of the story might be real too. His quest might really release Lady Eilís from the spell that had ensnared her. With that as the goal, there was no way that he was not going to finish the quest.

The possibility that this all might be part of his own personal destiny excited him. His mind raced as he kept reliving everything that had happened to him since he came to Afranor. All this—and the possibility that his many questions might actually get answered—made the time pass faster for him. Hours went by as he rode along, but he barely felt them.

And then he saw the second tower emerge from the mist. It looked much like the first tower. In fact, he wondered for a few moments if he had not somehow doubled back and actually returned to the first tower. He put that thought out of his mind since he had constantly had the sea to his left throughout the journey. It was impossible for him to be back at the same spot.

Wasting no time, he dismounted and walked around the tower. He saw the familiar iron arm up high, protruding out of the tower's wall. This time he would not have to waste any time figuring out how to get inside. He already knew. He retrieved his rope and scrambled up to tie it to the arm. He was then quickly back on the ground and tying the other end of the rope to the horse. In no time he had opened the hidden door to the second tower.

He carefully made sure the horse was secure and then walked to the entrance and peered in. He could see nothing but black. He braced himself mentally. The thought of what he might find inside both terrified him and tortured him with curiosity.

In the end, he thought to himself, *what could possibly lie inside this foul place that would be worse than meeting my two slain brothers and having to slay them all over again myself? After going through that, nothing again could ever be so dreadful. Surely, whatever tests I am to endure in the remaining towers, the worst of it must surely lie behind me. There is no point in being afraid now.*

And with that he slipped inside the entrance and into the inky darkness.

As before, he could see almost nothing, but at least this time his vision extended a bit farther because he had the dim light emanating from his blade. It gave him more of a feeling of security, not only because of the bit of extra light it provided but mostly because he knew it was an effective weapon against the Eidola. In contrast to his experience in the first tower, this time he felt much less like a victim in waiting.

Again, he followed the edge of the interior wall, all the time wondering if and when he would see something or when he might be attacked. As in the first tower, he was bothered by the fact that his sense of hearing was muffled. And this had the same disorienting effect as before. For some reason his sense of balance was upset by not being able to hear his own footfalls. He continued his progress along the wall, though, confident that it was only a matter of time until he would finally see something—or it would see him.

He then heard the sound. It was like a scream. Yes, he realized as the moments passed, it was indeed a scream. It was a woman's scream. And there was something all too familiar about it. It was difficult to tell exactly where it was coming from, but it was definitely coming from the deep interior of the tower, well away from the wall. He raised the sword and extended his arm in an effort to see as far into the interior as he could, but there was nothing to see. It was all perfect blackness. As the silence oppressed his ears, he began to wonder if he had imagined the scream.

He heard it again. It was a cry of terror. The sound of it made his stomach turn and sent a sickening feeling along the muscles inside his body, but he fought the fear and steeled himself.

If this is a test, thought Chrysteffor, *then I might as well go and be tested.* And with that he left the comfort of the wall he had kept close to and stepped cautiously toward the center of the tower's interior. He tried not to think too specifically about what he was heading toward. Still, he could not help but wonder who was screaming and—more worryingly—why she was screaming.

As the seconds passed in silence, he began to wonder if he was imagining things. He then heard the scream once more and louder than before. It seemed extremely close now. He kept trying to work out why the scream seemed familiar.

"No! No!"

Now he could make out words.

"Keep away! Keep away!"

I have heard this before, he thought. *And only recently.*

He quickened his steps toward the interior. *How*, he wondered, *can it be possible. It makes no sense. Am I losing my mind?*

The cries grew louder and closer together. This made it easier for him to move in the direction of their source. Before long he spotted a figure standing in the darkness. It was indeed a woman. Her back was turned to him. Was it really who it seemed to be? Chrysteffor's voice caught in his throat, as he numbly called to her.

"Lady Eilís?"

She did not turn around or otherwise behave as if she had heard him. Instead she cried out again, "No! No! Keep away!"

Those are the words she was crying in her sleep, thought Chrysteffor. *The words she was calling out in her fevered dream. But she is awake now. Why is she still calling them out? And how did she get from the castle to here? None of it makes any sense. This evil place must be driving me insane!*

He stepped closer to her. He extended his hand to touch her, to see if she was real or merely a figment of his imagination. As he came close enough to touch her, though, he could see what she was looking at—and why she was screaming in terror.

In the gloom beyond her, Chrysteffor made out a massive shape looming above the two of them. It was a hideous creature. Covered with scales, its mouth was gaping wide and displaying multiple rows of sharp teeth. It was not unlike a lizard but well beyond the size of an elephant. It let out a roar and flames spewed from its mouth.

A dragon! I have heard of them in tales, but not since I was a small child have I believed they truly exist. It must be some sort of illusion.

The prince laid his hand on Eilís's shoulder. She still gave no indication that she was aware of his presence.

In spite of the fearsome sight in front of him and of his own fear, Chrysteffor's heart leapt with something like happiness. He could not believe that, so unexpectedly, the woman he loved was in front of him. If only he could work out how and why she was there. That she was awake and beside him seemed much too good to be true, but any feeling of joy was overwhelmed by confusion.

"Eilís, how did you get here? Who brought you here away from the castle?"

She did not respond to him. She only released another scream.

Because the existence of the monster and its presence in that place seemed so unlikely, Chrysteffor did his best to convince himself that it was some sort of false apparition. No other explanation made any sense to him.

"It is all right, Eilís. It is not real. You do not need to be afraid."

In truth, he was unnerved to see Eilís so afraid. His first encounter with her had left him in no doubt that she was the bravest warrior he had ever met. He could never have imagined her being afraid of anything, even of a creature as large and fearsome as this one. He then saw the true source of her fear. She was manacled to chains that were bolted to the floor. She had no way to defend herself or to fight the creature. She was completely helpless.

"It is some sort of trick, Eilís," he said again. "It is not real. There is no need to be afraid."

Of course, these words were meant to convince himself more than her. As unlikely as it all was, at the same time it felt—and gave every indication of being—real. Chrysteffor did his best to stifle his fear and chose to rely on reason rather than capitulate to his overwhelmed senses.

The monster let out another roar and another ball of flame. It reached as far as the prince's arm, and his sleeve caught fire. He could feel the flame burning his flesh. He threw himself on the floor and smothered the fire under his body.

His arm ached where it had been burned. He studied the black area on his skin and the blisters that were forming around it.

If this is a mere illusion, he thought, *then it is an excellent one. This arm is no longer any good to me.*

And thus the prince realized he had no choice but to treat the monster as real—and to do his best not allow it to scorch him again. His first thought was to find a way to free Eilís. He had no doubt that she would be more effective at fighting the dragon than he, but the chains that bound her were too heavy for him to break without a blacksmith's tools. It was clear that he would have to be the one to fight this battle and he would have to do so alone and unaided. And the life of the woman he loved would hang in the balance.

The lizard reared its head in preparation for another burst of flame. Wasting no time, Chrysteffor darted off to one side—partly to draw the fire away from Eilís and partly to be in motion so as to avoid the blast himself. The river of fire inevitably erupted, and the prince was relieved to find that he had successfully avoided it altogether this time.

He could see that his main advantage over the monster was that, while it was very large, it was also lumbering and slow. As long as he did not tire, he should have no trouble keeping out of the way of its fiery blasts. The problem was that he would tire eventually, and then what? He had to find a way to attack the creature and wound it or, preferably, slay it. Given its size, that did not seem a hopeful prospect.

Eilís screamed again, "No! No! Keep away! Keep away!"

She keeps crying the same words, wondered the prince. *Why does she not recognize that I am here? Why does she keep calling out, as she did when she was dreaming?*

And then it dawned on him. As he danced across the floor to avoid another burst of flame, he finally worked it out. As fantastic as it sounded, Eilís was still dreaming. She was probably in fact still on the same bed in the castle where he had left her. By some sort of enchantment, he had entered into her dream. He had done enough dreaming in his own time to know that dreams never made much sense, and this one certainly did not.

Somehow he was taking part in her dream and he now had the opportunity to affect it.

So this is my second test then, he thought. *I must fight the battle that my darling Eilís cannot. And if I fail, then I suspect that there is no hope of her ever waking up. And if I succeed? Will she then find herself awake back in the castle? Will she remember me being in her dream and being her champion?*

He quite liked the idea of her waking and recalling him acting bravely in her dream. Then, suddenly, another burst of flame came unexpectedly close enough to singe the ends of his long blond hair and to make him realize that he had better stop imagining his future victory and instead focus on the task at hand—or else the only thing the princess might eventually remember from her dream was how she had witnessed him becoming a charred corpse. One thing of which he was fairly certain was that, if the dragon should kill him, his death would be no dream. He had no doubt at all that he would be just as cold and dead as if it were not happening in a dream.

Enough time passed between the bursts of flame to suggest to Chrysteffor that the dragon needed to rest a few minutes before exhaling more fire. Any attack on the creature would have to happen during one of those brief periods. When he saw the monster preparing to bellow again, he dashed across the floor, partly to evade the onslaught and partly to circle around and bring himself closer to the thing's feet. Worryingly, the creature seemed to be making itself more accurate in its outbursts.

The heat roared so close to Chrysteffor's head that his cheeks burned and turned sore. He did not let this slow him down. He raced to the toes of the creature and plunged his sword into its foot. His burned arm throbbed with pain, but he forced himself to ignore the aching. The dragon's reaction was immediate. It bellowed in pain and reared up on its haunches. Though no fire emerged as it roared, there was still a sickening heat blasting out of its gaping mouth. The prince feared that the sweltering air and foul sulfur smell might actually overwhelm him and cause him to pass out. That would surely be the end of him, and perhaps the princess as well.

By this point he was feeling foolish for having wasted precious moments in a daydream about rescuing Lady Eilís. He could see no way to defeat the monster and so far had only succeeded in provoking it into a mad rage. The dragon spun its head to one side and then the other in its anger. The prince quickly backed away to avoid being crushed by its stomping feet. He could see that another burst of flame was imminent and so ran as fast as he could to avoid being too easy a target. In the end he had to dive to the ground to avoid being seared over his entire body.

As it was, he felt as though, even through his clothes, his back was being burned.

His heart pounding in his chest, he was filled with terror over how close he had come to a painful death. At the same time he was now also angry. He was angry about being in this tower and about seeing the woman he loved being terrorized and, most of all, he was angry at the creature that was trying to roast him alive. He stopped thinking about strategy. He grabbed his sword and jumped to his feet and then charged at the dragon like a madman.

The creature was unimpressed. Though it had no flame to exhale for the moment, it was not about to hesitate. It quickly opened its jaws and thrust its head in the direction of the young man. Chrysteffor could see the deadly teeth coming straight for him, but he refused to be distracted by the threat. He continued his sprint right up to the foot of the creature and, with both hands, plunged his sword into it. He was not sure that his sword would penetrate the thing's scaly exterior, but somehow he had found a gap in the scales and the blade had found soft flesh underneath. The beast's roar was deafening, its rage palpable. The prince had to roll on the ground to avoid being struck by the massive foot as it reacted to the pain.

Chrysteffor was encouraged. The beast could be injured as long as he could force his blade between its scales. He leapt to his feet and jumped on top of the other foot. It would be only moments before the dragon would be ready to breathe more fire at him, but with any luck the flames would not be able to find him on the creature's own body. He began to climb the dragon's leg. It was not that difficult since its skin had the texture of stones. It was not unlike climbing a rocky cliff.

Did the creature even know that he was there? Could it feel him through the scales? It must have because it began twisting and gyrating its body in an obvious effort to shake him off. Chrysteffor tried to hang on for dear life, but the movement was so sudden and so severe that he lost his grip. He was sent flying toward the ground. The monster reared its head, and the prince knew that the fire was imminent. As fast as he could, he rolled his body as far as he could, hoping that in his so doing the flames would miss him.

He heard the roar and felt the intensity of the heat. For a moment he was not sure whether he had been burned. Would he even feel it, given the shock it would cause his body? A quick glance at his body assured him that he had avoided catastrophe—this time. He leapt to his feet and again charged the beast. One foot, the one he had stabbed, rose up. He made for the other one. He sprang off the ground and landed on the uninjured foot and immediately began a new climb up the leg. He did his best to make sure that every grasp he made on the creature's scales was as secure as he could manage. He did not want to be shaken off again.

Before he knew it, the prince had reached the main part of the dragon's body. His goal was to climb onto its back. Once there it would be easier to avoid falling and virtually impossible for the beast to burn him with its flames. The creature twisted and turned and did everything it could to shake him loose. At one point he had to stop climbing and simply do his best to maintain his grip. The beast did not seem to get tired. It was clearly hopeless to expect it to stop for a rest, so he carefully re-initiated his climb while doing his best not to lose his hold in the midst of all the turning and shaking.

His progress was slow, but eventually he found himself on top of what he took to be the dragon's spine. Still holding on as best he could with one hand, he reached carefully for his sword. He did not know how he could hope to drive the blade between the scales and keep a grip at the same time, yet he had no choice but to try. He would have to push the blade in with one hand while, at the same time, maintaining somehow his precarious hold on the scales beneath him.

He lifted his arm and prepared to strike with all the force he could muster, but his worst fear was realized. A sudden motion by the creature caused him to lose his grip on the sword. He watched in horror as it fell, and he feared to see it fall all the way to the ground. Luckily it lodged between the creature's scales just a small distance out of his reach. He moved himself into a better position to be able to grasp it. All the while the beast twisted and turned and did its best to make him lose his hold. If he had had the time to think about it, he would have surely concluded that his efforts were futile.

Chrysteffor laid his hand on the sword's hilt and pulled it toward him. He tightened his grip, determined not to let it slip from his hand again. He then worked his way back to his previous position in the center of the creature's back. He knew that, if there was any hope of stopping the beast, he would have to plunge his blade into its spine. He chose his spot and did his best to brace himself against one of the scales. He identified what seemed to be the most likely gap between the scales and placed the sword's blade into it. He knew that he would have only one chance to drive the blade in, and he furthermore knew that there was no hope unless he could drive the blade in with both hands.

He waited until the creature's motions had relented a bit in their suddenness, not something easy to discern since there was little pattern to its movements. When he thought he would have his best chance, he let go of his grip on the thing's body and grasped the sword's hilt with both hands and shoved the blade in as forcefully as he could. The skin underneath was more resistant than he had expected. He pushed all the harder, but he had only a moment to drive in the blade. The beast spun around and, now that he no longer had a grip on its back, he went flying through the air.

He landed on the hard stone floor with an agonizing thud. He prayed that he had not broken any bones in the fall. The shock of the hard landing left him unable to move. He lay there looking up at the monster, knowing that there would be no chance to avoid its flames now. His only hope was that he had managed to do it serious injury. The sound of his own gasps filled his ears as he lay waiting to see what would happen.

For a moment the dragon seemed to have frozen, as if it had been transformed into a giant statue. Suddenly it jerked and rolled over on its side. Its legs flailed, as if in pain. He had done it. He had wounded the thing seriously—perhaps critically. Though it was doing its best to thrash around, it had clearly lost control over most of its body.

The prince wondered if he too had been as seriously injured. He pulled himself up far enough to lie on his side. Despite the pain throbbing through the trunk of his body, he had the use of his arms and legs. He was going to be all right. It took a while to catch his breath. As he watched the beast writhe, he knew the danger was not yet completely vanquished. He forced himself to stand. After a few moments, he made his way to the giant body in front of him and clambered up its back. Despite his pain, the climbing was easy now that the monster could barely move.

He found his sword protruding out of its back. A river of thick liquid had oozed out of the wound. The prince reclaimed his sword and then followed the thing's spine right up to its neck and the back of its head. He was wary of the creature's mouth, in case there might be one last blast of fire to come. He picked a likely spot at the base of the head and placed the blade between the scales. With all his might he drove it in.

There was one final painful jerk of the dragon's body. Somehow Chrysteffor managed to hold on tightly enough to the sword's hilt in order not to be thrown off. He did not relish the thought of being flung again to the ground. More thick liquid oozed out of the new wound. The prince could feel the life go out of the monster's body. The battle was over.

His only thought now was of Eilís. He pulled his sword out of the creature's neck and climbed down off its body. He looked for the princess in the darkness. He no longer heard her cries. He looked everywhere for her, but she was not there. Finally, he found the chain and manacles that had restrained her. They were lying on the ground.

I have saved her, he thought to himself. *That is all I ever wanted to do. I have delivered her from the terror that was tormenting her.*

He wondered if his victory meant that she was now awake back in the castle. Would she remember her dream? Would she remember that he had been in her dream? Would she remember that he had been her champion and had saved her? His impulse was to head directly back to the castle and find out. After all, did he not have good reason to believe that he had now accomplished his mission and fulfilled his quest?

Reluctantly, though, he acknowledged that the prophecy must be something real and that it required him to go to all three towers. Even if Eilís were now awake—and he had no way of knowing if she was—all she would care about would be the deliverance of Afranor from the Black Sorcerer. And the only hope of that was to continue on to the third tower. As much as his heart longed to return to her, he knew what he must do.

He made his way back to the tower's entrance and, still in pain, forced himself through the opening out into the night air. If his quest were not yet over, he thought, he could at least take satisfaction in a second victory—one that had required of him resources he had never suspected he possessed. Despite the pain in his back and the still throbbing burn on his arm, this gave him confidence for the third and final test.

As he looked around, though, his heart sank. He spotted the tree branch where he had tied the horse's reins. He made out the animal's hoof prints in the ground. He walked in several directions looking in vain, but the seriousness of his situation eventually sank in. Resignedly, he sat down on the ground and disconsolately buried his head in his arms.

The horse was well and truly gone.

8
Aon Fhear

THE YOUNG PRINCE sat a good long time. It was the stubbornness of youth that perhaps made him think that, if he refused to accept his new plight, the reality might give in and change for him. Of course, no matter how long he continued to sit there, nothing was going to change.

His body hurt all over. Every ache from his battle and, especially, from being flung to the ground by the monster, was now plaguing him and tormenting him. The thrill of not only surviving the battle but of actually triumphing in battle had overwhelmed his pain. Now, though, it did not feel like a victory.

He did not want to contemplate his choices, but he had a decision to make. In which direction should he begin walking? He could head in the direction of the castle. It would be days before he would arrive there—assuming he could survive the journey on foot. And he would be arriving after having been to only two of the three towers. As satisfied as he was with himself for having defeated two supernatural warriors and having slain a dragon, he did not relish the thought of returning with his quest unfulfilled. Besides, based on his travels so far anyway, the remaining tower was almost certainly much nearer than the castle. On the other hand, his return journey would be all the longer from the third tower. Also, his provisions had disappeared with his mount. He no longer had any food. He would be weak with hunger after a day or two unless he could find something to eat.

Regardless of which direction he chose, he also had to contend with the fact that, without the horse, he would now be easy prey for the Eidola or any brigands whose path he might cross. Yes, his sword would give him more of an advantage than he had had when he first wandered into this country, but there was no guarantee he could triumph if he was badly outnumbered.

He forced himself to stand. As comforting as it was to sit with his eyes covered, he knew that he was better off walking. And he knew that there was really no question about the direction he should take.

I undertook this quest in the full expectation of not surviving it, he thought, *but I let my luck in succeeding in the first two towers tempt me into thinking that I would survive anyway. Allowing that hope to grow only weakens me. I must stick to my original plan. I will see this through. The only reward I can truly hope for is that Lady Eilís is or will be awake and will think kindly of me for my efforts.*

And then slowly he trod the road that followed the edge of the cliff.

If the journey had seemed long when he was on horseback, it seemed absolutely interminable now that he was on foot. Before long he found that he could not imagine any life ahead of him other than the tedious placing of one foot in front of the other. The panic and terror of fighting a dragon would be preferable to this boredom.

He still had the sensation of being watched. That had not changed. In fact, if anything, the feeling had intensified now that he was truly on his own. He found that he sorely missed the company of the horse. At least it was a fellow living creature. He had never felt so completely and utterly alone in his entire life.

He tried to calculate how far away the next tower was, basing his guess on the distances traveled to the first and second ones. But there was no calculating distances without knowing how much time he had spent traveling them. The lack of any sight of the sun or the moon made it impossible to know whether he had spent hours or days traveling. The journey would be that slightly more bearable, he thought, if he could just anticipate how much farther he had in front of him. Instead, every step felt as though it was being followed by another—without end.

As the time dragged on, he once again felt as though he might be losing his mind. He had no bearings or anything else his mind could work with. For a while he tried escaping into his memories—happy recollections of his childhood and times spent with his brothers. He thought of Lady Eilís and examined all of his memories of the brief time he had spent with her. He went so far as to try composing a song for her in his head, but he found that no words or melodies would come to him. For good or for ill, he realized, he had gradually come to stop caring about the possibility of being attacked, either by a man or a monster. He found that it no longer mattered to him. He focused only on placing one foot inexorably in front of the other.

He went on in this state for a good long time. His brain was about as numb as it could possibly be. So much so that he did not react when he first heard the noise.

The noise worked its way into his consciousness in a gradual manner. At first it seemed like something he was remembering from a past dream. It slowly dawned on him that it was a real noise that he was hearing—

something external to himself. It came from some far-off distance. He stopped suddenly. It felt strange not to be walking, as he had been walking without pause for as long as he could remember.

He stood as still as he could and tried not to breathe. He had heard nothing but his own breath for so long it seemed to fill his ears to the exclusion of everything else. He waited until he was at the point of having to exhale. He heard it again. He must have gone awfully stupid, he thought, because it was taking him a long time to work out something that was quite simple.

He took a breath and waited until he heard it again. It was the whinny of a horse. His heart raced. With any luck it would be his own horse. He had avoided speculating about what had happened to the horse. Had it worked itself free on its own? Had something frightened it so much that the power of its fear had enabled it to escape? Or had it been stolen? That is what he had truly not wanted to consider. Was someone or something about and aware of his presence?

He waited until he heard it one more time, this time to fix in his mind the direction of the sound's origin. Once he decided where it was coming from, he headed that way. He soon found himself at a makeshift camp site. The remains of a fire were in the center. And tied to the branches of some low bushes were two horses. One of them was his.

Elation at finding, against all hope, that steed—which was so precious to him not only because of what it meant to his own survival but because it belonged to his beloved Eilís—was quickly followed by wariness. He had no idea who had made this camp and he wondered for a few moments whether he should look for and confront the horse thief or simply take his horse and escape quickly. Although he saw only the two horses, he could not be certain how many men there were. He approached his horse and began to untie its reins. With any luck he would be gone before anyone knew the horse was missing.

"You!"

The voice was full of disdain and anger—and somehow strangely familiar. Chrysteffor spun around immediately and already had his sword drawn. He made out the shape of a man emerging from the mist.

"What the devil!" cried the prince. "Is it really you again?"

Chrysteffor blinked to better focus his eyes. It was the same black-haired brigand he had fought after he had come down from hiding in the tree the first day he had arrived in Afranor.

"I knew it was a mistake to let you live. I just never expected you to survive this long. And now you're stealing horses."

"I am not the thief here," replied the prince indignantly. "You cannot confuse me by telling lies. This is my own horse, and if you attempt to stop me from reclaiming it your life will be forfeit."

The black-haired man laughed but then snarled, "You have grown surprisingly bolder since our first meeting but, if you are expecting me to be merciful again, I am afraid that I have no mercy left these days."

Both men had their swords raised and began to circle each other cautiously. Seeing the brigand again brought back painful memories for Chrysteffor. He would never forget that this man had been there when Benet had died. Perhaps he was the one who had killed him. Despite his fatigue, the prince found his heart filling with a growing rage.

"You are the one who will be begging for mercy!" shouted Chrysteffor. "This is the day you pay for your crimes, which I am sure are many. This is your last day of life and you are looking at the man who is going to kill you."

As they continued their wary dance, the black-haired man replied, "You have changed a great deal in a short amount of time. I would barely know you are the same boy who senselessly and ineptly attacked me on the mountain road. I am afraid, however, that you are the one who is living his last moments here."

Chrysteffor could contain his anger no longer and thrust his blade forcefully at his opponent. The black-haired man dodged and twisted and pushed his blade surprisingly close to Chrysteffor's ribs.

"That is a very interesting blade you have," said his opponent, sounding intrigued. "You did not have it the other time we met. Where did you get it?"

You would like to have this sword, wouldn't you? thought Chrysteffor to himself, *but you shall not take it from me!*

The rage grew within him as he saw his foe, only a few years older than himself, smirking at him.

The prince threw himself into the fight, bombarding his opponent with one blow after another, but his enemy managed to deflect every one—though not without a considerable amount of effort. Chrysteffor did his best to stay on the offensive, but the other man was able to get in his own attacks as well.

Unfortunately for me, thought Chrysteffor, *this villain is not worn out from hours or days of walking. He clearly has the advantage. On the other hand, having resigned myself to die, my life is no longer precious to me. And the desire to avenge my brothers is a strong motivation.*

Remembering his brothers and how they died gave the prince a new spurt of energy. He shocked his opponent by roaring at him with an

75

unexpectedly loud voice and attacking him with renewed force, but the black-haired man was just as determined to be the victor. What was the brigand fighting for anyway? What was this thief's motivation?

As their contest dragged out, Chrysteffor had to accept that his opponent was the superior swordsman and that he would be slower to tire. If the prince was going to prevail, he would have to act drastically. He threw his entire body at his foe and caught him by surprise. The two of them tumbled to the ground with the blond-haired man on top of the black-haired man. They both still had their swords in their hands, but at such close quarters neither was in a position to use his against the other.

"So it's back to this," hissed the black-haired man.

It was true. This is how their previous fight had gone, and it had not ended well for Chrysteffor. This time the prince was determined not to let him turn the tables.

He used all of his body's weight to hold the brigand down against the ground, but it was not easy. His opponent had a bit of a weight and strength advantage. He could feel his muscles straining and struggling through both their clothes. Once again, the now-familiar smell of his breath overwhelmed Chrysteffor's nose, as did the odor of the sweat that was beading on his contorted face.

The prince's pale eyes were drawn to the brigand's black ones. As they wrestled, each man locked his gaze on the other. Despite the intensity of the struggle, Chrysteffor found his mind beginning to wander. *Everyone in this country,* he thought, *seems to have the exact same eyes. They all look so different from my own people. It is no wonder that they insist on remarking on* my *eyes.*

As the fight continued, Chrysteffor realized that he would not be able to restrain his opponent indefinitely and he could think of no way to take the advantage. He dared not release his hold on either of his arms. There was really only one choice left to the prince. He leaned back his head and then knocked it against his foe's as hard as he could. This only succeeded in making his adversary angrier than before, giving him an energy spurt. Before he knew it, Chrysteffor had been rolled over and found himself underneath the other man. He was completely pinned down and unable to move. All he could smell was the black-haired man's breath as it flowed over his face from his foe's angry gasps.

"I expected to run you through with my sword," panted the man on top of him, "but I think now instead that I will get more pleasure by choking the life out of you with my bare hands."

Chrysteffor was completely immobilized. All he could do was to keep struggling against the other man's hold and hope against hope that he would unexpectedly loosen his grasp on him or otherwise falter—and that seemed unlikely. Instead, he shifted his arm against Chrysteffor's throat. He was doing his best to cut off the prince's breathing.

"So tell me, my blond friend," hissed the black-haired man against his cheek, "what brought you down this road? No one ever comes this way. Were you following me?"

Chrysteffor did not have enough breath to answer. He was barely able to breathe. He feared he would pass out if he could not draw a decent amount of air soon. He tried to spit in his face, but the saliva ended up drooling down his own chin.

The prince felt the man's arm relax ever so slightly. Apparently, his curiosity had gotten the better of him. Chrysteffor could now draw a breath.

"Tell me! Were you following me? How did a hapless outlander like you come to be here of all places?"

The prince gasped, "You would not understand my reasons. You only live to rob and plunder. I am trying to save this country."

The black-haired man's hold on Chrysteffor relaxed more as he laughed heartily.

"Save this country! That is a good one! Save this country! Tell me, how does the likes of you ever hope to save accursed Afranor? Tell me! I would like to know!"

"What do you care? You are only profiting from this country's misfortune. The likes of you loves the darkness that has fallen over this land because it hides your evil deeds. You are part of the curse that plagues the good people who dwell here!"

The black-haired man reapplied the pressure from his arm and cut off Chrysteffor's air completely.

"You do not know what you are talking about! You do not know who I am or anything about me. Do not ever dare to tell me that I do not love my country! I will not listen to this from a shaggy-haired foreign pup who knows nothing of what he speaks."

Struggling for breath, Chrysteffor feared that he was about to pass out. Fortunately, his foe relented so that he could speak some more.

"Do you know the story of the three towers?" the prince choked.

"The three towers? Or course, I do. Every man, woman and child in this land knows the story. What of it?"

"Look at my eyes!"

"I have been looking at them for some time now. They are fierce ugly, so light and pale. What about your eyes?"

"Have you not noticed their color?"

"Did I not just say how ugly and pale they were?"

"They are different colors."

"Yes, they are. That makes them even uglier. Is everyone in your country as ugly as you are?"

"The prophecy. Do you not remember the prophecy? It is, after all, your own country's story, not mine."

Chrysteffor detected a glint of recognition in his opponent's eyes.

"Listen, blond boy, you have now truly piqued my interest. Tell you what, I am going to release you so that you may sit up. If you try anything funny, I will run you through with my blade faster than you can say brown and blue. Understand?"

The prince nodded. Carefully, the other man lifted himself off him and quickly drew his sword into position so that it was aimed at his chest. Chrysteffor pulled himself up into a more comfortable sitting position.

"Go on now. Tell me what *you* know about the old prophecy."

"I have been told that it was prophesied long ago that a man such as myself, with eyes of two colors, would save Afranor at the time of its greatest peril. I did not believe this story when I first heard it, but lately I have come to think there may be something to it."

"And that is why you are on this road? To visit the three towers?"

"Yes. I have been to two of them. I am now on my way to the third, but I have been considerably delayed because my horse was stolen."

"I found that horse abandoned, in the middle of nowhere. It was tied to a tree. If I had not brought it with me, for all I could tell, it would have starved. Or be attacked and eaten. It seemed like a waste of a perfectly good horse."

"Stop telling me your lies. The horse was not abandoned. I was there, inside the tower. The horse was waiting for me, and you stole it, you miserable thief."

"So tell me, what did you find inside the first and second towers?"

"Why? Are you hoping that there was something of value that you could steal? Is that all you think about?"

The listener became angry again and pushed his sword's blade right up to Chrysteffor's neck.

"Stop calling me a thief! Why do you keep saying that?"

"Maybe it has something to do with the way we met. You and your fellow brigands killed my brother and tried to make me pay a ransom anyway. You must think I am completely stupid. Have you no shame?"

"You *are* completely stupid. I was not with those brigands. I was fighting them. I was trying to help you and you attacked me!"

Chrysteffor thought back to the encounter. It was true, he realized. This man had been fighting the bandits. He had only assumed that he was one of them and that it was a fight among themselves. It had not occurred to the prince that this man was a passer-by, not unlike himself.

"Is that true? You had nothing to do with those vile robbers? But how can I be sure that what you are telling me is the truth?"

"Use your head, boy. Why would I have been fighting them if they were my comrades? Though you and I seem to fight every time we meet, I am really a very peaceful person. Usually, I try to avoid a fight."

"If you are not a brigand, then who are you? Why do I keep meeting you?"

"I am just a wanderer. I travel the roads. I have not had a lucky life. I have lost my home and my family. There is nothing left to me but to seek revenge against the one who is the cause of it all."

"The Black Sorcerer?"

The black-haired man looked impressed.

"Most people are afraid to speak that name out loud. You are either very courageous or more of a fool than I thought you were. So tell me, what did you find in the towers?"

Chrysteffor was still not certain if he could trust this man.

"At least tell me your name first. You could at least extend me the courtesy of telling me whom I am talking to. I am Chrysteffor, crown prince of Alinvayl. I came to this country with my two brothers, who are now dead. I did not seek the quest I am now on, and I knew nothing about your prophecy. But circumstances have tied my destiny to Afranor's."

The black-haired man looked impressed. He lowered his sword.

"My name is not important. I have given it up until my land is free. In any event, it has been a long time since anyone has had a need to call me by any name. I have been biding my time in the most shadowy corners of the land until I can learn how and where to strike back at the villain who has brought the darkness here."

"Now that is just silly. What am I supposed to call you then? I cannot very well call out 'ugly black-haired Afranor man' every time I want your attention, can I?"

For the first time, Chrysteffor saw the man smile.

"Some people I meet on the road have taken to calling me Aon Fhear. It is not a name. It is words in the old language for something or someone who has no name. You can use that if you need to call me something. Now will you tell me what you found in the towers?"

"I promise you will not believe me. I scarcely believe it myself."

"Enough drama. Out with your story already, Prince Chrysteffor."

"In the first tower I encountered my two dead brothers. They were doing the bidding of some evil force—like the Eidola. I had to fight and defeat them lest I perish myself. It was the most difficult thing I ever did. That is where I acquired the sword that you admire so much."

"That truly is difficult to believe. How could your brothers have ended up in that tower? And how did you enter the tower anyway?"

"There is a mechanism that opens an entrance. I will show you at the third tower if you want to come with me."

"And the second tower?"

"That was more incredible. You truly will not believe what I found there."

"Just tell me then. I will be the judge of whether it is credible."

"The enchantment of the second tower is that I actually entered someone's dream."

"Whose dream?"

"Princess Eilís."

Aon Fhear looked as though he had been struck in the head.

"Eilís? How do you know Princess Eilís?"

"She came to the aid of my brother Benet and me the first day we arrived in this country. She invited me to Castle Aill Stoirm. That is how I learned about the Black Sorcerer and the prophecy."

"And why did Princess Eilís not accompany you on your quest to the three towers? It would not be like her to stay safely at home while others go to fight for her country."

Chrysteffor was surprised at how well Aon Fhear seemed to know Eilís.

"I am afraid that Lady Eilís fell under an evil enchantment. I left her in the castle sleeping and unable to wake. The dream that was tormenting her in her sleep is the same one that I entered through the sorcery of the second tower."

"Tell me. What happened in the second tower? Tell me now!"

"She was being menaced by a dragon. To make a long story short, I slew the dragon."

Aon Fhear looked stunned.

"Not Eilís! How dare he do this to her! I will kill him for this, I swear!"

Chrysteffor was taken aback at how upset this news had made the other man.

"I had no idea that Eilís had fallen under such a spell," he continued. "This is terrible news. Do you think your intervention released her from the enchantment?"

"I have no way of knowing. All I know is that to complete the quest I must continue on to the third tower and confront whatever awaits me there. And I have been delayed because someone stole my horse."

Aon Fhear sat quietly for a few moments.

"I have no way of knowing if you are telling me the truth. Your story is nothing short of incredible. Can it really be true, or are you merely a madman roaming the roads of my country? But I suppose anything is possible. We have seen all manner of unbelievable things since the Black Sorcerer unleashed his evil on this land. I have no choice but to believe you."

Aon Fhear stood and spoke gravely.

"Prince Chrysteffor, I shall accompany you to the third tower. Furthermore, I shall give you any aid and support that I can in your quest."

To Chrysteffor those words seemed too good to be true. After all his trials and difficulties, he now had an ally—and perhaps even a friend—in his quest to save his beloved Eilís.

Still, something troubled him. It was the look in Aon Fhear's eyes when the name Eilís was mentioned. He knew her—and obviously quite well. It made a certain kind of sense. Aon Fhear and Eilís were clearly kindred spirits. In her travels on the roads of Afranor she must have met this young man. They might be friends. But no, the look in his eyes was not mere friendship. He loved her. This man was without a doubt her lover.

Whatever glory his quest might earn him, the prince was beginning to realize, he would not be earning Eilís's heart as a prize. He now suspected strongly that it was already taken. His own heart sank but, still, he was no less determined to see his mission fulfilled.

"Aon Fhear or whatever your name really is, here and now I am willing to call you friend. I gratefully accept your offer of aid. I cannot promise that we will emerge alive from the final tower. In fact, I can all but assure you that we will not, but I will happily face whatever test remains now that you are with me."

9
The Final Tower

THE TWO MEN rode side by side on the road to the third tower. They made a stark contrast. Chrysteffor's pale skin and long blond hair could not have been more different from Aon Fhear's olive complexion and head of curly black hair. But they both exhibited youthful strength and the sort of confidence that young men affect naturally in one another's presence.

Despite all he had been through, Chrysteffor now felt, for the most part, physically restored. Having a companion made all the difference to him. The atmosphere was still as oppressive as ever, but at least now it was no longer magnified by the weight of loneliness. It was a relief to no longer be facing unknown dangers entirely on his own. Perhaps there was still a bit of doubt as to whether he should completely trust his new friend, but he took comfort in the fact that Aon Fhear was as skilled a fighter as any man he had ever met. After all, he had survived out in the wilds for who knows how long on his own. He was definitely a good man to have at one's side in whatever perilous situation might emerge.

"You know," said the dark-haired man, breaking the silence, "even though I have heard the story of the prophecy all my life, I confess that I stopped believing it a long time ago. I suppose, when I got to an age where I questioned things, I simply came to assume that it was merely a story made up to console children. After all, no one—not in this country anyway—had ever seen a man with eyes of different colors before."

"Well," replied Chrysteffor, "I only heard the story for the first time a few days ago. Imagine how strange it sounded to me. I would never have considered it anything other than nonsense... if I had not actually gone to the towers and lived through the fantastic events myself."

"Were you long in Castle Aill Stoirm?"

"A few days, I think. It is hard to be certain, given that day and night are one in this country."

"With whom did you speak?"

"Mostly with Lady Aigneis. She is old, but in a way she has the most strength of any of them."

"Did you see the king?"

"Only briefly. I am afraid he is a broken man. He is very aged—probably well beyond his actual years, by my guess. The enchantment that fell over Lady Eilís seems to have broken his spirit completely."

Aeon Fhear's face darkened.

"And how was Lady Eilís? I mean, before the enchantment."

Chrysteffor glowed.

"She is wonderful. I have never seen a more proficient warrior. She spends all her time trying to help those in need."

"Yes," said Aon Fhear with a faraway look in his eyes, "she is truly wonderful. There is no one like her."

Chrysteffor had no doubt—even if his new friend did not say so outright—that Aon Fhear not only knew Eilís but that they were very close. His suspicion that they were lovers only became more plausible as time went on. This did not bother him as much as he might have expected. At least not at this particular moment. Not as long as the black-haired man offered some hope that the prince might actually survive his sojourn in Afranor. He still believed that the most likely outcome was that he—and probably Aon Fhear as well—would be dead soon. Unrequited romantic love at the moment seemed a small price to pay for not having to face death alone. On the other hand, he also acknowledged that, if by some stroke of unanticipated good fortune he and Aon Fhear both survived, he just might feel differently about it.

The two rode on quietly for a good while before either one spoke again. It was Chrysteffor who broke the silence.

"May I ask you a question?"

"Yes?"

"How do you do it?"

"How do I do what?"

"How do you, well, how do you keep going? How do you not become overwhelmed by the enormity of the world in which you find yourself? Do you not ever lose hope?"

Aon Fhear did not respond for several moments. Chrysteffor thought perhaps he had not heard the question or was choosing to ignore it. Finally, the black-haired man replied.

"I do not think much about hope. I am motivated by, eh, less lofty emotions. It is the desire for revenge that keeps me going—the idea that one day I will see the foul villain—the one who has caused so much pain for me and for those I love—die. And that I will be the one to make him die. It is not very pretty, but there it is. That is what keeps me going."

"And is that feeling of hate sufficient to, well, to keep you from being afraid?"

This is a question that Chrysteffor could never have asked either of his brothers. To admit fear to them or to any man he knew in Alinvayl was to invite ridicule. Aon Fhear was different. He barely knew Aon Fhear and Aon Fhear scarcely knew him, and the two of them might well be on the road to dying together. The grim experience they were sharing gave the prince the confidence to speak more openly and honestly than he ever had before with any man.

"There is no point being afraid," said the black-haired man. "Fear is of no help. It can only undermine you. If it is death you fear, you will be better able to avoid death by not worrying about your fears. Strangely, your fear is only more likely to bring about that which you are fearing."

"But…"

Chrysteffor struggled for the right words. Though the two of them might soon be dead and Aon Fhear's opinion of him would not matter one bit in the grand scheme of things, he still did not want the older man to think badly of him.

"But?"

"But how do you keep from being overwhelmed? Overwhelmed not only by the knowledge of all the dangers that you are aware of as well as by all the dangers you do not even know to suspect? Do you not look around you at all the darkness and all the perils that lurk just out of sight and calculate your odds of survival and then ask yourself, what is the point? I confess that the only thing that has kept me going since I arrived in this country is the certainty of my death—that nothing I do is of any real consequence, that it is all well past caring about."

The black-haired man kept his silence for a good while. Chrysteffor was sure that Aon Fhear was embarrassed by the prince's admission, that he was regretting his offer to accompany the prince on the final leg of his quest.

"Congratulations, my friend, on discovering the secret."

"The secret?"

"Yes, the secret that is kept by every warrior, every hero, every champion there ever was. There is no man who is not afraid—at least in the darkest recesses of his heart late at night when he is alone. This is also true of the bravest fighter on the field of battle surrounded by his comrades. Those of us who talk bravely and who show no sign of wavering in the face of battle are really only covering up our deepest terrors."

"Do you mean to tell me that you too feel fear? That you feel an overwhelming horror in your heart—the same as me?"

"Every man does, I am quite sure."

"But you do not show it. You have never given any indication of being anything but stalwart and courageous. There is nothing about you that betrays any dread or distress."

"Nor have I seen anything like that in you. If you had not spoken, I would never have suspected that you were plagued by such doubts."

"But it must be written all over my face. Surely, someone as courageous as you must see that my show of bravery is nothing but a charade. You must hear it in my voice and see it in the way that I carry myself."

"I assure you that to someone else you appear as steady as any veteran warrior. It is the façade that all men must master. It is what is expected of us."

Chrysteffor was dumbfounded. It had never occurred to him that he was not the only man who was plagued by doubts and dread. Yet here was the bravest man he had ever met telling him that this was indeed so. He looked on Aon Fhear with new respect. What's more, he was surprised that in such a short time he had come to love this new friend as a brother. In fact, he could never have opened his heart to his brothers the way he had been able to Aon Fhear. His feelings of affection were only enhanced by the fact that his curly black hair and intense black eyes constantly reminded him of his beloved Eilís.

"You are wise and kind, Aon Fhear. I clearly misjudged you in the beginning, but I now find your words are an inspiration to me. I will speak no more of fears and terrors and will devote myself only to the task at hand. I will follow your extraordinary example and acquit myself as a man and a prince should. Indeed, you yourself have more princely qualities than any man I have ever known. This is proof that character is not a simple matter of a man's station at birth."

The black-haired man was not much given to smiling, but he smiled widely at Chrysteffor's heartfelt compliment. In fact the prince was certain he had heard a soft chuckle.

There was little conversation after that. Both men seemed content to dwell in their own particular thoughts as they followed the road along the sea cliff. The hours passed by, but for Chrysteffor at least they passed more quickly than they had during his journeys to the first two towers.

The mere fact of having a true comrade alongside him made the darkness and the tedium more bearable.

At long last, the familiar shape of the next and final tower revealed itself through the swirling mists. It looked little different than the other two.

"Well, this is it then," said the prince from Alinvayl. "We are here. I suppose there is no point in delaying. I will make the tower reveal its entrance to us."

"I never knew there was a way to enter the towers. How did you learn the secret?"

The question flattered Chrysteffor. The trick now seemed so obvious to him in hindsight that he could not believe he was the first to discover it.

"There is lever high up on the tower wall. If it can be pulled downward, the opening will appear."

"You are an amazing fellow," said Aon Fhear, "to have figured out such a thing."

Chrysteffor dismounted, gathered up his rope and approached the tower. He looked for the dangling piece of iron that he had seen at the other two towers. As he walked around the tower and studied its walls, he was disconcerted not to see the same piece of iron on this structure.

"This is strange," he said. "I swear to you that the iron piece was there on the other two towers."

He worried that Aon Fhear would think that he had invented the story about his experiences in the other two towers. In his confusion, he himself began to wonder whether he might have only imagined those experiences, but his companion did not seem to doubt him.

"There is no reason that this tower should be exactly like the others. It may only be that there is a different riddle to solve here."

Chrysteffor made another circle around the tower, studying it more closely this time.

"I remember hearing a tale as a child," said Aon Fhear, trying to be helpful. "In the story the hero had to call out a particular phrase to make the door open for him."

"There was no magic involved in entering the other towers," said the prince, as he continued to pace around the structure. "The mechanism for opening them was a marvel, but it was not magic. It followed the laws of the natural world."

He circled the tower one more time, his eyes continuously focused at a certain height. He settled on a particular spot and leapt onto the side of the tower's exterior. Grasping carefully with his hands and lodging his feet where he could, he climbed up the stony surface. He kept going until he was at about the same height as he had found the iron piece before. He probed the crevices among the stones.

"I think I may have solved the mystery," he called down to Aon Fhear, who stood on the ground below watching intently. "There is no riddle. Only a fault in someone's clever invention. The lever is here all right, but it has broken off. We need to find a way somehow to make it work as it was intended."

"Tell me what I may do to help."

"I do not know if there is anything either of us can do to make it work. This may be the end of my quest. I may not be able to complete it if I cannot find another way into the tower."

The prince grabbed at the remnant of the lever every way he could, but there was no way to move it. He gave up and scrambled back down to the ground.

"This is disappointing," he said. "I, we, have come so far. Surely, it cannot end like this."

"We know there is an entrance," said Aon Fhear. "Can we not locate it and force it open?"

Chrysteffor was doubtful. He reasoned that the complex mechanism that was meant to force the door open would, if not activated as designed, serve to prevent the door from opening. He racked his brain, desperate to think of a way to make the entrance appear. No solution presented itself.

The prince walked partway around the tower. He knew where the entrance had appeared, in relation to the lever, in the other two towers. He focused his attention on the spot where the entrance should be for this tower. As uneven as the surface was, it all seemed to be of one piece. He could not discern where there might be a gap or even two joined pieces.

"It must be here somewhere," he said. "It has to be."

Aon Fhear said nothing. Chrysteffor wondered if he might not be losing confidence in him.

At his wit's end, the prince unsheathed his sword and held the blade close to the stone, hoping its ghostly light might reveal something he could not see in the darkness. When the blade passed over one particular part of the exterior, he was surprised to see the blade's glow seemingly reflected from within a crevice. At first he thought his eyes were playing tricks on him, but as he moved the blade around it was clear that something about the sword was provoking a reaction from within the stones. He placed the tip of the blade into the crevice. He was surprised at how much of the blade disappeared into the crack.

Aon Fhear was mesmerized. "How strange," he said in a whisper.

Chrysteffor tried pushing the blade farther into the stone, gently at first. When it met resistance, he pushed a bit harder. He used the full strength of his arm to force it in. He stumbled backward a step when a bright light shone suddenly in a beam out of the now apparent crevice.

"You said that there was no magic involved in opening the door," said his impressed companion. "I would not be so sure of that. I have never seen anything like this before."

"We are not inside yet, my friend. I do not know what this means, but there is clearly more to this sword than the fact that it is quite helpful in killing the Eidola."

Encouraged by what he had seen, Chrysteffor pushed harder on the hilt of the sword. It resisted any further progress. He tried shifting it in one direction and then another. It seemed well and truly stuck in the crevice.

"My friend, come help me shove this weapon into the hole. Maybe with the strength of both of us we may force it in farther."

The black-haired man joined him and entwined his arms around the blond man's. They braced their bodies in order to put their combined weight into the pushing.

"On the count of three…" said Chrysteffor. "One, two, three!"

At first it seemed fruitless, but the two did not cease applying as much force as they could.

Then, suddenly, they felt the resistance give way and the sword sank into the stone right up to its hilt. To their astonishment, they found themselves bathed in a burst of bright light. The sudden shock of it caused both of them to fall back, sitting on the ground. Unaccustomed to the light after having spent so much time in darkness, they found themselves blinded for a few moments.

As their eyes returned to normal, they blinked continuously in an attempt to be certain of what they were seeing. The stones in the wall of the tower had indeed parted. There was now a gap wide enough for a man to pass through. Aon Fhear rose to his feet first and approached the opening. He tried to see what was inside, but all he could see was inky blackness within. The entrance might as well have been nothing more than a surface painted black.

"There is indeed enchantment at work here," said Aon Fhear, "and you and your amazing sword appear to have mastered it. There is no way to see what lies inside, but at least the way is open to us."

Chrysteffor stumbled to his feet and looked for himself. It looked no different—and no more inviting—than the entrances to the other two towers. He shuddered at the memory of what he had found within those structures.

"Well, I suppose this is it, my friend. This is what we came for. Nothing stands in our way. I have committed to this quest and I have come to accept that the prophecy refers to me. You are under no obligation to follow me inside to encounter who knows what. Indeed, since the tests have been so specific to me, I have no idea if the enchantment will allow you inside."

Chrysteffor was surprised to hear his own words. It was as though he was listening to someone else. Someone much braver and more confident than he. The thought that Aon Fhear would be at his side was the only thing that made this final test bearable to him. He did not want to go in alone, but he also knew that his words were true. This was clearly his own quest.

"I gave you my word, Prince Chrysteffor, that I would see this to the end with you. And I do not give my word lightly. Having come this far, I will not be left behind. There is no getting rid of me now, my friend."

The prince's relief was immense. So much so that he feared it was readily visible and he would appear to be wavering. To steady himself he impulsively embraced the other man.

"Forgive me, Aon Fhear. I cannot tell you how much your friendship and your loyalty—which I have yet to properly earn—mean to me. I have so recently lost my two brothers, but I now feel that I have found another brother who is as good as any man. The truth is that I undertook this quest not expecting to survive. And to be honest, I still do not expect to survive, but at least now I have hope that I might survive. And that is entirely because of you. In the event that I do not get the chance later, I want you to know how grateful I am."

Aon Fhear did not smile or show any emotion.

"Prince Chrysteffor, I am the one who is grateful to you. You have done more than any man to liberate my land from the curse under which it suffers. This would be remarkable for any man of Afranor, but you are not from this country. Whatever happens now, I have no doubt that your name will be remembered—indeed sung—for generations. But enough talk. It is only delaying us. I am eager to have this over. In the short time we have known each other, the bond we have formed is such that we do not need a lot of words to know what is in each other's heart. Let us wait no longer. Let us go and fight evil."

Chrysteffor nodded grimly, and Aon Fhear nodded in return. Then, with no further hesitation the blond man stepped inside the tower. The black-haired man followed immediately. And as quick as that, the inky darkness within had swallowed them up.

10
Into the Maelstrom

THE DARKNESS was so thick that, at first, Chrysteffor felt completely alone. For a moment he wondered if the other man had followed him in at all. His worst fear had been that the tower would somehow prevent anyone other than himself from entering. He extended his hand in the dark until he felt Aon Fhear's arm.

"There you are," he whispered. "For a terrible moment I felt as if I were again completely on my own."

"I am definitely here, my friend," the other man whispered back to him. "And I shall follow wherever you lead."

Reassured but by no means sanguine, Chrysteffor proceeded, as he had twice before, along the interior wall of the tower. He did his best not to think about what he might eventually encounter. He held up his sword to see what might be revealed by the bit of dim light that emanated from it. As he knew all too well from experience, it showed him nothing—not yet.

The prince said nothing and listened intently, recalling that the last time it had been somebody's cries that had alerted him to the challenge at hand. And he continued to peer into the darkness, wondering exactly when the moment would come, the moment when the inevitable danger would present itself. As he took one step after another, the wait felt endless. The silence and the darkness made him feel as alone as ever. He had only his own trust to assure him that Aon Fhear was indeed behind him, as there was no way verify it without speaking again. In the suffocating atmosphere of the tower he could not hear footsteps or breathing, and he dared not look behind him—in case he might be distracted at the very moment that a threat suddenly presented itself. The longer this went on, though, the more he was plagued by the feeling that Aon Fhear was no longer there, that he had vanished or wandered off or simply turned around.

He wondered why his friend did not speak, but then he realized that he was undoubtedly keeping quiet for the same reasons that Chrysteffor was. The prince had now spent so much time in darkness that he truly hated it. He promised himself that, if he survived this adventure, he would in the future reward himself by furnishing his own home with no fewer than a hundred candles—burning constantly day and night. For the rest of his life the dark would hold nothing but terrible memories for him.

He had to fight to keep his mind from wandering. He tried to empty all thoughts from his head, lest one of them distract his attention at the wrong time. He blinked his eyes, gritted his teeth and redoubled his concentration. He tried not to calculate how much time had passed since they had been inside the tower.

Finally, he heard the sounds.

At last, he thought, *it is here. The final test. There is no mistaking the noise. It is coming for me, for us. This is the moment that everything has been leading to. This is the final test.*

Chrysteffor stopped dead in his tracks and peered in the direction of the sounds. He stole a quick glance to his side to assure himself that Aon Fhear was there. He was relieved to see that he was. The black-haired man was staring in the same direction as Chrysteffor, braced for battle, his sword at the ready.

The noises grew louder.

This is no warrior or two, thought Chrysteffor, *nor is it a dragon or any other single beast. Whoever or whatever is coming, there are many of them. A great many of them.*

Before he knew it, the noise was deafening. He felt his heart sinking to the pit of his stomach. He glanced again at his companion, hoping that he could draw strength from the black-haired man's courage and determination. While Aon Fhear stood steadfast and ready, his face betrayed the same panic that Chrysteffor was feeling.

The two men then saw what they were facing. The hordes were illuminated by torches that some of them were holding above their heads. As far as the pair could see in the distance and as far as they could see from one side to the other, they were coming. It was the Eidola. More of them than had attacked Chrysteffor and his brothers on their first day in Afranor. There was no end to them. There were more of them than could logically fit inside the tower. In the darkness, the interior of the tower appeared to go on forever in every direction. And in every direction the interior of the tower was filled with monsters.

"There is no way we can hope to fight all of them!" shouted Chrysteffor over the din.

Aon Fhear stared ahead, grim and resolute.

"No!" he shouted back. "There is no hope! There is no way we can survive these odds, let alone prevail against them! I fear, my friend, this is truly the end of your quest!"

As the hordes advanced, the prince swallowed hard. He had to shout ever louder to be heard above the tumult of the creatures.

"I am so sorry that I brought you here! You might have had a chance to save your country if not for my folly! Now we will both be dead, and it will all have been for nothing! I am so very sorry!"

Aon Fhear raised himself up with surprising determination. He had only a few remaining moments before his last words would be drowned out by the roar.

"Save your apologies for all the Eidola that are going to die today! I may be going to the afterlife this very hour but, by the gods, I swear that so will as many of these abominations as I can bring with me!"

Aon Fhear raised his sword high and strained his neck screaming his final words.

"For Afranor! And for Eilís!"

Inspired by his friend's courage, Chrysteffor lifted his sword and screamed the same words—only now they were completely drowned out by the roaring pandemonium. He himself could not hear the sounds coming out of his own mouth.

The first creature that approached Aon Fhear met the black-haired man's blade and summarily lost its head. The second one met the same fate. And the third. Impressed and encouraged, Chrysteffor attacked any or all monsters that came near him. He had an easier time of it, as his blade killed the Eidola much more readily than any ordinary sword. As he saw the cadavers pile up in Aon Fhear's wake, Chrysteffor became infected by his friend's zeal. He felt as if he were going mad with rage and bloodlust. He surprised himself by how forcefully he was killing all the foes around him. In his delirium he felt as though there was nothing he could not do, no obstacle he could not overcome. His passion could surmount anything.

In his manic frenzy, Chrysteffor actually came to believe that he could slay all the creatures that were coming at him. After all, they were slow and lumbering and had no intelligence. All they had was brute strength and a mindless devotion to killing the two men. They were not bothered by the numbers of their kind that had fallen. They knew no fear. They had no doubts. They did not question why they were there or why they were sacrificing themselves in such numbers for no apparent purpose. They were not plagued by questions of the rightness of their motivations or the logic of their behavior. They did not wonder how they came to be in that dank, dark place and why their whole existence had come down to these few hours of carnage. They were no more bothered by the absurdity of it all than pebbles that roll down a mountain and become part of a landslide.

The same could now be said of Chrysteffor as his mind became increasingly numbed by his frenzied attempt to survive. He no longer felt entirely in control of his own body. As he strained and maneuvered to avoid being killed and to be more efficient at killing, he felt as if it was someone else engaging in the combat. He no longer felt like himself. He no longer recognized himself.

He was surprised that he was not tiring. As soon as the thought of exhaustion entered his mind, though, he did his best to banish it. The less thinking he did, the better off he would be. To consider the inevitable was to weaken himself. He had to allow himself to become like a machine that performed and did not think. He had to become like the animals in the wild. He had to become, well, like the Eidola. The hope of defeating them was to become as much like them as possible.

The battle raged on. It seemed to go on forever. Indeed it went on for hours, but there was no way to know how many. And it was better not to think on it. In Chrysteffor's mind the battle had always been going on and would always be going on. This was now his reality. There was no past and no future. There was only the immediate moment. And the immediate moment was the battle, the brutal war with no end.

The prince's skin was wet with sweat. He felt like shedding his clothing, that it was only restricting him, only making the damp heat more oppressive. He felt he should be naked like an animal because that was what he was now. He knew that his clothing afforded him a certain amount of protection, but that did not matter to him any more. In fact, he would have willingly torn his clothes asunder and discarded them if it would have not been a distraction from his main purpose of killing every creature that he could. So he bore his clothing like a burden, one additional intolerable thing that plagued him.

Everywhere around him the cadavers were piled high. The numbers of creatures attacking them and the number of creatures vanquished were staggering. The highest stacks, of course, were of the creatures' main bodies. There were also smaller heaps consisting of limbs and, in no small number, heads.

It is funny, thought Chrysteffor. *One severed head is horrific. Twenty of them in a pile is just a clump of unpleasant rubbish.*

At first the fetid smell of their bodies threatened to overwhelm Chrysteffor. As the odor worsened and intensified, though, it somehow became easier to ignore. No doubt the sweat from his own body, as it

94

soaked into his filthy clothing, was no small part of the odors assaulting him. It did not matter. All smells had become one, and it all was the smell of life at its most primal and, most of all, of death.

Inevitably, Chrysteffor noted that his movements were slowing. He did not want to admit it to himself, but he was finally tiring. He stubbornly avoided pondering the implications of this fact. After all, even if his conscious mind did not want to contemplate it, at some level he knew that this meant the beginning of the end. He would become increasingly tired. Eventually, he would find himself not moving quickly enough to avoid a blow or an injury. In his exhaustion he would begin to make mistakes and misjudgments. It would only be a matter of time until he was knocked to the ground and one or more of the creatures would deal him the fatal blows. There was no other way this could end.

He glanced over at Aon Fhear. So far the black-haired man had shown no signs of tiring or slowing down. He continued to fight like a maniac, lopping off heads and arms to one side and then to the other. If these had been men they were fighting, those men would have fled in terror at the sight of him and his fury and his unstoppable rampage. But these were not men. They merely looked on with uncomprehending eyes and followed one another into the attack on the two men, with no regard for their own safety or survival.

Seeing Aon Fhear fight gave Chrysteffor hope. His friend did not appear to be losing heart. Clearly he was not dwelling on the inevitable end to this battle, on the impossibility of their survival. He was living entirely in the moment and giving it his all. And he would continue to do that without question or pause. His friend's example gave him inspiration and somewhere Chrysteffor found new energy to launch himself into the battle with redoubled force. He had made the mistake of thinking ahead. He would fight the temptation to do that again and only think of the moment now.

The battle went on a good bit longer. Eventually, Chrysteffor was taken aback by a pain in his chest. At first he thought he had been struck unawares, perhaps from behind, but then he realized that it was his own breathing that was causing the pain. The soreness extended along one of his arms. He felt a cramp in one of his legs. His body was reaching its limit. The wonder is that it had taken so long to complain.

He glanced again in the direction of Aon Fhear. Each time he had felt himself faltering, the sight of his comrade had renewed his spirit. He hoped it would do so now again. This time, however, he saw a different look on the black-haired man's face. It was an expression he had not seen before. He too was exhausted. His eyes flared with desperation and panic.

His movements were no longer as graceful as they had been before. Every swipe with the sword was now clearly an effort. Chrysteffor's heart sank as he saw him struggle not to lose his footing.

Strangely, this gave the prince a unexpected jolt of energy he did not know he still had. For hours Aon Fhear had kept his spirit up by his example and the sight of him wavering was more than Chrysteffor could bear. Now the prince had an overwhelming need to be the other man's inspiration. He did his best to appear as though there was no problem continuing the fight. He swung around with renewed vigor as he lopped off more heads with the glowing blade.

His effort appeared to pay off. Once Aon Fhear saw him still fighting, the black-haired man threw himself into the battle with renewed force.

Yes, thought Chrysteffor, *we can do this. We can keep fighting. We can do this forever if need be. There is no future. There is only now. And as of now we are still alive. We are still fighting. That is all that matters.*

That moment of resurgent hope was all too short-lived. Throughout the length of the battle Chrysteffor had felt he had an advantage in that the creatures moved so slowly, but now they seemed to be moving with increasing speed. He could not be certain whether they were truly moving faster or if it only seemed so because, in his exhaustion, Chrysteffor was slowing down. Whatever the explanation, he could no longer avoid every blow that was aimed at him. No sooner had he sliced through one creature than another was battering him on the back with a rough club. And as soon as he had swung around to dispatch that monster, a third one was pounding him from another direction with a blunt stick. In their endless numbers, they were closing in on him and restricting his range of motion.

He looked in his comrade's direction and saw that Aon Fhear was faring no better. Chrysteffor was losing sight of him as the hordes surrounded and obscured him. Chrysteffor screamed as loud as he could manage. One or two of the things paused in reaction—but only for the briefest of moments. The prince summoned up all his resources. He refused to accept that the end might be drawing near. He threw himself into the battle with everything he had, but it was not enough. The arms and bodies of the creatures were everywhere. Every movement was frustrated by the numbers pressing in on him.

Of all the things I feared and imagined we would encounter in this tower, thought the blond prince, *somehow I did not expect this, simply to be overwhelmed by monsters. The first two towers did truly seem to be tests, not only of my endurance but of my very soul. There is no test here, only endless battle and unavoidable death. It is as though this supposed quest was nothing more than an elaborate trap, a ruse to lead me to my doom after exhausting my spirit. Well, I did know and accept all along I was going to my death, so it is no one's fault but my own that I began allowing myself to have hope. I only regret that I have caused Aon Fhear to die with me.*

He stole another look in his friend's direction. He could only see the top of his head, the mass of thick black hair jerking in one direction and then another. Soon he could not see him at all. Everywhere he looked the creatures were pressed next to him, above him, and under him. It was as though they were a thick black inky sea that was flooding the room and taking up all available space. He found it increasingly difficult to get a breath of air. He strained to catch his breath. He longed to kill just one more of them—one last enemy dispatched—but he could not raise his arm. He could not move at all.

He strained against the mass of bodies. He struggled for one more breath. In desperation he even tried biting one of the creatures in the arm, though he was sure that their flesh was likely poisonous. It did not matter. He did not even have the freedom of movement to do that. Still, he did not relent. He did not give up. He kept straining but, no matter what direction he tried, movement was impossible.

When it finally became clear that all his straining and resisting were making absolutely no difference, he stopped. Straining or not straining, it did not matter. Either way his body could not move. He could see nothing. He closed his eyes. He closed them tight. He conjured up an image in his mind. He brought forth the face of his beloved Eilís. He imagined her in front of him, smiling and laughing. He saw her reaching toward him with her hand. He saw her face draw closer. He saw her lips so near that he could kiss them. He remembered what kissing her had felt like, and he imagined that he was kissing her again.

Then everything went black.

11
The Sorcerer's Lair

CHRYSTEFFOR WAS dreaming. They were not the sort of dreams one remembers upon awakening. Rather, they were the kind of dreams that leave one with a vague but profound sense of unease for most of the following day.

In the middle of his dreams, he heard a voice. The voice was different from everything else. The voice was somehow real, whereas everything else was not. Gradually, the dreams melted away, and only the voice was left in the darkness. He did not question why everything was dark. As far as he knew, it had always been dark and would always be dark.

The voice did not belong to anyone he knew. It was the voice of an old man, who was speaking slowly and quietly. He sounded tired. He was not speaking to Chrysteffor. He was at some distance, talking to someone else. Chrysteffor wondered if it was some visitor of his father's. Yet if there was a visitor in the castle, the prince wondered, why was he not helping his father to entertain him? The prince was sorely confused. All that he knew for certain was that he was exhausted and had no energy.

It dawned on the prince that, if he opened his eyes, it might no longer be dark. And so, with a huge amount of effort, he managed to open his eyes. He did not recognize where he was, but it came to him that he could not possibly be in his father's castle. He was not in his own country. He recalled Castle Aill Stoirm. Is that where he was? He tried to sit up, but he could not move. He tried again, only to realize that he was securely bound to a table by ropes.

He strained against the cords. The act of straining reminded him of something. It brought back painful memories—his most recent memories. He remembered straining before. All too slowly the fragments of memory came back to him. He remembered having entered the third tower and having been overwhelmed by an army of monsters. He wondered how he could have survived the battle. He wondered if he *had* survived.

Could this be the afterlife? he wondered. If so, it was certainly not the afterlife he would have expected. But then, he reasoned, the afterlife was always bound to be a surprise. After all, no one had ever returned to describe it.

Or perhaps, he thought to himself, *this is how the Black Sorcerer turns the dead into the Eidola.*

He turned his head in an attempt to see who was talking. He could not catch sight of him. The prince did his best to listen intently, in the hope that he could make out what was being said.

"This is quite extraordinary," said the old man in a voice that was only slightly louder than a whisper. "It has been a very long time since anything surprised me. Yet I am surprised by you. I never expected to see you again."

His voice was achingly tender.

"You cannot know how good it is to see your face again. I know you will not believe this, but I do love you. I have always loved you. You will never know how much it has pained me, the way things happened."

His voice was strangely soft and filled with melancholy. Chrysteffor strained harder to move his head, but the old man was just beyond his line of sight. He tried to call out to him, but he found he had no voice. All he managed to do was to make a grunting sound.

"Eh?"

The old man had heard him. He walked slowly over to the bound prince, and Chrysteffor was at last able to get a look at him. His face was quite long and, in a strange way, it reminded him of a horse. Moreover, his face was extremely wrinkled. The wrinkles were so deep that his skin seemed to droop over his skull. It was almost as if his face had frozen in the process of melting. The eyes were well hidden under bushy eyebrows. His hair was long and straight and the color of cold embers from the previous night's fire.

The old man, whose shoulders were draped by a well-worn brown robe, looked tired. His movements were languorous but deliberate, as though he had little energy to spare and had to make the most of every movement. He stared intently at Chrysteffor's face, as if he were trying to figure something out about him.

"You have done quite well to still be alive," he said in a tone that was almost kindly.

The prince tried to speak, but his mouth and throat were completely dry. He did his best to salivate so that he could get his voice back.

"Where...?"

"This is where I work," said the old man matter-of-factly. He addressed Chrysteffor the same as he might a small child.

"Who...?"

"I am Leannain. I apologize for leaving you bound, but you are clearly a very dangerous young man. I thought it prudent to take no chances until I knew a bit more about you. This country has become full of dangers in recent years and, as you can see, I am no longer a young man. You have me at a complete disadvantage, I fear. I neither know who you are nor what your motives might be. I am quite frail and would be no match at all for someone as young and strong as you."

Chrysteffor remembered the name Leannain from Lady Aigneis's story. This man was the Black Sorcerer. He was nothing like what the prince had expected. He did not seem dangerous at all—notwithstanding the fact that Chrysteffor was completely helpless and at his mercy.

"Aon Fhear?"

"What?"

"Aon Fhear. Where is he?"

The question made Leannain laugh.

"Is that what you call him? You realize that that is not his name? Indeed that is not a name at all."

"Is he alive?"

"Oh, yes, the two of ye survived that terrible battle. I am not certain how, but ye did. Without a doubt anyone else would be well dead. Most impressive, I must say."

"Where is he?"

"Oh, just here. Do not worry. You are both quite safe here together. Please, tell me about yourself. Who are you? Where do you come from? Clearly, you are not from Afranor."

"Water. Please."

"Of course. Sorry. I should have thought of that myself. Just a moment."

Leannain shuffled out of Chrysteffor's sight and then after a few moments returned with a cup. He put it to the prince's lips. Some of the water spilled on his chin. He choked as he tried to swallow it. All the while, Leannain patiently held the cup while lightly stroking the prince's hair. He seemed fascinated by its pale blond color. His eyes also kept darting toward Chrysteffor's eyes.

"Tell me," said the old man, still speaking barely above a whisper, "were your eyes always two different colors?"

He took the cup away so that Chrysteffor could speak.

"From birth. Does that signify something to you?"

"I find it curious. That's all. It just goes to show that nature continually surprises us."

The sorcerer carefully set the cup down on a table.

"So, tell me, my young fellow, what is your name?"

"Do you really not know? Do your supernatural powers not allow you to divine that information?"

The old man laughed again.

"I do not know what you have been told about me. Do I really seem that powerful to you? I am afraid I am little more than what you see. I am simply an old man passing his last years laboring away in a humble workshop. Obviously, someone has been trying to give you reason to fear me, to make me seem somehow more formidable than I am."

"Well, I am the one who is tied up, while you get to ask the questions. That did not happen because you are so old and frail. The fact that you are holding me against my will is more than enough proof of your malign intent."

"Ah, yes, you are quite clever, so you are. You would like to trick me into releasing you. To give you all the advantage in the situation. Your attitude demonstrates that I was more than right to be cautious. I assure you that I mean no one any harm. Certainly not a fine young man whom I have never set eyes on before."

"Those creatures in the tower, the Eidola. Do you mean to tell me that they were not doing your bidding? Are you not the one behind the continual darkness that afflicts this land? You cannot fool me by playing the kindly old grandfather."

Leannain seemed nothing but genuinely amused. His eyes suddenly twinkled at the prince's words.

"Ah yes, I see they have done quite a good job of making you believe that I am somehow solely responsible for all the misfortunes that have befallen this woebegone country. Tell me, do you always believe everything you are told without question or requiring any proof at all?"

The prince found it difficult to argue with the sorcerer. For one thing, his head throbbed with a dull pain and he found it difficult to think. He had not expected to be engaging in a debate over the veracity of everything he had been told since he had arrived in Afranor. On the other hand, it now occurred to him that all he knew—or thought he knew—was what he had been told by Eilís, Aigneis and Aon Fhear. He had come to trust all of them, however, and could see no reason why they should mislead him.

"If you are not the villain you have been made out to be, then release me. If you have only the best interests of Afranor at heart, then you and I want the same thing. Unbind me as a show of good faith."

Leannain smiled.

"I am quite confident of my own good faith. It is yours that is in question. You have not answered my queries. Who are you and where do you come from?"

"I am Chrysteffor, crown prince of Alinvayl. My brothers and I ventured into this land on our way home from distant lands when we were waylaid by those creatures. Now my brothers are dead, and I am the only one left. Do you really mean to tell me that the Eidola are not under your control? Are you really telling me that you are not responsible for the deaths of my brothers?"

"I am very sorry to hear of your loss. This is the first I have heard of those unfortunate deaths. Until now I did not know that you were abroad in this land. I assure you that you have my sincerest sympathy."

"I do not want your sympathy. I want to be released. If you are as innocent as you claim, then set me free. If you mean no harm then you have nothing to fear from me."

"I wish I could believe that, but everything you have done and said leads me to a different conclusion. I will need a token of good faith before I can trust you."

"A token? What sort of token?"

"Tell me everything you have seen and heard in your travels in this country. I need to know everything that you know. For a start, what were you doing in the towers?"

"You seem to already know Aon Fhear—or whatever name it is that you have for him. Why do you not ask him. Is he bound as well?"

"He has not awakened. He may be more injured than you are. If you are an honest man, you will answer my questions. Your hesitation only confirms that I was right to be cautious with you."

Chrysteffor strained again at the ropes. He did not like feeling so helpless. He did not know what to make of the old man. He was not at all what the prince had been expecting. Still, the prince knew that appearances could be deceiving—especially where magic was concerned.

"I was told there was a prophecy, that I might be able to save this country if I went to the three towers. I thought I might be able to save Lady Eilís."

Leannain eyes widened involuntarily when he heard the princess's name.

"So you know Eilís! Tell me, how is she?"

"I think you know how she is. When last I saw her, she was under an evil enchantment. I believe that spell was your handiwork."

Leannain closed his eyes and looked pained.

"It is difficult to converse with you when you keep insisting on reciting the lies you have been told by others. I do not know where to begin unraveling all the untruths that you have absorbed. I can assure you that I never wanted any of these things to happen. They have all effectively been out of my control. It was my brother and sister who must bear the responsibility for all that has happened."

The old man paused. He looked sincerely distressed and seemed to be taking a moment to choose his words carefully.

"I am not saying that I am blameless in all this. You see? I can see their side of it as well as my own. But I assure you that I never wanted for any of this to happen. In this moment I want nothing more than for you to help me to put things right. You cannot know how much the things you have recounted to me have pained my soul."

The old man seemed so sincere that Chrysteffor could not, in spite of himself, help but have some sympathy for him.

"So," said the prince, "you say that I have been duped, that I have had my mind poisoned against you. If this is true, then the best way to correct that is for you to give me some direct answers to some simple questions. For example, did you or did you not bring never-ending night to this land?"

"It is true that I unleashed the supernatural power that allowed that to happen, but I was not the one who triggered it. That was my brothers. They bear the responsibility."

"Did you or did you not create the Eidola? Do they or do they not do your bidding?"

"What you call the Eidola are a manifestation of the same force that took away the sun. One is a consequence of the other. I never wished for those foul creatures to roam my land."

"But they do indeed carry out your bidding, do they not? Did they not bring me and Aon Fhear here to you?"

"If not for my intervention, they would have killed the two of ye. I saved your lives. It took every ounce of my wizardry to pluck ye away from certain doom. Those creatures follow no master but their own base impulses. If there were a way to cease their existence, I would eagerly make it happen."

"And Lady Eilís? Was it not your hand that put her under an evil spell? Are you not the direct cause of her sleeping fitfully without end?"

"I did not know of this spell until you told me just now. What you must understand is that, while I have mastered certain supernatural skills, the magic that has been unleashed can manifest itself in reaction to the impure attitudes and beliefs of others. That witch Aigneis is more responsible for poor Eilís's plight than I am, I assure you. She may not realize it, but my sister's antipathetic spirit has caused more misery in Afranor than anything I have ever done."

The old man's words and the sound of his voice caused Chrysteffor's head to hurt more.

"You confuse me. Explain. Explain how the king and Lady Aigneis can somehow be responsible for the neverending night and the spell on Lady Eilís. It makes no sense. You are the sorcerer. It is your magic that makes these things happen, is it not?"

"I did not expect you to understand. The world appears simple to the young, but the world is much more complex than you realize. I do not know if I can help you to comprehend all the causes and effects that are in play. Let me start with this. You do not need to be a sorcerer or wizard to set evil in motion. Often what happens is that the magic one unleashes with all the best intentions is influenced and twisted by the strong negativity of other people's spirits. Yes, I am responsible for unleashing sorcery in Afranor, but it was not doing my bidding when it caused all these terrible things to happen. Can you not see? Can you not think for yourself instead of simply parroting the arguments of those who would manipulate you?"

The sorcerer looked down at him with sadness in his eyes.

"You seem such an intelligent, fair-minded young man. Surely, if you use your own reason instead of relying on the negative arguments of others, you can reason the truth for yourself. I beseech you. Open your mind and your heart."

The throbbing in Chrysteffor's temples had only grown worse while the old man spoke. His talk was making the pain increasingly worse.

"I have no way to judge one way or the other whether what you are telling me is true. How am I to decide if your version of events is more credible than other versions? I am in an impossible position."

"I know, I know," said the sorcerer sympathetically. "How can any of us know what the real truth really is. All we can do is look into our own hearts for guidance. What does your heart tell you?"

The prince was confused. Strangely, fighting a dragon or the Eidola seemed easier—well, maybe not easier but simpler—than arguing with a sorcerer. All he really knew for certain was that he wanted to be released from the ropes that were binding him. He did not like this feeling of helplessness.

"Sorcerer, you are doing my head in. Just tell me what you want of me. What do I need to say in order for you to loose these ropes."

"Ah, you see, there is the problem," said Leannain. "It is not simply a matter of you reciting the right words. I have to know that you believe my version of events. You have to make me believe that you accept what I have said as truth. Convince me that you sincerely believe me."

"But I do not know how to do that. Whatever I say now, you will say that I am merely telling you what you want to hear. I do not know how to convince you. Not as long as I am completely at your mercy."

"To the contrary, Prince Chrysteffor. If your heart has changed, I think I will know it. If you really believe me and you say that you believe me, I will know that it is true. All you must do is open your heart."

By now the throbbing pain in his head was all but unbearable.

"If I could talk to Aon Fhear, I think that I could resolve all this in my head. I would like to hear what he has to say. He and I fought for our lives side by side. I trust him completely. If I could hear his counsel, I think I could sort through my thoughts and feelings. Is there any chance that he will wake soon?"

"I fear that he will need some time before he will be recovered enough to talk to either of us. He suffered terribly in the battle within the tower. I am afraid that you are altogether on your own for the time being."

The sorcerer stroked Chrysteffor's hair tenderly.

"Except for me, of course. I am here with you. I would dearly like to be your friend. I know enough now to judge that you are a good person. I have every confidence that you will make the right decision. I think that we will be great friends and allies. We have much in common, you and I. You have lost brothers, and I have lost brothers. We could be very helpful to each other."

Chrysteffor wished that the throbbing would cease.

"I heard you talking to Aon Fhear. You seem to know him well. Tell me, what is he to you?"

Leannain sighed deeply.

"He is my own flesh and blood. I had hoped that he would be by my side through all my trials and tribulations, but he was rebellious. He was determined to find his own way, but now he has come back to me. I think he might be ready to be by my side again. I would love nothing more than to have the two of you by my side. Will you join me? Will you help me? Will you help me put things in Afranor to right again?"

By now Chrysteffor was well and truly confused. First, he had thought Aon Fhear was a brigand. Then he came to believe that he was a patriot, fighting for the liberation of his country. Now he was being told that he was the Black Sorcerer's flesh and blood. Was that true? Could he be

Leannain's son? Had he been roaming the roads of Afranor not because he wanted to save his country but out of an act of rebellion against his own father? If this was true, was it not possible that he would eventually rejoin his father? After all, in Chrysteffor's experience, nothing was stronger than blood in determining a man's ultimate loyalty. If Chrysteffor insisted on opposing the Black Sorcerer, might he not eventually wind up opposing Aon Fhear as well?

It was all confusing and not least because of the continuing throbbing in his head. It was as though the more he thought, the more his brain ached. The only way to assuage the pain seemed to be to stop thinking.

"I am willing to consider your side, Leannain. First, however, I must know what it is that you would want me to do. And whatever I do, Lady Eilís must be released from her spell. Do you understand me?"

"Oh, I understand you perfectly, Prince Chrysteffor. You and I want exactly the same thing. If we work together, I have no doubt that Eilís will be back to herself and Afranor will once again be a sunny and happy place. All I ask of you is that you go back to Castle Aill Stoirm and tell them that I am returning. Tell them that it is time to put all of our sad history and disagreements behind us. Tell them that we will all be one family again and the darkness will be left in the past. That is all you have to do. May I rely on you, my young prince?"

Chrysteffor tried to find fault with what Leannain was saying, but he could not see anything wrong with what the sorcerer was asking. Was it not better for the king and his brother to settle their differences than to continue on the way things had been?

"Yes, Leannain. I will do as you ask. I will carry your message to the castle and tell them to make ready for your return. It is time for everyone to put this all behind them. It is time to choose peace instead of war. You may count on me. I will return to Aill Stoirm in the name of peace."

Suddenly, the ropes holding Chrysteffor loosened and then fell away. With effort he lifted himself off the table and stood on his feet. He was a bit unsteady, a bit wobbly, but he was delighted to find that his headache was suddenly gone. He felt better than he had for quite some time.

12
In the Name of Peace

FOR THE FIRST time the prince could now see the sorcerer's workshop in its entirety. It was by no means a large room, and it was extremely cluttered. Its many shelves were stuffed with old books of every size and description. Most of them were covered with a thick layer of dust, and many had bindings that were barely attached to the spines. On the tables were numerous jars containing liquids and powders of varying colors. Scrolls were spread out here and there haphazardly. Chrysteffor wondered how the sorcerer could find anything at all with the way things were left.

His eyes were drawn to one table in particular. That was because lying on top of it, completely motionless, was Aon Fhear. The black-haired man's eyes were closed. A trail of dried blood ran from his mouth and down his chin. His face was bruised and his hair looked as though it had been pulled in several different directions. He was bound to the table with ropes, just as Chrysteffor had been. The prince drew near to him and placed his hand gently on Aon Fhear's arm.

"He is hurt," said the prince with concern. "Why do you keep him bound? He is no possible threat to you in his present condition."

"Yes, but *only* in his present condition. You see, I know him all too well."

The wizard sighed heavily.

"He will wake soon enough and I expect he will be spoiling for a fight. I will need time to reason with him before I set him free. The time he has spent in the wilderness has given my enemies—and his own rebellious nature—ample opportunity to turn him against me. It is terrible what poisonous words can do to a young and trusting mind. It has pained me to see him become so bitter. I hope that, in addition to his bitterness, he has also accumulated some wisdom in his travels and his experiences."

Leannain looked the prince straight in the eye.

"Prince Chrysteffor, you have obviously grown and matured because of your own recent experiences. It is clear to me that you are not only clever but also wise—despite your youth. I daresay your father would be proud of you."

The prince found himself bothered by the sorcerer's reference to his father, although he was not sure exactly why.

"So we are agreed," said Leannain. "You will return to Castle Aill Stoirm and inform them of my imminent return. You will convince them not to oppose me. We will settle our differences once and for all. Peacefully."

"Yes, I will carry your message. There has been too much fighting and too much death. It is time for peace. I will tell them. I will make them understand."

"Yes, that is exactly what I want. The same thing everyone wants. I just want to see peace. And you are the one who can make it possible. I cannot thank you enough for your help."

"Just one question, Leannain."

"Yes?"

"How will I find my way to the castle? I have no idea where I am."

The sorcerer chuckled.

"Why, you will go back the same way you came."

"But I do not remember the way I came. I was unconscious when I was brought here."

"Yes, of course. It must be confusing for you. You see, you came directly from the third tower. There is a tunnel from there to my humble dwelling."

"A tunnel?"

"Yes. Where did you think all those creatures had come from? How did you think that they had gotten into the tower?"

"They all came through a tunnel? From here?"

"Why, yes. They had been waiting for you. For quite a while, in fact. We were beginning to wonder whether you were ever going to arrive. And we never expected that you would be coming with my dear, dear boy here. It was an amazing stroke of luck that you met him and convinced him to join you."

"You knew I was coming? But how?"

Leannain smiled.

"Well, I may be an old man, but I do know a few tricks. I have a few powers that compensate for my advanced age. I knew you were coming as soon as you entered the first tower."

"But how did you know? Did you have some sort of magic orb or crystal ball that allows you to see wherever you want?"

The sorcerer laughed.

"That would be very nice, now wouldn't it? But no, I have nothing so marvelous or handy as the kind of magic orb you describe. The fact is that the three towers are the source of my power. They have always been a resource of vast mystical energy, but no one knew how to tap them. Not until I unlocked their secrets. It is only natural that, when an interloper wandered into one of them, I would be able to sense it. I knew immediately what was going on. You see, I too grew up with tales of the famous prophecy—the very one that you so obviously were trying to fulfill. Certainly, there was a kernel of truth in the tales that old wives handed down from generation to generation, but back then people were too primitive to fully grasp the true meaning of what they were recounting. I had always known that it was only a matter of time until some young fool..."

Leannain stopped himself.

"I'm sorry. I am not calling *you* a fool, you understand. You are different from most other young men and certainly from most young men in Afranor. I always knew that some young lad would attempt to go to the three towers because of that prophecy. And I always knew that it would likely end in his death. I am glad, though, that it was you who came. You, after all, had the wiles to survive the towers. Just as you have the intelligence to bring peace at long last to this country."

"But tell me something. If the prophecy was, as you suggest, not really true, what about this one very specific detail? The part about the country's savior having eyes of two different colors?"

The sorcerer stroked his chin thoughtfully.

"Yes, well, that *is* a fascinating coincidence. I cannot begin to calculate the odds of that having happened, that a random man such as yourself would match such an unusual detail in the story. I suppose it just goes to show that the universe has a sense of humor. But I assure you, it is nothing more than a coincidence."

"So I am to follow the tunnel back to the tower and from there make my way back to the castle?"

"Yes, yes, exactly. I trust you will find your way with no problem."

The prince glanced wistfully at his unconscious friend.

"I would make the journey with more confidence if Aon Fhear were at my side. Shall I not wait just long enough for him to wake so that he may accompany me?"

The sorcerer shook his head.

"I am afraid that we cannot spare the time. And we have no idea what state he might be in when he does wake. We do not know if he will be fit for the journey. No, it is better if you take your leave immediately. You will be fine on your own."

Chrysteffor sensed that it would be futile to argue with Leannain, and so he reluctantly resolved to make the journey by himself.

"As you say, then," said the prince. "So I will just be needing my sword and to be shown my way to the tunnel, and I will depart."

The sorcerer shifted his gaze away from the prince.

"You will not be needing a sword. You will be quite safe. I give you my word. Besides, do I not see a fine mace hanging there from your belt?"

This was not a question on which Chrysteffor was willing to concede.

"How can you guarantee my safety out there in the darkness, with all the creatures and brigands and who knows what roaming about? I would be mad to go out there without my sword. Or is it your intention that I be killed on the road back?"

The sorcerer smiled as kindly as he could manage.

"My dear lad, if I wanted you dead, I could have ended your life easily while you were still bound on my table and at my complete mercy. Why would I possibly go to the bother of sending you into a trap, only to accomplish what I could have done faster and more easily right here? You have my word. You will be absolutely safe."

Chrysteffor was feeling more and more uneasy about the sorcerer's plan. He wished that Aon Fhear was awake and able to take part in the discussion. He would really like to hear his friend's opinion and his own version of events. Most of all, though, he wished that Aon Fhear was going with him back to the castle. The more he thought about it, the more his head began to hurt again. In fact, it was now hurting so much that he found it difficult to think clearly. He just wanted to be gone out of the sorcerer's lair and on his way back to the castle and to Eilís.

"But how can you promise that I will be safe if I take to the road unarmed? How can you ensure that no man or creature will cross my path and attack me?"

"My good prince, you forget that I have certain abilities. My power can protect you. A sorcerer is a much better friend to have than any weapon you might possess. You need only to trust me. Believe me when I say that you have not survived this long only to meet some ordinary meaningless death on the road to Castle Aill Stoirm."

The prince's head throbbed. He wanted nothing more than for the pain to stop. And he strongly suspected that it would stop if he could just get away from the sorcerer's lair. And it was clear that he would not be leaving with his sword or with his friend.

"Very well. I am not happy about this, but it seems I have no choice in the matter. Show me the way to the tunnel."

Leannain led the prince out of the room. Chrysteffor followed him down a narrow and winding staircase that was built into a rough stone wall. As he watched the hunched figure step gingerly and slowly on one step and then another, all the while leaning on his staff, he marveled to think that this was the man who had spread so much fear across an entire kingdom. It occurred to the prince that he could end the old man's life in an instant by giving him a sudden shove as he walked behind him. But he was no longer afraid of the sorcerer. He no longer saw him as a threat. He saw him only as an old man, one who could not possibly have many more years to live. Chrysteffor laughed at himself for ever having thought that this man was dangerous.

When they reached the bottom of the stairs, the sorcerer led the young man down a dark and windy corridor. The farther they went, the narrower the corridor became and the lower the ceiling was. Chrysteffor wondered if they would not soon be on their hands and knees. Before that happened, though, the corridor ended at a heavy oak door.

"I am afraid I must ask you to open it," said Leannain. "There is no way I can do it myself. Normally, I would have one of my helpers do it, but today I have instructed all of them to stay out of sight."

Chrysteffor examined the door. It was barred by a heavy wooden beam across the front of it. He had to strain to lift it out of its holder. He realized that he was still weak from his battle with the Eidola, but at least he was fit enough to manage a heavy object like the beam. He pulled the door open and felt a gust of chilly damp air rush over his arms and face. He looked into the inky blackness inside. The seemingly endless depth of the darkness made him shiver.

"Well done, young prince. Now I have something for you. Something to bring with you to the king and his family."

Leannain pulled out of his robe a large shiny gemstone. It was attached to a chain, as if it were meant to be worn around the neck as a pendant. He took Chrysteffor's hand and placed it in his palm. The stone was surprisingly heavy, even given its large size.

"This stone has a long and storied history in our family. It is very precious to me, and I am loath to let it out of my possession. Now, though, I feel that I must—as a gesture of my sincerity to the king and the others. When they see this, they will know that it could have come only from me and that it means that I have put my trust in you and in them. They will know that I mean to let bygones be bygones and, I hope, it will assure them that burying the past is the right thing for all of us. May I rely on you to keep it safe and deliver it only to my brother?"

"You may, of course," said the prince. "I will guard it with my life."

The wizard's eyes brightened with satisfaction.

"There is one more thing. I want you to carry a verbal message as well. I want you to memorize a few words from the old language. When you recite them to the king and his family, all possible remaining doubts in their minds will be erased. They will know that the gesture is from me and that it is sincere and heartfelt. Will you do that, Prince Chrysteffor?"

"I do not know if I can, Leannain. What I have heard of your old language sounds strange to me. I do not know if I will manage to remember any of its words."

"Nonsense, my dear boy. You learned the words *Aon Fhear* well enough. What I will now teach you is only a bit longer. There is no doubt that you are a quick learner. Listen carefully and repeat after me. *Dóigh i ifreann.*"

"Duh e frun."

The sorcerer smiled.

"A good first attempt. Now try it again. *Dóigh i ifreann.*"

"Doy if run."

"Brilliant. You nearly have it. Really you do. Now try it one more time. *Dóigh i ifreann.*"

"Doigh i ifreann."

"Very good. That will do nicely. Say it in Castle Aill Stoirm just as you have said it to me just now. Your words will definitely have their intended effect. No doubt at all. I cannot thank you enough for what you are doing for Afranor. It is certain that you will be long remembered in this land forever—and indeed in many others."

Chrysteffor kept repeating the words in his head so that he would not forget them. He put the chain holding the gemstone around his neck, as that seemed the easy way to carry it. He looked one more time into the inky depths before him and shuddered. As he stood there, the sorcerer took a piece of a tree branch that was hanging on the wall and held it up in front of him. The top of the piece of wood burst into flame.

"Here," he said. "Use this for light. You should have no trouble finding your way. After you reach the tower and go outside, you will find your horse waiting for you. You will be back at Castle Aill Stoirm in no time. May we meet again soon and under better circumstances."

Chrysteffor took the torch from the old man and held it in front of him as he peered into the tunnel. The torch's flame revealed little. He did not particularly fancy making his way through the darkness by himself, but the prospect of soon being outside again and having his horse underneath him did cheer him.

"Just one more thing, my boy. Promise me that you will not say the words again until you are in the castle. I know Reicheart and Aigneis can be very suspicious. I do not want the words to sound overly rehearsed. Just speak them naturally, as you are after doing."

"I will keep my word, Leannain. I will carry this stone and your message to them. I will do my best to bring peace to this land."

With that he began his walk through the tunnel. He had not gone far before he heard the sound of the oak door closing behind him. He wondered how the old man had managed to do that so quickly. Was he actually stronger than he pretended to be? Or had one of his "helpers" been lurking nearby all the time?

Chrysteffor knew there was no way he would have been able to walk the length of the tunnel without a torch. Of course, it was so narrow that there was no chance of becoming lost, but it would have been too disorienting for his mind. Even with the torch's light, the complete darkness around him had the effect of giving him vertigo. At least he did not have to feel his way the entire distance by constantly touching the walls. He frequently stumbled on objects on the ground. He did not take the time to look at them, but he assumed they were stones. Part of him, though wondered if they were not bones or skulls. After all, the typical users of this passage would be the Eidola. He wondered if the remains of some of their victims wound up here.

Time passed slowly in the tunnel. His journey seemed to go on forever. It reminded him of the journeys between the towers, alone and in the darkness. During those journeys he at least had had the horse for company. The smallness of the space felt oppressive. The stone hanging from his neck seemed to grow increasingly heavy. It slowed him down and made his neck and shoulders sore. At least there was one bright spot. He no longer had the headache that had been bothering him when he was with the sorcerer.

He could not wait to reach the end. Minutes felt like hours. Hours felt like days. As so often happened since he came to Afranor, time felt completely distorted. He tried to think of things to make the time pass more quickly. He thought of Eilís and that gave him comfort—but only up to a point. After all, it occurred to him that, in the event that he did succeed in ending the war between Leannain and the others, it would likely result in Eilís and Aon Fhear being reunited. And the two of them would almost certainly end up married. It was a painful irony to him that the success of his quest would likely mean losing the one thing that he desired most in the world.

Eventually, the walking and stumbling went on so long that Chrysteffor became convinced that there actually was no end to the tunnel. He came to believe that he had walked into a trap that the sorcerer had set for him—an enchantment that would force him to walk and stumble in the darkness for eternity. And yet his only hope was to continue forward—even if it meant doing so forever. That is what made it the perfect trap.

His spirits were lifted when he felt a breeze on his face. He knew it must be air coming from beyond the end of the tunnel. He picked up his pace, only to stumble and fall to the ground, but that did not matter. He quickly scrambled to his feet and resumed walking, as fast as he could. The farther he went now, the fresher the air—although it was only fresh in comparison to the stale air he had been breathing for hours in the tunnel.

At last he came to the end of the tunnel. He was met by a pile of rocks. He held the torch aloft and looked up. As far as he could make out, there was an opening above. He clenched the base of the torch between his teeth while he used both hands to climb the rock pile. When he got to the top, he found himself emerging from a hole and standing on a floor. Despite the darkness, the place was familiar. He was back in the third tower. As he explored with the torch in his hand, he saw the corpses of the Eidola that he and Aon Fhear had killed. He was staggered by their numbers. The agony of the combat came flooding back to his mind. He was amazed all over again that he had survived the battle.

The stench of the cadavers was overwhelming. He almost preferred to be back in the tunnel. At least down there the draft created by the opening in the tower's floor had deceptively made the air seem fresh. He put his free hand over his nose and mouth and resolved to find the way out with no delay. He stepped over the bodies carefully, doing his best to avoid falling or stepping on something sharp like a stick or a monster's tooth. He made his way rather nervously. He worried that one or more of the creatures might actually still be alive and might spring up if it detected a prey. He did his best to proceed in a straight line, knowing that he would eventually come to a wall. When he did find the wall, he followed it, knowing that it would eventually lead him to the tower's entrance.

The thought of being out of the tunnel at last and, soon, out of the tower lifted his heart. He looked forward to being in the open air. As oppressive as the darkness and mist would be, at least the air would be fresh and he would not feel entrapped. In his anticipation, his attention wandered, but then he suddenly became alert and his heart began to pound. He detected a movement. Thinking he might have imagined it, he proceeded cautiously, holding the torch as far in front of him as he could. He strained his eyes, trying to see anything ahead of him that might pose a danger.

Just ahead of him he saw it clearly. A figure was standing there-- upright. He froze, waiting to see if it actually moved. He was certain that he saw it shift its weight from one leg to another. It then lifted a weapon. Chrysteffor cursed himself for having let Leannain convince him to travel without his sword. What an absolute fool he had been. He tightened his grip on the torch, preparing to use it as best he could to strike the thing if need be, while at the same time reaching for the mace. Thus having armed himself as best he could, the prince stood waiting for his adversary to make the first move.

The prince stood waiting for what seemed like an awfully long time. That made him think that he was not dealing with one of the Eidola. As far as he had observed, they never hesitated. Perhaps this was a brigand who wandered into the tower when he saw the opening. Or maybe it was an assassin sent by the sorcerer. Despite Leannain's unexpectedly mild manner and talk of peace, Chrysteffor still was not certain whether he could be trusted.

The figure spoke.

"Identify yourself! What are you doing in this tower?"

Chrysteffor was dumbstruck. He knew the voice. And he could not believe that he was hearing it. Surely, he was yet one more time the victim of some strange enchantment.

The person standing in front of him was Eilís.

13
Dóigh i Ifreann

"EILÍS? IS IT really you?"

The prince heard a gasp.

"Chrysteffor? Have I really found you?"

The prince dropped the club. He came close to dropping the torch as well. He scrambled heedlessly over the bodies that were in his way and made his way toward the princess as quickly as he could. He silently prayed to himself that it was not some spell or enchantment or hallucination. When he reached her, he stared at her face in the torch light, studying every feature to reassure himself that it was really her. What convinced him that it was not an illusion was the detail of the thin scar that ran down from her eye to her cheek. As odd as it may have seemed, he loved that scar. For some reason it made her beautiful to him, and the more he stared at it the more he wanted to kiss her.

"Eilís, are you really here? Is this a dream? Am I in your dream again? Are you a mere apparition? Please. Speak to me."

She laughed. It was the same laugh she had made when he first kissed her. That was enough to reassure him that it was really her.

"Chrysteffor, I cannot believe I have found you. I have been searching for you ever since I woke from the spell that befell me. I was incredulous when they told me how long I had been asleep. All I could remember was a terrible dream. Something about a dragon. And you were there. You fought for me when I could not fight for myself. It was Aigneis who told me that you had gone to the three towers. I could not believe that you would have done something so foolhardy. I had to find you. I had to know that you were all right. I rode to each of the three towers. I knew I had found you when I found my own horse waiting next to the third tower."

For a moment Chrysteffor again felt every bit the callow youth he had been—not so many days earlier—when he had first met Eilís and had failed to impress her. For just an instant he was dumbstruck and overwhelmed and did not know what to say.

Now, however, he saw something different in her eyes. She was no longer looking at him as someone younger and less experienced than herself, someone who amused her. She was now looking at him with respect and perhaps admiration. As she looked up at him, there was something in her eyes that told him that she now saw him as someone worthy of esteem. Everything he had been through since the beginning of his quest to find the three towers had led to him having more confidence in himself than he had ever had before. Having faced death squarely and having survived gave him a much better idea of what was worth worrying about and what was not. He realized that he was no longer concerned about what she might think of him. He was only concerned about how he felt about her. As he looked at her—and she met his gaze with apparent affection—he leaned forward and did what he had been thinking about for endless days. He put his arms around her and kissed her as if it was the last thing he would ever do. She did not laugh and she did not protest. She put her arms around him and held him as tightly as he was holding her.

When their long kiss was finished, the princess smiled mischievously.

"You have much improved since the first time you tried that."

"I am not the same, Eilís. So much has happened."

She turned more serious.

"I know, Chrysteffor. I can see it in you—the way you stand, the way you speak. I can only imagine what you have been through since we last met. In Afranor, we have all had to mature beyond our years. None more than you, though you have been here only a short time."

"There is so much I want to tell you. I do not know where to begin. But I have good news. The Black Sorcerer is not a threat. Afranor is going to be at peace."

The princess looked confused.

"What? How? What do you mean?"

"I will explain, but we need to return quickly to Castle Aill Stoirm. We have to tell them. We have to tell everyone. I must show them the stone and tell them the words."

"You're not making any sense, Chrysteffor. What are you talking about?"

"I'm sorry. I'm not explaining things clearly. It's just that so much has happened. I have learned so much. I will tell you everything, and let me begin with the most important thing."

"Yes?"

"I love you. I love you more than life itself. I have thought of nothing but you since I first laid eyes on you."

117

At this the princess did something that Chrysteffor had not seen her do before. She blushed.

"But," said the prince, "I suspect that there is someone else that you favor. In fact I have met him. He is a fine man. He is my friend. We have fought side by side. He has become like a brother to me. If he is the one you prefer, I promise I will not stand between ye."

"Chrysteffor, by all the gods what are you talking about?"

"I have met him. In fact, I know him well now. And I know that he knows you. And I know that he loves you. I am speaking of my friend, Aon Fhear."

"Aon Fhear?"

"Yes."

"Uh, you do realize, don't you, that that is not actually a name?"

"Yes, yes, I know, but that is what he asked me to call him. He did not tell me his true name. He clearly has his reasons for not wanting to be called by his own name. Surely you must know of whom I speak. He is so obviously very close to you."

"Can you bring me to him?"

"Yes, but we must go to the castle first. I have to deliver Leannain's message so that we can end all the misunderstandings."

"What message? What are you talking about?"

The prince held up the heavy stone hanging from his neck.

"I have brought this. You do recognize it, don't you?"

The princess studied it intently.

"No, I am afraid I do not. What is it?"

"This gem is important to your family. Surely, you must know it or else know of it. Leannain gave it to me to bring as a sign of good faith."

"Chrysteffor, I have never seen this stone in my life. And I have never heard of anything like it. Please. Tell me from the beginning everything that has happened."

"Aon Fhear and I fought the Eidola. It was a ferocious battle. It happened here in this very place. You can see the casualties all about us. It was a miracle we survived. We were captured and brought to the Black Sorcerer's abode. Then he explained things to me. He told me how the spells and the curses and the fighting were all part of a misunderstanding. He let me go so that I could carry the message to your father. He gave me this stone as a sign of his faith. He even had me memorize a phrase in your own language to recite to your father. To prove that this indeed comes from Leannain and how sincere he is. Everything is going to be all right, Eilís. Don't you see? Everything is going to be all right."

Chrysteffor had expected the princess to be relieved and happy to hear this, but she was neither. In fact, she was clearly perplexed.

"Do I understand you correctly?" she asked. "You were in the sorcerer's lair. You spoke with him. And then he let you go. You did not fight him. You did not attempt to kill him. Is that right?"

"There was no need to fight him, Eilís. He explained everything. It was all a misunderstanding. There is no need to fight anymore."

The prince felt the pain in his head returning. The same pain he had felt in the sorcerer's lair. Eilís looked at him with concern.

"Chrysteffor, are you all right?"

"Yes, of course, I am all right. There is nothing wrong with me, but we need to get back to the castle as soon as possible. Once everything has been put right, we can return to the sorcerer and see Aon Fhear again."

The pain in his head grew worse.

"I do not like the color of your face, Chrysteffor. You do not seem well. Please, come outside and we will find a place to sit."

"Yes, let's leave this foul and terrible place, but I do not need to sit. I need to get to the castle as soon as possible. I do not understand why you want to delay."

The two made their way to the opening in the tower wall and emerged into the dark night air. Chrysteffor took a deep breath, glad to have fresh air again in his lungs. He was happy to see, just as the sorcerer had assured him, that his horse was there waiting—next to Aon Fhear's and a third horse, the one that must have brought Eilís. The prince looked around with a quizzical air. He set down the torch, which was still burning after all this time, on a large flat stone.

"Strange. I would have thought that he would have removed the spell that keeps this land in darkness. After all there is no need for it anymore. Why does he not lift it? Well, I suppose he has his reasons. The sooner we get to the castle, the sooner everyone in Afranor can see the sun again."

"Chrysteffor, I do not like the look of you. You do not seem well. And I do not like the way you are speaking. There is something not right about it."

"You are the one who is not well. Why do you keep questioning me, doubting me?"

"I do not doubt you, dear Chrysteffor. I am simply worried about you. You are exhausted. And that stone around your neck is clearly a terrible weight. Why do you not set it down? You might feel better without all that pressure on your neck and shoulders."

"No! I swore an oath to bring this gem to Castle Aill Stoirm, and I will not rest until I have done so. Why are you so interested in getting it away from me anyway?"

"Chrysteffor, you're not making sense. I am not interested in that stone. It is you I am concerned about. Please set it down. Just for a few moments."

"No, I will not. Not for you or anyone else. Not until I have brought it to the castle. Stop asking me. It is almost as if you are trying to thwart the reconciliation that I am going to bring about. I doubt that the real Eilís would be doing anything other than helping me get back to the castle as soon as possible."

"The real Eilís? What do you mean?"

"Are you the princess at all? After all, I have seen so many strange things in this country, so many evil enchantments. Perhaps you are a demon sent to stop me from bringing peace to this land. Is that it? Is that your aim? Perhaps you are the one who is causing my head to hurt. Yes, that makes sense. You are trying to keep me from my new quest. My quest for peace."

Eilís changed her tone as she put her hand gently on Chrysteffor's shoulder.

"You have it wrong, Chrysteffor my love. I only want to help. So no more delays, I promise. Let us mount this very moment and be off to Aill Stoirm."

Chrysteffor was glad to hear her being more reasonable, although he continued to be wary of her. He put his foot up to mount the horse, but it took a great effort.

"Chrysteffor, that stone around your neck is weighing you down. There is no need to wear it like that all the time. Put it safely in your saddle bag. After all you have been through, the last thing you need is the extra burden on your neck and shoulders."

The prince knew this was good advice, and he did as she suggested before preparing to mount again. Eilís drew near to him.

"Here, allow me to help you mount. I amazed that you have managed to keep going after all of your battles and your injuries. There is no shame in accepting a little help in mounting your horse."

The prince was pleased to feel her touch as he again put up his foot, but he was taken completely by surprise when she did the last thing he expected. She gave the horse a violent slap on its haunches and sent it galloping. She chased after it, screaming at it. Quickly the princess and the steed had disappeared into the mist. Chrysteffor was so astonished that he could only stand there and stare for several moments before running after them.

When he caught up to them, he found Eilís beside the horse, which was standing on the edge of the precipice. The roar of the sea rose up from the depths below. The princess's face was contorted in anger.

"Say the words, Chrysteffor!" she shouted at him. "Say them now!"

For a moment the prince was completely dumbstruck.

"What words? What are you talking about?"

"The words that the sorcerer told you to say. Speak them now!"

"Eilís, what is wrong with you? What has come over you? Or was I right? Are you not my beloved Eilís at all? Who—or what—are you really?"

"I am not going to discuss this with you, Chrysteffor. Just do as I say. Speak the words that the sorcerer had you memorize. Say them now!"

Chrysteffor feared for the safety of the horse. Eilís did not seem in her right mind, and one well placed slap would send the poor creature over the edge and to its death.

"I do not understand. I would have told you anyway. You did not need to do this. It's just that Leannain was insistent that I not say them until I was in the castle. I only wish to honor his request. It seems a small favor to grant him. And what difference does it make anyway? Please, Eilís, come away from the cliff and let us talk about this like reasonable people."

The princess became more agitated. She did not seem to be in her right mind. Chrysteffor was convinced that this could not be the real Eilís. He regretted not having his sword, but he still had Benet's mace hanging from his belt. The sorcerer had not taken it from him.

"I am warning you, Chrysteffor. Say those words this very minute. Say them! Now!"

Why was it so important for her to hear Leannain's words, he wondered. Did they contain information that could be used against him and the real Eilís? Because they came from a sorcerer could she use them for her own evil purposes? His instinct was to not say the words, not here, not now, but only in the castle as Leannain had instructed him.

The woman who appeared to be Eilís raised her hand, intending to slap the unfortunate horse. Her face grew more twisted and more determined. The prince considered grasping the mace and striking her down. If she was as quick and ready as the real Eilís, she would have no trouble countering him with her own weapon. And the poor horse would be doomed for sure. Moreover, he was not at all certain that he could manage to raise a weapon against her. There was just enough doubt in his

121

mind that, however mad she had gone, this might be the real Eilís. He could not take the chance of injuring or killing the woman he loved. In the end, he decided to risk saying the words he had sworn not to utter until the right time and place.

"Very well. Have it your way, but you have clearly gone mad. These are the words I was told say. *Dóigh i ifreann!*"

The prince had no sooner spoken the words than the princess brought her hand down fiercely on the horse's haunch. The frightened animal reared up in pain and then, in a motion that seemed to the prince as though time itself had slowed, tumbled over the precipice. Chrysteffor watched in horror as it vanished into the dark. Its terrified cry rang in his ears. He fell to his knees. He had seen much death since he came to Afranor, but the senselessness of the horse's death, of the mount that had been a loyal companion through his darkest days was too much. He stood up and began swinging the mace. Clearly, the thing that had done this could not possibly be Eilís.

Before he was able to say or do anything, he was thrown to the ground by a terrible shaking of the earth beneath his feet. It was the most powerful jolt he had ever felt. A rumbling roar rose up from the sea below. A blast of fire shot up from beneath the cliff's edge and far into the inky sky. The heat from it was hot enough to inflict on his face a painful sensation of being singed. He shut his eyes to protect them. When he opened them again, he saw billows of smoke rising, obscuring the remaining light from the terrible flame.

Chrysteffor's heart raced with fear, and it took him a good while to catch his breath. He sat up with his arms resting on his knees. He warily surveyed the black vapors mixing with the mist. He put the back of his hand over his nose in an attempt to stop the acrid odor. And he dearly hoped that there were no more explosions to come.

"By the gods, what was that?" he coughed.

Eilís had also been knocked off her feet, but she was now already again standing erect. She stared grimly into the remnants of smoke wafting from below. Although she did her best to stay steady, she was every bit as shaken as the prince.

"That, my dear Chrysteffor, is the sorcerer's idea of peace."

14
An Emotional Reunion

STILL DUMBFOUNDED, the prince stared at Eilís awhile before rising unsteadily to his feet.

"Did you do that? Did you cause that terrible explosion with some supernatural power of yours?"

She glared back at him in exasperation.

"No, of course not," she said grimly. "How could I have possibly caused something like that?"

"If not you, then who or what?"

"Are you really so slow? No, you are not. I would say that your thinking has been clouded by some enchantment of the sorcerer. That is the danger of trying to confront him face to face. He can do things to your mind."

"What are you talking about?"

The prince was feeling increasingly confused.

"Do you not see? That devastation was caused by the stone you were carrying. Imagine if you had brought it inside my father's castle and spoken those evil words there. Everyone in or near the castle would be dead. Every last one of them."

Chrysteffor did not want to believe her but, the more he thought about it, the more her words made sense to him. What else could explain it? What an incredible fool he had been. He had not only agreed to carry an evil, powerful gem back to the people who had given him refuge but he had carefully and obediently learned the ungodly incantation to unleash its cursed power. He had been a fool, and now it was all so clear. Why could he not have seen things as clearly when he was with the sorcerer? He felt imbecilic and guilty and humiliated. As terrible as he felt, though, there was at least one thing he was glad of. His headache was at last gone completely.

"My darling Eilís, please forgive me. I have been so incredibly stupid. When I think what might have happened..."

"The important thing is that the disaster was averted. Thanks be to the gods. I only regret that I had to sacrifice the horse. It was a noble animal and did not deserve to die. I had that horse for a very long time and it carried me faithfully for many miles. Sadly, I could see no other way to get the stone away from you."

"How did you know…?"

"And how did you *not* know? No, that is not fair. You have not lived through this nightmare your entire life the way I have. You are still learning what true evil is, whereas I have had a lifetime of instruction. I only needed to know that the stone came from the sorcerer to know that it could only mean death and destruction. Still you must have a strong mind and a solid character not to have gone completely under the wizard's sway. A lesser man would have been compelled by the spell to kill me rather than lose the stone. You had enough will to hesitate just long enough for me to do what needed to be done."

"You flatter me. A better man would not have been seduced by the sorcerer's pretty words in the first place."

"None of that matters now, my dear Chrysteffor. We must decide what we will do now. The sorcerer surely knows that his plan has failed, and he will not be one bit happy about it. We are in grave danger."

As the prince's mind grew ever clearer, he was alarmed by a sudden memory.

"Aon Fhear!"

"I told you that that is not a name."

"Yes, yes, so you said. But he is my friend and the evil one has him. If the sorcerer is in a rage over the failure of his plan, he may well punish my comrade for it. I have to go back for him."

"Are you mad? The sorcerer let you live because he thought he could use you to destroy all his enemies at once. Now that his plan has failed, you are of no further use to him. He will seek only your death. The last thing you should do is put yourself back within his grasp."

"But my friend…"

"Think, Chrysteffor. Are you certain your friend is real? The wizard was playing with your mind. Could he not have created this friend as an illusion or hallucination in order to manipulate you?"

"No, he is real. He is as real as you or I. We talked. We fought each other. I felt his body against mine, and he was as real as any creature of flesh and blood. And we fought together against the Eidola. He was no phantom. He was a real man. That is his horse there. Why would that horse be there if he were not real? And he knows you. In fact, by all appearances, he loves you deeply."

"Chrysteffor, I honestly have no idea of whom you are speaking. How could he know me and, as you say, love me and yet I do not know him?"

Chrysteffor pondered her words. He had believed the sorcerer's words about the stone, and he had not been able to see through his deception. Was it possible that Eilís was right and that his memories of Aon Fhear had been placed in his mind? After all, where sorcery was concerned, was not anything possible? How could he know for certain?

The prince turned toward the tower and made his way to the entrance. The princess watched as he went back inside, and then she followed him. She found him standing just inside. He had picked up the torch, which was still burning after all this time, and was using it to survey the endless numbers of cadavers.

"I killed a good many of these monsters," he said, "but I did not kill all of them. No one man could have. Most of them were killed by Aon Fhear. This is the proof. And now he is a captive of Leannain. I must rescue him or die trying. I am certain he would do the same for me."

"Chrysteffor, you are mad."

"You are probably right. But at least, unlike before, I can see things clearly now. I know what I must do, and I must do it not because it is sane or reasonable. I must do it because it is right. I know the way back to the sorcerer's lair, and I will now return and do what I should have done the first time."

"Can I not talk you out of this?"

"No. I will not leave here without Aon Fhear. And I have another reason for going back."

"Yes?"

"That villain has my sword. It is an extremely powerful sword with its own magical properties. And, more than that, it means a great deal to me. I had to fight my own dead brother for it. I definitely mean to get it back."

Eilís did not know whether to despair or to be impressed. She knew all too well what the wisest course of action was. Yet she found Chrysteffor's purposeful determination strangely infectious.

"You are most definitely mad, Chrysteffor. Yet perhaps madness is exactly what is called for in the situation. Your plan, while incredibly risky and foolhardy, certainly has the element of surprise. It is definitely the last thing that the sorcerer would ever expect. I surrender to your madness. Please show me the way to his lair."

The prince had not actually expected Eilís to be convinced. Perhaps somewhere deep in his mind he was hoping that she would succeed in stopping him. In any event the die was now cast. This would almost certainly mean their deaths. He did not mind so much for himself. After all, he had completely resolved himself to a premature demise quite a few days earlier. That he had survived this long was actually something of a pleasant surprise, but he would have preferred that Eilís not die along with him. On the other hand, if he was to have any hope of surviving this day, his chances would be significantly better if she were at his side. In the end, it was this selfish thought that stopped him from arguing with her.

"It is a long passage that is dark and very confined," said the prince. "We had best get started and run its length as quickly as we can—if we want to have any hope of benefiting from this element of surprise."

The last thing Chrysteffor wanted to be doing was traveling again the entire length of that narrow, dank tunnel, but by this time he had more or less ceased to care about his personal comfort or safety. With a head that was now clear, he had a goal.

He led her to the hole in the floor, and they climbed down the rocks to the passage below. Then, without allowing himself any time to dwell on it and holding the torch aloft, he simply stared straight ahead into the darkness and proceeded through the tunnel as quickly as he could with Eilís close behind. The fact that she was with him made tolerable the intolerable.

As they made their way, slowed only by the occasional stumble on the uneven floor, it occurred to Chrysteffor that there would be a heavy wooden door at the other end of the tunnel. He had no idea how they would get past that obstacle—or the army of Eidola that were more than likely waiting on the other side of it. He was past worrying much, though, about the future—even if the future was relatively near and drawing nearer with every step.

"Why do you keep looking back at me? Surely, we can move faster if you do not keep doing that."

"I am sorry. It's just that, well, I still cannot believe you are here. I keep fearing that, when I look back at you, you will be gone."

"Well, then the solution is to stop looking back. After all, if your fear is of looking back and seeing I am not here, then there is no chance of that happening if you do not look back. Does that not make sense?"

"No, Every moment that I do *not* look back, you vanish constantly. In my mind, I mean."

"You are a funny man, Chrysteffor. I promise you that I am here and that I shall continue to be here—even when you do not look back. Now please keep moving with no further delay."

The prince did as he was told, although at times he found it more than he could bear not to sneak a backward glance. Instead, however, he merely imagined in his own mind that he was looking backward at the princess. Keeping her image in his mind—just as he had done all the time when he was entirely alone—kept his heart up and gave him the motivation to press onward. It also had the effect of somehow making the time pass more quickly for him.

Before he was ready for it, their passage came to an end, just as he had known it would, at the heavy wooden door.

"And how do we get past this?" asked Eilís.

"That, I fear, is an excellent question," said Chrysteffor, as he pulled uselessly on the chain that was mounted on the front of the door.

No matter how he strained at pulling the chain, the door did not move in the slightest. It gave every appearance of being barred on the other side. As pointless as they were, the prince continued his efforts, as he did not know what else to do.

"Was this door not here before?"

"Yes, yes, it was."

"And did you expect it to be open?"

"No, not particularly."

"So then, what exactly was your plan to get past it?"

"I had no plan. Only a goal."

"And how do you expect to achieve your goal now?"

Although he did truly love Eilís with all his heart, Chrysteffor was now finding that she could be annoying. He tried pushing on the door, instead of pulling, but the result was similar. He pounded against the door in order to test its strength and solidity.

"Do you really think the sorcerer will open the door if you knock politely?"

"Do you have any ideas? Or can you only criticize?"

"This is not *my* plan. Sorry, I mean, my *goal*."

The prince looked around until he settled his gaze on a good-sized stone.

"Here. Hold this, if you will," he said, as he handed the torch to the princess.

He then picked up the stone and forced it with all his might against the door. The wooden obstacle did not budge in the slightest.

"With all this noise you are making, the sorcerer will surely hear it and come to invite us in."

"At this point I am past caring. If he dares to open that door, he will get the biggest—and final—surprise of his wretched life. We should be making more noise."

"Be careful what you wish for, Chrysteffor. He used charm on you before. You have not seen him when he resorts to violence."

"Let him do his best. He has not seen violence until he has met me again. Come open this door, you coward! I dare you to face me! Hiding will do you no good!"

"He is hardly hiding. He does not even know we are…"

"*Dóigh i ifreann!*"

The prince had shouted the words so suddenly and forcefully that the princess's jaw hung in mid-sentence. She watched in wonder as the door slowly but steadily turned on its hinges and opened wide.

The two of them stared through the doorway apprehensively, wondering if anyone or anything would be coming from the opposite direction. Chrysteffor took the torch back from Eilís. The princess raised her sword in preparation. As the moments passed, they relaxed—but only a bit.

"What made the door open?" whispered the princess.

"There is no explanation. Unless…"

"Unless?"

"Unless it was the words that I spoke."

"What made you say them?"

"I don't know really. It was an act of desperation. I suppose I thought that, if they had power over that cursed stone, then they might have power over this as well. Perhaps I am becoming a bit of a sorcerer myself."

"Or else the real sorcerer is the one who caused the door to open and he is now toying with us. So now what?"

"So now we have only a staircase to climb and we will be in the sorcerer's lair."

Without hesitating further, Chrysteffor set off to retrace his steps back to where he had awakened on the table. The princess followed, watching warily in every direction. She could not believe that this curious young foreigner had actually led her into the home of her lifelong enemy.

The prince crept cautiously up the stairs. He was surprised that Leannain had not appeared, and he was in dread of the possibility of encountering the Eidola at some point. Surely, if the sorcerer was as powerful as he had been led to believe, he must surely know by now that he and Eilís were there. Yet they encountered no man or thing to hinder their progress up to the room above. At the top of the stairs, Chrysteffor softly drew a breath before quickly passing through the doorway. He found the table where Aon Fhear had lain. He was not there. The ropes that had bound him lay in a tangle on the floor. Nor was there any sign of anyone else in the room.

"My friend is gone. The sorcerer has moved him somewhere else."

"He is probably dead. The sorcerer is not known for his mercy."

"I do not think so. There was some connection between them. Leannain actually seemed to be strangely fond of him—in spite of the fact that Aon Fhear wanted nothing more than to destroy him."

"So if your friend is not here and the wizard is not here, your efforts in coming here may unfortunately have been in vain."

The prince's face lit up.

"Not at all. It was more than worth the journey back," he said as he crossed the room to a table in the corner.

To his delight he had spotted his sword. Scarcely believing his luck, he grasped it and held it aloft. It was no trick of the eye, he was sure, that the blade gave off a soft glow at the moment he first touched it.

"With this in hand I will not hesitate to scour the entire castle or, for that matter, all of Afranor. I am now ready for Leannain and anything else that awaits."

"Well, I like your confidence anyway."

"Come. We must find my friend."

And with that the prince raced out of the room. Despite her apprehension, Eilís saw no better course than to follow him.

Chrysteffor had not previously appreciated how large and complex the sorcerer's castle was. There were so many corridors and stairways and rooms with multiple entrances that it felt like being in a maze. As the pair raced down one hallway and emerged into yet another chamber, the prince wondered if the layout of the castle were not shifting by some magic. Noting that he had never seen a way to exit the castle—apart from the underground tunnel—he in fact wondered whether the castle would ever allow them to leave. He chose to put that thought out of his mind in order to focus on the immediate task at hand, which was to find his friend.

As he strode down yet one more corridor, he noticed a heavy door that was barred. It had a small window with iron bars, giving every appearance of being a room that held a prisoner. As he approached it, a voice could be heard from inside.

"Release me, you coward! You cannot keep me here forever. It is only a matter of time until we will have our reckoning."

Chrysteffor's heart leapt as he recognized the voice of the man he was seeking.

"Aon Fhear! It is Chrysteffor. I have come for you."

"Chrysteffor! I was certain you were dead."

"Stand ready. I will release you."

The prince attempted to lift the bar that was across the door, but it would not budge. As much as he strained, it would not move an inch. It was as though it was held fast by an enchantment. Chrysteffor stood back and stared at the door and said, "*Dóigh i ifreann!*"

Nothing happened. Frustrated, he made another angry attempt at lifting the bar, but to no avail. It then occurred to him to try something else. He inserted the blade of his sword under the bar and attempted to pry it.

"Chrysteffor! You will break your blade," said Eilís.

"Who is that?" said Aon Fhear.

To Chrysteffor's relief, the bar flew off, as if of its own accord, when pushed by the glowing blade. The beam of wood landed on the floor with a thud, and the door began to swing slowly open.

"That is indeed some sword," said Eilís, impressed. "I can see now why you were so keen to get it back."

The prince pulled on the heavy door to open it further. To his delight, his curly-haired friend quickly emerged. Still looking bruised and battered, he was at least walking under his own power. He grinned in a way that Chrysteffor had never seen him do before, as his eyes squinted at emerging from the total darkness of the room. He immediately embraced the blond prince.

"You did it, my friend. You survived the battle with the Eidola and you succeeded in releasing me from this stinking hole. I will be forever in your debt."

Eilís stared with her mouth agape at the dark-haired man who had appeared before her. She let out a loud gasp.

"This is impossible!"

Aon Fhear looked over at her and likewise gasped.

"You! Here!"

Neither said another word. Chrysteffor, suddenly feeling quite invisible, stood back as Eilís ran to Aon Fhear and threw her body against his. The two of them embraced as if neither had any intention whatsoever of ever letting the other one go.

15
A Terrible Vision

CHRYSTEFFOR STOOD awkwardly for what seemed to be an eternity. He was all too aware of the fact that any delay might risk their lives. Yet he could not bring himself to interrupt the passionate reunion he had brought about.

"I never dreamed I would see you again."

Eilís's voice was a whisper, as if she were showing reverence in a sacred place. Chrysteffor had never before heard her sound so tender, so vulnerable. As happy as he was for these two people, both of whom he loved so much, the sight of them together sharing such profound emotion and so much common history was making his heart break. He knew there was no possibility of his ever being able to come between them. It was clear to him that rescuing his friend had meant losing the only woman he could ever imagine loving.

As Eilís gazed up into Aon Fhear's eyes, she said, "Why did you not tell us? How could you not let us know? That was so very, very cruel."

"It was the only way I thought I could keep ye safe. I could not let him know that I was alive. The only hope I could see for defeating him was to do my best to let him think I was well and truly dead."

Chrysteffor decided that he could wait no longer. They had already delayed more than was prudent. He had no choice but to intrude into their conversation.

"My dear friends, I wish the circumstances were better for this sweet meeting, but I fear we must press on with all haste. It is clear how much the two of you love each other, and I pray that you will have many happy years together ahead of ye. For now, however, we must find Leannain before he finds us—and dispatch him, once and for all. My dearest Eilís, as for any of the silly things I might have said to you before I knew of Aon Fhear, please feel free to disregard them. I understand now how things are."

"By all the gods, what is he talking about, Eilís?"

"I do not know. And what ever possessed you to tell him to call you Aon Fhear?"

"I could hardly tell him my right name, could I?"

"Perhaps then," interjected Chrysteffor, "Eilís's beloved could at long last tell me his true name?"

"My beloved?" laughed the princess. "Chrysteffor, this is my brother. His name is Feidhlim."

Chrysteffor's heart nearly leapt out of his chest.

"Feidhlim? The one who fell from the cliff while battling the sorcerer? But did Feidhlim not perish?"

"So all of us thought," said Eilís. "Tell me, brother, how ever did you manage to survive a fall from such a height?"

"I myself can scarcely believe that I lived to tell of it. It was pure good fortune that I missed the rocks below and hit the water in a place that was deep enough that I did not smash against the sea floor. I thought my lungs would burst before I could swim to the surface. It was such extraordinary luck that I truly believed that fate spared me for a purpose. And that purpose could only be ridding our land of the sorcerer. It occurred to me that, if he believed I had died, it might possibly give me an advantage over him. Sadly, however, all my attempts to locate his hiding place while maintaining the element of surprise failed miserably. It was not until I met this young foreign prince here, who had actually heeded the old legend of the three towers, that I found my chance."

"But I only knew of the legend of the three towers from your aunt, Lady Aigneis," said Chrysteffor. "Did she not speak with either of ye about it? Why did no one else attempt to visit the towers?"

Eilís and Feidhlim looked at one another somewhat sheepishly.

"The fact is," said Eilís, "that everyone always considered our dear aunt Aigneis, well, not quite right in the head. For many years now she has lived in her own world."

"We should have paid her more heed," mused Feidhlim. "It appears she may have been wiser than all of us. As for now, Chrysteffor, you are right about haste being paramount. Time is of the essence. It worries me that there is no sign of the sorcerer here in his own lair. What do you suggest we do?"

The young prince was still absorbing all that he had just learned, but he quickly turned his head to the task at hand.

"We must search this place from top to bottom," he said, "and assure ourselves that he is truly not here. If we do not find him, at least we might learn something useful in the search."

"Shall we split up to save time?" asked Feidhlim.

"No," said Chrysteffor. "The sorcerer will be a match for all three of us, let alone for any one of us. Our best hope is to stick together—even if it prolongs our task."

With that the three of them continued the search that Chrysteffor and Eilís had begun, inspecting every corridor and every room in the wizard's labyrinthine castle. It was not the easiest of undertakings, as there were times when the trio could not be certain they were not searching rooms and corridors where they had already been. There were also times when they felt completely lost and wondered whether they would ever find their way back out again. Eventually, they were satisfied that they would not find Leannain anywhere. The mystery was, where had he gone? And what did his absence mean?

They made their way back to the room where Chrysteffor and Feidhlim had first been brought. As they pondered their next move, Chrysteffor spotted something he had not noticed before—the entrance to a smaller room off to one side. Cautiously, the blond prince stepped inside to see what was there. There was no sorcerer, but there was something there that amazed the young man. On a table sat a large glass orb. Chrysteffor began to laugh.

"Are you all right?" asked Eilís. "What could you possibly find so funny here?"

"That evil old trickster. His words are definitely not to be trusted. Or rather, his words are only to be trusted in the sense that they will always be false. He specifically told me that he did not have a magic orb. And what do I find here but an orb that gives every indication of having some kind of supernatural properties. He must have been having a great laugh at my expense—all the while playing the simple and sincere old man."

"And what do you imagine this orb does?" asked Feidhlim.

"I suspect this is his eyes and ears. Or at least his eyes. If I can only figure out what makes it work."

"What makes you think it does any work at all?" asked Eilís skeptically. "Perhaps it is only a decoration."

"Somehow I think not," said the blond prince determinedly.

As they discussed it, the orb gave off a constant low glow. Every so often, of its own accord, it would brighten and then dim again. Chrysteffor tried waving his hand in different directions across the glass surface, but this had no effect. He tried placing his hand directly on the globe. Nothing happened. He slid his hand across its surface, but then jumped back when he felt a light shock to his palm.

"Did it hurt you?" asked Eilís.

"No," said Chrysteffor, "it startled me, that's all. This orb definitely has some sort of power. If I only could comprehend it."

The young prince placed his hand once again on the globe, closed his eyes and murmured, *"Dóigh i ifreann."*

As he spoke the words, the orb glowed brighter than at any time he had so far seen, but that was all. He waited a few moments to see if anything else would happen, but nothing did—except for the orb's glow dimming again. The prince drew his sword and was only mildly surprised to see that it was glowing at the same intensity as the orb. He placed the sword's blade against the surface of the globe. He felt a steady energy pulsate through the sword's hilt and into his clenched hand. The energy spread until he could feel it throughout his entire body. For a moment, he wondered if he had made a dreadful mistake. Would there be some terrible price to pay for meddling in things he did not understand?

"Chrysteffor?"

The prince did not understand why there was such concern in Eilís's voice. That was because he could not see what she and Feidhlim saw. They saw the orb's glow merge with that of Chrysteffor's sword and then expand to envelop Chrysteffor's entire body. They watched with disquiet as the orb and the prince together shimmered so much that they could no longer be seen clearly.

As for Chrysteffor, his attention was directed entirely at the orb. He was amazed to see things inside it, as if he were looking through a glass and seeing outside of the castle. It was all hazy at first but, the more he studied it, the more distinct it became. It was as though he was peering through swirling mists and, the more he willed it, the more the mists parted. Moreover, his vantage point was seemingly from the sky, the way a bird in flight might see things. In the distance he could make out the distinct shape of Castle Aill Stoirm, silhouetted against the dark sky atop its sea cliff. Chrysteffor was amazed that, in spite of the swirling mists, he could see it all so clearly. It was as though he were truly soaring above the castle.

He was alarmed, though, by what else he saw in the orb. At first it seemed to him as though the ground were moving, but the more he studied it, the more he realized that it was not the earth in motion but hordes of creatures on the move. It was the Eidola. More of them than he had ever seen before, all marching in one direction. They were marching toward the castle. And leading them, atop a large black stallion, was the sorcerer himself. He no longer looked old and feeble. He looked like a man much younger than his years. Alarmed by what he saw, Chrysteffor pulled his sword away from the orb and felt the strange energy drain from his body. He felt dizzy and faint as he stood there, the globe's glow and the visions receding into memory.

"Chrysteffor! Are you all right? Why did you not answer me?"

The words seemed as though they were coming from a great distance, though they were spoken by Eilís, who was standing close to his side.

"I'm sorry. I did not hear you. Did you see it? Did you see what I saw?"

"See what?" asked Feidhlim. "All we saw was you trapped in some kind of strange light. It looked as though you might be carried away to another world. This is a dangerous business you are playing at, Chrysteffor. Do you have any idea what you are doing?"

"Then ye did not see it? Ye did not see the castle? The Eidola?"

"What are you talking about, Chrysteffor?" asked Eilís.

"I saw it. I saw it in the orb. The Eidola are marching on Castle Aill Stoirm, led by the Black Sorcerer. There are so many of them. The castle will not be able to withstand the assault. We have to go to their aid. We have to go now."

"I do not understand," said Eilís. "How could you see that from here? Are you sure it was not just a hallucination brought on by the sorcerer's malign instrument?"

"No, it was real. I can feel it in my bones. I do not know how it is possible, but I know for a certainty that I was seeing what is happening at this very moment."

"Could it not be some sort of prophecy?" asked Feidhlim. "A vision of the future? How can you be so certain that it is happening now?"

"I just know," insisted the blond prince. "I cannot explain it any better than that. While we debate this, we are losing precious time. Lives are at stake. Will ye follow me back to the castle? There we shall all see the reality."

The other two agreed, but mainly because returning to the castle would have been the logical course in any event. Chrysteffor led the way back down the stairway and into the tunnel. As tired as he was, the blond prince was able to travel the length of the tunnel faster than the previous two times. He found that the glow from his sword's blade lit the way for him so that he was more sure of foot. Moreover, the sword in some way seemed to be a source of energy for him. Eilís and Feidhlim found it was all they could do to keep up with him. When they emerged from the third tower, the two horses were waiting there.

"I will have to ride with one of you," said Chrysteffor, "as I no longer have a horse."

"Ride with me," said Eilís matter-of-factly. "That only makes sense, as I am lighter than my brother."

The blond prince sorely wished that he had his own horse. On the other hand, he did not exactly mind sharing Eilís's horse for the length of the journey. After all, it required him to hold onto her tightly. And that he did, perhaps a bit more tightly than was absolutely necessary. The brother and sister knew the road well and were able to make good time with no delays. Chrysteffor prayed that the vision he had seen in the orb was not true, but he was certain in his heart that it was. He dreaded what they would find at the road's end.

For once, he thought to himself, *the longer the journey the better.*

Despite the dire situation, he was in no hurry to dismount and to have to let go of Eilís. As they rode along, it was easy enough to lose himself in an imaginary world containing only himself, Eilís and the horse beneath them. None of the three riders spoke. Each was lost in his or her own thoughts.

In the end—and contrary to every expectation—the journey passed all too quickly for Chrysteffor. It was no time at all before they had passed the second tower. And after that it was not much longer until they had passed the first tower, the one where Chrysteffor had fought his brothers and had acquired his sword. Once this last milestone had been passed, the prince could no longer hide in his timeless dream world. Instead, he became alert and on edge, waiting for any sign of the catastrophe he had seen in the sorcerer's orb. He had no doubt that at any moment they would come upon the hordes of the Eidola he had seen marching toward the castle. Now his entire body was becoming more tense with each passing mile.

Thus he was genuinely surprised when they eventually arrived at the castle and there was no sign of either a siege or a battle. Everything looked the same as before. Still the young prince was cautious. As quickly as he dismounted, he placed his hand on the hilt of his sword. He stared attentively in every direction. He listened for any unusual sounds. Feidhlim took note of his determined vigilance.

"Easy, my friend. I do not doubt what you saw, but is it not possible that what you saw was merely an illusion summoned up by the sorcerer? To unsettle you? To put fear in your soul? It was likely a mere conjurer's trick. Besides, I am the one who should be nervous in this situation. I have not been back to this place in years. What sort of reception can I expect from my father, who believes me dead?"

"It will be the first joy he will have known in as many years, brother. His only regret will be all the time that has been lost."

The three approached the castle's entrance. Eilís greeted the guard.

"What news, Conn? Anything strange here?"

Conn stared with wide eyes at the dark-haired man with Eilís. He looked as though he might faint.

"Prince Feidhlim? Do my eyes deceive me? How can this be? By what witchcraft…?"

"Steady, Conn," said Feidhlim. "It is a long story, but rest assured it is indeed myself. I have come home."

The three entered the castle and strode down the corridor. They were quickly spotted by an incredulous pair of young eyes.

"Feidhlim! Is it really you?"

The lad sprinted to his cousin and wrapped his arms around him.

"Goodness, Ruaraidh, I hardly knew you. You were just a wee fellow the last time I saw you. You are nearly a man now."

"He *is* a man, Feidhlim. He was the first one I saw when I woke from the spell that had been placed on me. He had been standing vigil over me for days. I was told that he never left my side the whole time. I could not have asked for a more loyal guardian."

"Feidhlim, I am so happy you are back," said the lad as he gazed up into the older man's eyes. "Everything will be all right now, won't it?"

"Yes, Ruaraidh, you and I and Eilís and Chrysteffor we will all do everything we can to make everything right again."

There were now four walking down the corridor, and they did not stop talking until they arrived at the door of the king's chamber. In response to the noise they were making, Lady Aigneis emerged quite cross from the king's room.

"What is all this clamor? The king is not well. He needs his rest. He…"

The old woman stopped short when she noticed that the noise was coming from Eilís and Chrysteffor, who had returned. She saw the tall dark-haired man with them and her jaw dropped.

"Can it possibly be…? Is this some sort of cruel trick?"

"No, dear aunt, your eyes do not deceive you. I have indeed returned."

Lady Aigneis looked as though she might fall down, but instead she collapsed into the black-haired prince's arms, sobbing.

"I cannot believe it. I cannot believe it," she whimpered. "All hope is not lost. All hope is not lost."

Under other circumstances, Chrysteffor would have been more moved by the outpourings of emotion at Feidhlim's unexpected return, but he could not shake the feeling that all was not right. His heart was dominated by an overriding dread. He could not banish the vision of Eidola hordes from his mind. The tearful Lady Aigneis extended her hand and put it on the blond prince's shoulder.

"Thank you, Prince Chrysteffor. Thank you for bringing back our dear lad. You do not know what this means to us."

Distracted, Chrysteffor continued to glance in one direction and then another.

"I fear this happy reunion is to be short lived. Danger approaches. We must be ready."

"Danger?" asked Aigneis. "What do you mean? What danger?"

"There is a horde of Eidola making their way to the castle. I do not know when they will arrive, but I fear it will be soon."

Lady Aigneis looked up at her nephew.

"Is this true, Feidhlim?"

"I... do not know," said the black-haired prince. "I do not know what to believe. Prince Chrysteffor saw something in an orb in the sorcerer's castle. I do not pretend to understand exactly what it means."

Lady Aigneis looked concerned.

"But in all these years, Feidhlim," she said, "those creatures have never attempted to attack this castle directly. Would they really do so now?"

Lady Eilís put her hand gently on the blond prince's arm.

"Chrysteffor, the sorcerer confused you before. Remember? He nearly made you bring that terrible stone here. Could this not merely be yet more of his perfidy? After all, we rushed back here at your urging and found nothing amiss."

Chrysteffor found himself becoming increasingly agitated.

"No, this is different. With the stone, my mind was clouded. My head ached. I am thinking clearly now. Believe me. I know what I saw and, though I do not know how to explain it to you, I know that what I saw was real. Even if it is not happening at this very moment, it will happen. And I fear it will happen soon."

The other four looked at Chrysteffor uncertainly.

"You must understand, my friend," said Feidhlim, "this is confusing for us. What would you have us do?"

"We must rally every able-bodied man and woman in the castle and prepare for the siege," said Chrysteffor agitatedly. "You must send word to every nobleman who is loyal to the king to come quickly and join the defense. And this must be done now. Without delay."

"They will think us mad," said Eilís. "Not without more reason than simply the urging of a young foreigner."

Chrysteffor felt a deep frustration. He understood perfectly how unreasonable his words sounded. He might well have said the same thing if he were in Eilís's place. Still, it bothered him that she did not trust him anyway, did not have faith in him—however blind that faith would have to be.

"What do I need to say to convince ye? I will go outside myself and join the guards and wait with them for the invasion to come. Will none of ye come with me?"

The silence was awkward until another voice spoke with determination.

"I will go with you, Prince Chrysteffor. I will follow wherever you lead."

It was young Ruaraidh.

"You kept your word and freed Lady Eilís from the evil enchantment. You brought Prince Feidhlim back from the dead. You went to the three towers and came back alive. Prince Chrysteffor, I will follow you wherever you lead me—without question."

Chrysteffor was deeply moved by the boy's loyalty but, of all of them, he was the one the prince did *not* want to bring with him.

"The lad is right," said Feidhlim. "You have earned the right to our trust and loyalty—even if you have gone mad. And my darkest fear is that you have not gone mad. I will do as you ask."

Before anyone else could speak, a terrible cry came from above.

"That is the watchman in the tower," gasped Lady Aigneis. "He sounds as though he has seen his own ghost."

Feidhlim immediately raced to the nearest stairway, and Chrysteffor and Eilís followed close behind. When they reached the tower, they found the guard unable to speak. His face was drained of all blood, as he kept pointing into the distance. The three peered into the darkness. They could make out an eerie light in the middle of the fog. As they studied it, they could make out more detail. The light was coming from torches—scores of torches. They could just make out the shapes holding them aloft—and all the other shapes as well. It was Chrysteffor's vision, seen from a different perspective.

The Eidola were coming. And leading them on a great black stallion was the sorcerer Leannain.

16
The Final Battle

"IT IS TRUE!" gasped Eilís. "If only it were not, but it is."

"Quick!" said Feidhlim. "Let us send riders to the other castles, as Chrysteffor advised. Those creatures are fearsome, but they are lumbering. With luck, their progress may be slow enough that aid may yet arrive before all is completely lost."

Eilís's face darkened, and her gaze was determined.

"There is no point waiting for them to arrive at the door of the castle. Feidhlim, can you send the riders and gather everyone within the castle for its defense? I myself will go out and meet them. I will not be able to slow them down much, but I will do what I can. By all that is sacred, I will make them pay the highest price possible to reach the castle door."

"Eilís," said her brother, "that is certain death."

"Maybe so, but I would rather meet death out there than wait for it inside these walls. All that I ask is that you do not waste my efforts. Do all that you can to prepare for the onslaught here."

"I will go with you," said Feidhlim. "I will not let you make this sacrifice alone."

"No. One of us is needed here. It should be you. Our father does not yet know you are alive. Go to him—while there is still time. I am quite happy with my plan. Now leave me to it."

Chrysteffor was never more in love with the princess than he was at that moment.

"Eilís, you are right that Feidhlim's place is here," he said, "but mine is with you. I will go with you. We may yet be lucky if the two of us are fighting the enemy together. And if not and if today is indeed the day that I die, then know that I will be much happier dying at your side than living the rest of my days without you."

The princess smiled sadly.

"Ah, there are those pretty words of yours again. Well, you did promise to write a song about me, did you not? It sounds to me as though you have already made a good start on it. Very well then, man of Alinvayl, join me in my folly. You can sing my song while we kill monsters. I challenge you to compose a melody that is as sweet to my ears as are the screams of the dying Eidola."

"No more delay, my love. I cannot wait to teach that unholy chorus to sing to our tune."

With that the two of them raced down the steps, leaving Feidhlim with his mouth agape.

"They are mad, the two of them," he said to Ruaraidh who, he was only now noticing, had followed the three of them to the tower.

"Eilís and Chrysteffor are the bravest people I know," said the lad, "except for you, of course, cousin Feidhlim. Chrysteffor once told me that he plans to marry Eilís. Do you think he really will?"

"Nothing that fellow does surprises me anymore. May we all live to celebrate such a happy day. But that is for another time—if ever. Come, Ruaraidh, we have much to do and, I fear, precious little time to do it."

And with that they ran down to the king's chamber.

Chrysteffor and Eilís rode as fast as they could toward the oncoming horde.

"Are you certain these horses will not throw us in panic once they encounter the Eidola?" shouted Chrysteffor over the noise of the wind. "I had a bad experience with my horse when I encountered these creatures on my first day in Afranor."

"Do not worry. These animals have had the fear bred out of them. They will keep their heads when under attack."

"That is good to know. Now I must ask you to let me take the lead in the fighting. I know that is not in your nature, but I have a good reason."

The princess gave him a cross look.

"I have never deferred to anyone in my life. And I am not about to change my habits today."

"How well I know that! Indeed, I would gladly and prudently defer to you in the fight—but for one thing. I have a particular advantage when dealing with these creatures. This sword I acquired in the first tower is endowed with some sort of enchantment. It can kill the Eidola much more easily than can an ordinary weapon. It is only for that reason that I ask you to let me take the lead."

The princess gave no sign of being impressed.

"I am glad to hear of your marvelous weapon. If it is truly magical, then it just might allow you to keep up with me."

With that she gave her steed the command to gallop faster. Chrysteffor struggled to make his horse keep up. All too soon they came upon the front line of the monsters' swarm. Chrysteffor scanned the line up and down looking for their leader, the Black Sorcerer, but there was no sign of him.

"Die, ye spawn of hell!" cried the prince, as he lopped off his first adversary's head with his glowing blade. He beheaded one after another.

"Do you see what I mean about the sword?" he called over to the princess, who was busy with her own fight.

"You call that a sword?" she yelled back at him. "It is like something I might use to clean beneath the nails of my fingers."

The prince had to admit to himself that she was really doing just about as well in the battle as he was—and with a weapon that, as far as he knew anyway, had no supernatural properties. He also had to admit that, despite the advantage his blade gave him, it did nothing to mitigate the advantage the enemy had in its sheer numbers. He had no sooner decapitated one creature than two or three or more took its place. There was no end to the killing and, despite the energy he drew from the frenzy of battle, after an hour or two, he could feel himself tiring. Whenever he felt himself flagging, though, he had only to look over at Eilís to give himself the determination to continue the fight. She was every bit an inspiration as a battle comrade as was her brother.

As in the battle of the third tower, the corpses of the Eidola piled higher and higher the longer the carnage continued. And yet the numbers of the enemy did not give any sign of dwindling despite their mounting losses. Worse, given that Chrysteffor and Eilís could only fight so many enemy at a time, there were large numbers that simply ignored them and continued on toward the castle. There were simply too many for a mere pair of warriors to stop, but Eilís and Chrysteffor kept up the fight, knowing that every monster they killed on the field was one fewer for the castle's defenders to confront.

The longer the battle continued, the more Chrysteffor was aware that the flood of creatures was gradually forcing him and Eilís backward in the direction of the castle. It was only a matter of time until they would be fighting at the castle's gates. Still, they did their best to put off that eventuality for as long as possible. Striking at the enemy from atop their steeds gave them an advantage but, as the numbers of Eidola around them seemed to multiply from one minute to the next, the abhorrent creatures continually attacked the noble animals until Chrysteffor and Eilís were forced to abandon them.

As they slowly ceded more and more ground, the prince wondered how long he and the princess had been out there fighting. Was it hours? Could it be days? His mind was so exhausted he could not be sure. He only hoped that they had delayed enough invaders for enough time that the defenders within the castle had had sufficient time to prepare. And he prayed that there had been time for reinforcements to arrive from other nearby castles. He had no way of knowing, however, what the situation actually was, and he had to face the prospect that he might never know.

When Chrysteffor's lungs began to burn from exhaustion and his arms became so sore that he imagined them wanting to tear themselves from his shoulders, he glanced behind him and despaired. He and Eilís were nearly at the door of the castle. Many of the creatures had already placed themselves up against its walls, probing for weaknesses. Several were pounding together against the main door. Defenders on the turrets were firing arrows down at the invaders, but these seemed to have no effect.

Then, as he turned his head back, Chrysteffor spied something that truly horrified him. Eilís had plunged her blade into the torso of one of the creatures, and the creature was not slowed. It frantically twisted its body as the princess held a firm grip on the sword's hilt, and then it turned with such force that the blade broke. Eilís was left holding nothing but the hilt and a jagged remnant of the blade. She was now defenseless.

The prince screamed at the top of his lungs, but his roar was lost in the din of the ferocious battle. He maneuvered himself as best he could in Eilís's direction. She was doing her best to avoid being struck by the creatures while attempting to stab them with her little bit of a blade. Chrysteffor knew that she would not last long. He screamed one more time as loudly as he could. This time she heard him and turned her head. The look in her eyes was without hope. In his fear for her, he flung his own sword in her direction. Surprised, she instinctively reached out and managed to take hold of it, despite the onslaught all around her.

"Take it!" yelled Chrysteffor. "You will do more good with it than I will!"

She flashed him a look of annoyance before she quickly became occupied with defending herself. She did not look in Chrysteffor's direction again. He could tell she was amazed at how much easier it was to kill the creatures with the enchanted weapon. She threw herself back into the battle with renewed vigor.

Now Chrysteffor was the one without a sword. He grasped the mace from his belt and began batting his assailants with it. He was thus able to fend off any fatal blows, but he knew that there was no hope of killing any of the enemy without his sword. His strategy was now merely to escape the battle without losing his life. He did his best to dodge blows as he slowly made his way around the outside of the castle. He was finding

143

that the Eidola were not particularly interested in him. Their main focus was on the castle itself. Once he was not standing in their way, they paid him little heed. Soon he found himself standing on the edge of the cliff on the far side of the castle. He now actually had a moment to watch everything going on around him without having to worry much about the creatures. He scanned the mob of invaders, trying to spot Eilís or anyone else he knew, but he could see no living man or woman.

He looked up the walls of the castle and saw a sight that made his heart go cold. He saw the body of a guard fall from one of the turrets to the ground. He looked up at the turrets and despaired when he saw no men above. He saw only the Eidola. They were inside the castle. And any defender they found, they threw to the ground. He had little time to ponder what this meant because one or two of the creatures near him were now turning their attention toward him. Following the example of their brethren in the turrets, they clearly meant to toss him over the cliff. The prince looked around helplessly. There was no hope of getting past the hordes blocking his way. And there was no way he could stop the creatures from forcing him over the edge.

So this is how it finally ends, he thought. *Well, I've had a good run. I lived much longer and survived more tests than I ever expected to. Still, I am not quite ready to die. These past few days I've found that I quite rather enjoy living—no matter how bad things get.*

He glanced down in the direction of the sea and the rocks below. He chuckled grimly at the memory that, not so long ago, he had stood in this same spot and considered throwing himself over—for no better reason than he was horribly frightened. How silly he had been. How much he had learned in such a short time. He then remembered something else.

Did not Feidhlim go over this cliff's edge? And did he not live to tell of it? The plunge does not necessarily have to be fatal. With a bit of luck and, if I can keep my wits about me as I near the water, I just might repeat his feat. But, thought the prince, *could I really throw myself off this cliff? Where will I find the courage? It is such a long way down.*

He laughed at himself heartily. Had he not well and truly learned the lesson of courage by now? Was this not the one time when there was absolutely no reason to fear death—because death was all but certain? He laughed again, louder than before. One of the creatures looked at him sideways.

He has surely never seen a man laugh before, thought Chrysteffor, and that made him laugh more.

And then he threw himself over the edge.

17
An Old Friend

CHRYSTEFFOR REMEMBERED the descent through the cold, damp air. He was surprised how long it took to reach the bottom. He was all but convinced that he would never hit the rocks or the water or whatever it was that awaited him. He found it unsettling that he could not see what lay beneath him. It would have been better, he thought, if he actually saw the rocks or the water rushing up toward him. Not knowing when the impact would come was the worst part. The sea's surface suddenly appeared and he saw the water rushing toward him. He saw rocks as well. He tried to shift his direction to avoid them, but there was little he could do by that point. He closed his eyes and held his breath and then felt a blow as if he had been thrown against a stone wall. After that he felt himself plunging through water, and that seemed to go on longer than his plunge through the air. Fortunately, he kept his wits about him enough not to open his mouth—as much as he wanted to. Finally, he stopped plunging and he felt himself rising—but slowly. He kicked his feet, trying to make himself rise faster. His body was unbearably cold. He feared his heart would stop, and he feared that he would not be able to hold his breath long enough to reach the surface. He was afraid of losing consciousness at any moment. After a while, he felt as though he could hold his breath no longer, but he forced himself to keep his mouth closed. Things seemed to be going black, as if he were falling asleep.

Well, it was worth a try...

Suddenly he felt air on his face as his head pushed through the surface. He gasped for breath. The air made his body feel even colder than the water had. After that he remembered nothing more.

When Chrysteffor woke, he had no idea where he was. It reminded him of waking up in the sorcerer's lair. His first thought then had been that he was in his own bed in Alinvayl. He wondered if he was in Alinvayl now, but he did not think so. He wondered then if he was back in Castle

145

Aill Stoirm. That did not seem likely either, although he was having trouble working out why.

He was aware of people around him. He sat up with a terrified start. Were they Eidola?

"Easy there, Chrysteffor," said a voice that was strangely familiar. It was a voice that did not belong there. He was completely confused.

"By the gods, Chrysteffor, you were the last thing I ever expected to fish out of the sea. And here of all places."

It was a woman's voice. And she was speaking his own language—or at least one close enough to it that he knew it like his own. He followed the sound of the voice and was surprised to see a face that he knew. A face with flashing green eyes, framed by wind-tossed flaming red hair.

"Valloniah? Is it really you? But how?"

"It is indeed, Chrysteffor, but tell me, what is going on? What are you doing here? Where is Adryan?"

The prince lay back down. He could see that he was on the deck of Valloniah's ship. His heart sank at the news he had for her.

"Adryan is dead, Valloniah. Benet too. They are both dead. They died nobly but unjustly. I am so sorry to have to tell you this."

"Adryan dead? It cannot be! Tell me who is responsible. He or she shall taste the wrath of the Pirate Queen!"

Chrysteffor was all too familiar with Valloniah's famous temper. The lovers' rows between her and his brother were notorious up and down the entire southern coast. The prince stumbled to his feet.

"You and I shall have our revenge together. I promise you," said Chrysteffor. "But tell me, how did I manage to wake up on your ship?"

"We have been sailing up and down the coast for days. A few weeks after ye three parted company with us in Portfrith, we were preparing to set sail when all three of your horses wandered into the port—riderless. They were half-starved and frightened out of their skins. I knew that something terrible had happened. I could only conclude that your pig-headed brother had decided to head back to Alinvayl by way of Afranor. By the gods, that man could be stubborn. What a foolhardy thing to do."

Chrysteffor thought he could see the beginnings of a tear glistening in one of her eyes, but it could have been a trick of the light. The Pirate Queen had never been known to shed tears—at least not in front of her crew.

"Anyway," she continued, "there was never any question of landing on the coast of Afranor. The crew are superstitious, and none of them would have gone ashore. Besides, we had no idea where to begin a search. It was only luck that I decided to stay off the coast here—on the chance we might spot something or hear some news. The problem was that it was so bloody difficult to see anything in all the gloom that smothers the land. Every so often a random gust of wind would reveal more of the shore, but there was little to see. When we heard the sounds of battle ashore, we drew closer to get an idea of what was going on. Clearly the castle was under siege. Luckily for you, the mist cleared just enough at the right moment and I myself saw you plunge from the castle's promontory into the water. Of course, I had no idea it was you at the time. We managed to fish you out of the water before you sank for good. You are an extremely lucky man, Prince Chrysteffor of Alinvayl."

"I am indeed, but I have to get back to the castle. I have to find out if anyone has survived the siege. I have to find Eilís and Feidhlim. I have to go to their aid."

"I would not advise going back there. From what we can see, the castle is completely overrun with ungodly creatures. Horrible things. Even at this distance it is clear that they are beings never meant to exist in nature. What manner of sorcery holds sway in that accursed land? Let us bring you home. Your father must be frantic with worry by now."

"No, I cannot leave. Bring me to the shore. And lend me a weapon. I must go back."

The Pirate Queen gazed appreciatively at the young prince, as if she were seeing him for the first time.

"My, you have changed, Chrysteffor. You are different from the boy I knew only a few weeks ago. It is as though you have aged several years in just the span of a fortnight or two. To be honest, I never had much hope for you, but now I find myself impressed indeed."

"Will you please do as I ask, Valloniah? Lend me a weapon and bring me to shore."

"There is no point, Chrysteffor. That castle is lost. I have cannons on board. The wisest course at this point would be to fire on the castle and level it. Believe me, there is no saving any man or woman in that place."

"Cannons…?"

"Yes. Do you not remember my cannons? They are the scourge of the home ports of the southern corsairs. No rampart has ever withstood their fire for long."

"Yes! The famous cannons of the Pirate Queen! Of course. Why did I not think of it sooner?"

"Say the word and we will demolish the castle. I wager not many of those unholy creatures will survive that assault."

"No, no, not the castle. I have another target for you. I have three targets for you."

"What are you on about?"

"Just trust me, Valloniah. Follow the coast northward. In memory of my brothers, I need you to do this. The reason is a bit complicated to explain, but the task itself is straightforward."

"Whatever you say, Prince Chrysteffor. My ship and my crew are at your disposal. And when this is over, we shall do a great amount of drinking in memory of your brothers."

Chrysteffor paced anxiously up and down the deck, as the ship made its way up along the coast. He peered intently into the mists. Finally he spotted the thing he was looking for. At the top of the promontory he saw the first tower, the one where he had fought his brothers and won his sword.

"That's it!" he cried. "Blast that tower with your cannon. Demolish it to the smallest bits of pebbles you can."

"Why on earth do you want to do that?" asked Valloniah. "What difference will that make to the castle down the coast?"

"If I try to explain, you will think me mad," said the prince. "Please just do it. If it makes it easier for you, think of it as an indulgence for a madman grieving for his brothers."

"Whatever you say, Chrysteffor. It makes no difference to me whether that tower stands or falls."

The Pirate Queen's crew loaded the cannon and fired at the target. By the third volley, only a pile of rubble was left.

"Are you satisfied now?" asked Valloniah.

"That was brilliant! Now I need you to do the same again two more times."

Valloniah shook her head and laughed.

"If it makes you happy, Chrysteffor. The crew can always use the target practice."

As the ship continued up the coast, the prince studied the sky. He could not be sure whether it was his imagination or not, but he definitely thought that it was no longer quite so dark. And the mist was not quite so thick. After the pirates leveled the second tower, they continued on toward the third one.

Yes, thought Chrysteffor. *The darkness is definitely lifting. I can see miles in every direction, much farther than I was ever able to see here before. At least that was one thing the sorcerer did not lie to me about. The towers really were the source of his power.*

After the third tower was demolished, Valloniah noticed the dissipating darkness.

"Well, the fog has lifted," she said. "I could have sworn that it was the middle of the night, but it turns out that we are in the middle of a rather nice day."

Standing at the ship's prow, Chrysteffor's heart soared as he felt a fresh clean breeze against his face and the warmth of the sun on his skin. He could see the coast of Afranor for the first time properly. It was a beautiful green land bathed in sunshine, and the sea was a deep azure color. For the first time he understood all that Leannain had taken away from the people here.

"You have done a marvelous job, Valloniah! Now please take me back to the castle. I only hope that your good work did not come too late for everybody."

As the ship sailed back southward, the men and women of the crew buzzed in conversation about the sudden and strange turn in the weather. Chrysteffor held onto the ship's railing with all his strength, trying to will the vessel to move faster. He watched the coastline until the castle again appeared. His anticipation about what he would find there was a mixture of hope and dread. Most of all, he did not know if he could withstand finding that Eilís had not survived.

When the ship arrived below the castle, the anchor was dropped.

"It will be just a short while to lower a rowboat so you can go ashore," said the Pirate Queen.

"Never mind the boat," said Chrysteffor. "I will swim to shore."

And with that he dove into the water and headed for the land.

When he reached the rocks at the base of the cliff, Chrysteffor clambered up out of the water and only then took time to catch his breath. He sat there for a few moments to enjoy the sunlight and the warmth. It was a fine spring day, and he did not mind that he was soaked to the skin. He studied the rocks to decide on the best course for making his way back up to the castle. It occurred to him that, because he had so impetuously abandoned the ship to come back without delay, he had brought no weapon but the mace. That weapon would be of limited use to him if he met an enemy, but he was willing to gamble that would not matter.

Somehow I do not think the Eidola will bother me or anyone else again, he thought. *Surely, it was only the sorcerer's power that kept those monsters going, and the source of that power has been cut off. I only pray that I am not wrong about that.*

In truth, though, he had no idea what to expect when he got back to the castle. He began the slow, determined climb up the cliff's rocky face. It felt like forever until he neared the top, and he wondered if it would have been faster to swim the additional half-mile along the bottom of the cliff to the dock at the end of the winding path from the castle. In any event, he was now almost to the top.

At least I can now judge better the passing of time, he thought. *What a relief to see the sun's progress in the sky.*

He raised his head over the top of the cliff, and he could now see the field in front of the castle. What he saw was not exactly a surprise, but it was still shocking. The field was littered with piles of carcasses. The numbers were so large that there was scarcely anywhere to walk. In the daylight the monsters appeared even more hideous than they had looked in the dark. And the rotting, stinking smell was overwhelming. It was as though the cadavers had been decomposing for days instead of mere hours. As the prince lifted himself onto the edge of the field, he covered his nose and mouth in an attempt to block the smell. Though these bodies were all of the enemy, the sight of so much death left him overwhelmed.

He staggered around them as best he could in the direction of the castle entrance. It made him feel ill to look at them, but he forced himself to scan the heaps of dead on the chance he would see a body that was not one of the Eidola. As he neared the castle, he saw the first bodies of the men of Afranor who had died defending the castle. The farther he went the more human bodies he saw. Some of the faces were familiar to him, their eyes frozen in various expressions of terror. When the number of dead defenders became more than a handful, he stopped counting. He feared to keep looking, terrified that he would find Eilís among them, but then he saw something that nearly stopped his heart altogether. It was a body that was a bit smaller than the others. Lying face down, the hair on his head was the color of rust.

"No!" wailed the prince, as he dropped to his knees.

Gently, he pulled the body close to him and cradled it in his arms. Tears flooded from his eyes as he stared into the lifeless face.

"No! No!"

He rocked back and forth, hoping against hope that somehow he could make Ruaraidh wake up—even though he knew from the moment he touched the cold, stiff body that there was no life in it. Chrysteffor simply continued to rock back and forth, sobbing.

He sat like that for a long time until he finally accepted the fact that he needed to find out what had happened to the others. Was there anyone at all left alive? He held Ruaraidh in his arms as he struggled to his feet and proceeded to carry the lad toward the castle. Through the tears he studied the dead as he walked past them, praying that he would not see anyone else he knew.

When he reached the door of the castle, it was wide open and appeared to be unguarded. Chrysteffor walked through it, still carrying Ruaraidh's body. Once inside, he was surprised to be suddenly challenged by a very startled man.

"Easy, Conn. It is only myself, Chrysteffor. I found poor Ruaraidh on the battlefield. I am sorry I could not do more. What tidings have you?"

"Ah, Prince Chrysteffor," said Conn, looking relieved. "It was terrible. It was the most terrible day I have seen in my life. Ah, poor Lord Ruaraidh. He was such a good lad. I saw him on the battlefield. His father would have been so proud of him. What a terrible day. And yet here I am to tell of it. It was like a miracle, Prince Chrysteffor. We held out as long as we could. We put up a good fight, I swear we did. But then it was all over. We were only waiting for the inevitable. The fighting had stopped, and the Black Sorcerer had gone into the castle. We did not know what was going to happen. Only that it was going to be bad. There was nothing to stop him from slaughtering the lot of us. I thought for certain we were all done for, so I did. Then the most amazing thing happened. The sun came out. The sun! It has been so many years since anyone can remember seeing the sun. At that moment these monsters just stopped in their tracks. They all collapsed and began stinking and rotting—as though they had been dead for a long time. I never saw anything like it."

"If only it could have happened sooner, Conn. If only it could have happened in time to save this poor lad here—and all the others who are out there lying dead. But tell me, what of Lady Eilís and Prince Feidhlim? What news of them?"

"Prince Feidhlim is alive and well, I am happy to say. There are a few of us who survived the day but, sadly, not nearly as many as who perished. It was a terrible day. They are in the large hall. They will be very happy to see you, Prince Chrysteffor."

Conn turned his gaze back out toward the castle entrance. He had resumed his watch. Chrysteffor carried Ruaraidh's body into the hall, the same place that Lady Aigneis had given him a meal the night he had first arrived at the castle. Inside there was a gathering of men and women. The prince was surprised to see so many of them but, as Conn had suggested, their number was small compared to those who were absent. Feidhlim was the first to notice him. His face lit up.

"Chrysteffor! My friend! You are alive!"

Feidhlim then saw the boy's body and the smile vanished. He walked silently over to the blond prince and took the lad's body into his own arms.

"I would have traded my life for his—without a moment's hesitation. On a day of too much death, this one is the hardest of all to bear. Thank you, my friend, for bringing this brave lad home."

Feidhlim carried the boy to another chamber. In the meantime, Chrysteffor scanned the hall anxiously for any sign of Eilís, but he did not see her anywhere. When Feidhlim returned, the blond prince summoned the courage to ask about her.

"Eilís?"

"By the gods, she fought bravely. She fought them on the battlefield. She defended the castle's door. And when they were inside the castle, she fought them there as well. I swear, I will never be half the warrior my sister is. I did not see her fall myself, but it was recounted to me later by more than one astonished witness. Every man and woman was in awe of her valor and strength. Many wept openly when they saw her struck down."

"So then Eilís…?"

"They carried her to her chamber. In the middle of everything I knelt down at her bed and wept openly over her myself. If only it had been me and not her."

"I must go see her at once."

Just then there was a commotion coming from the entrance to the castle. Feidhlim's eyes flashed with anger as he immediately headed in that direction, his sword drawn.

"By the gods, do not tell me that some of those monsters survived. Is the battle not over yet?"

Chrysteffor followed.

"These strangers are asking for Prince Chrysteffor," shouted Conn. "Frankly, I do not like the look of them."

The blond prince was relieved to see that it was only Valloniah and some of her crew. Apparently, now that the sun was shining in Afranor, they had overcome their fear of coming ashore.

"Do you not know who I am, little man?"

A man of average height, the guard did indeed appear small next to Valloniah. She towered over the trembling Conn.

"They call me the Pirate Queen, and I am accustomed to going where I please. And I do not yield to the likes of you."

"It is all right, Conn," said Chrysteffor. "They are friends. They not only saved my life but they are responsible for bringing the sun back to this land and destroying the sorcerer's power."

At that moment one of the nobles appeared, requesting Feidhlim's attention. He was quite insistent that the prince join him and the others in what he assured him was an urgent conversation. Feidhlim reluctantly took his leave from Chrysteffor.

"But wait a moment, my friend," said the blond prince. "We have scarcely had time to talk. You must tell me, what happened to Leannain? Did he survive the battle?"

"My friend, waste no time worrying about that villain. There is so much to tell you. And I shall. If I can only get a moment for myself. You and I shall speak soon, and I shall tell you all. I swear."

"I will hold you to that promise," said the blond prince. "But in the meantime I scarcely have the patience myself for talk. I cannot let one more moment pass before seeing my beloved Eilís."

He rushed to her chamber, the same one where he had previously seen her lying under the sorcerer's evil spell. His heart broke upon entering the room and seeing her laid out and so completely still, half her face covered in blood. He fell to his knees at the bedside and, for the second time that day, began to weep. He was so lost in his grief and anger that he was only vaguely aware that someone had followed him into the room. He did not care who it was or that they were seeing him in a moment of such weakness. A well-tanned arm passed in front of him and gently touched the princess's shoulder. He heard Valloniah's impatient voice.

"She is still alive," said the Pirate Queen. "Why is no one tending to her? If that wound is not cleaned straight away, it will soon be festering."

The prince could scarcely believe his ears. He had been certain she was dead. He put his ear next to her breast and realized that Valloniah was right. He could detect the slightest sound of breathing and a weak heartbeat. Valloniah sent two of her crew outside to look for any grass or herbs that they could find and another to search the castle for water. At that moment Chrysteffor noticed that Eilís's saddle bag was on the floor near the bed, and he picked it up.

"I think I once saw her take some sort of herb out of this bag. She used it on me when I was injured. Is there anything here you can use?"

Valloniah examined the contents and was impressed.

"This woman of yours is well prepared for any contingency. This should do nicely."

The Pirate Queen then began the careful process of wiping away the blood from the princess's face and cleaning the gash. It occurred to Chrysteffor that, in a strange coincidence, the wound was in the same place as the scar he had admired the first time he saw her.

"This is not good," said Valloniah grimly. "She has lost the eye."

18
A New King

"TELL ME what I can do to help," said Chrysteffor, frustrated that he was clearly being no help at all.

"Just hold her hand and talk to her. She is a strong woman, nearly as strong as myself. If we can keep this wound from festering, she has a good chance. If I have anything to say about it, she will live. She will sorely miss having that eye, though."

Chrysteffor stayed at the princess's side long after Valloniah had finished her work. He was there when night fell and the room became dark, and he was there still when the light returned and he knew that the sun had risen.

How beautiful, he thought, *to again know when it is day and when it is night.*

A few times during his vigil, Feidhlim visited the room, but each time, with much reluctance, he soon took his leave again. Like Chrysteffor, he had believed his sister dead and had been overjoyed to learn of his error. The blond prince was anxious for Feidhlim to stay long enough to recount all that had happened in the battle and to answer his many questions. To his frustration, though, there was never enough time for anything more than for Feidhlim to hear a brief update on Eilís's condition and then leave again. For the time being the prince of Alinvayl resolved to put aside his questions and give all his attention to the ailing princess.

"I am afraid," said the black-haired prince sadly during one of his visits, "my time is already being taken up with plans and discussions. They are not even allowing time for grieving. The nobles are keen to begin rebuilding the country and they are anxious, after so many years, for leadership from a new and younger king."

Feidhlim sighed with a heavy heart.

"If only there were a way to convince them that I was dead again."

Chrysteffor could not honestly tell whether or not his friend was joking.

At long last came the moment Chrysteffor had waited for. Lady Eilís awoke.

"Where am I? What has happened?"

"Thank the gods, my love. You have survived. We have both survived. Too many died defending Afranor, but you and I and Feidhlim are all here."

"Chrysteffor?"

Eilís visibly struggled with her confusion. "Chrysteffor? Is it really you? I was sure and certain you were dead. Thank the gods you are not. I so desperately wanted to see you again. I cannot see well with all these bandages. Help me remove them."

"Not just yet, my love," he said softly.

"Do not be daft. Help me."

She began tugging at the bandages. As gently as possible—and much to Eilís's annoyance—the prince took hold of her hands and pulled them away from her head.

"My dear, dear Eilís, you must leave the bandages for a while longer yet. You were badly injured. I am afraid that… you have lost your eye. The important thing, though, is that you are alive."

She stopped struggling against him, and a single tear slowly trailed below her uncovered eye.

"It is all right," said the prince quietly. "Do not fear. You are still beautiful. And with an eye patch I swear that you will be more beautiful than before."

At this Eilís's temper flared.

"You fool. Do you really think I am worried about how I look? Do you not understand what this means? How will I be able to judge distances with only one eye? I will be useless with a bow and arrow and severely disadvantaged with a sword. This is terrible."

The prince quickly put his arms around her. At first she bristled at his touch, as if she resented the attempt to comfort her, but then she relented. In the end she welcomed his embrace and indeed was glad for it. They did not speak for a good few moments. While he regretted deeply the circumstances, Chrysteffor felt relief and happiness to be holding her close.

"How is it possible that you survived, Chrysteffor? I was so certain I had seen the last of you."

"And I too was certain that you had seen the last of me. I plunged from the cliff—the same as your brother. And, like him, I was lucky enough to survive the descent. I would have surely drowned had I not been quickly found by Valloniah."

"Who?"

"An old friend. My brothers and I have known her for years. Adryan and Benet were once in a fierce battle in the Eastern Lands, and by chance it happened she and they were fighting on the same side. They were all fast friends ever after. In fact she and Adryan became lovers. Well, off and on anyway. Their relationship was always tempestuous at best."

Chrysteffor felt a sadness come over him as he recalled happier times. Looking at him, it occurred to Eilís how much there was about the young prince and his family that she did not know.

"And the Black Sorcerer? What of him? How did the battle end? I trust that the fact that you and I are here means that the Eidola were somehow defeated."

"I have many of the same questions as you. I have been waiting for your brother to have the time to recount the end of the battle. What I myself can tell you, however, is that the Eidola were completely and utterly vanquished. Leannain's power was extinguished when Valloniah's cannons destroyed the three towers. In that moment the sun returned to Afranor and the Eidola collapsed and lost whatever force was animating them."

The princess closed her eye and said nothing more as she took it all in. After a while she spoke.

"My country owes you so much, Chrysteffor. I do not know how to begin thanking you for all that you have done on our behalf. Frankly, when I first met you, I would have never dreamed that you of all people would be the kingdom's savior. You seemed so young, so uncertain, so…"

"Yes, well, that seems a long time ago now. We have both changed a great deal in a short span of time. My dearest Eilís, I am afraid there is much bad news along with the good. The saddest of all—and it breaks my heart to tell you—is that your cousin Ruaraidh perished in the battle."

A look of pain came over Eilís's face. She shut her eye tightly, as several tears trickled down her cheek.

"I know," she said. "I saw him die."

Seeing her sorrow, the prince relived the anguish of finding the boy's body all over again. He embraced her more tightly. In that moment he would have given anything to be able to take away her pain.

"It was terrible, Chrysteffor. There was nothing I could do. I could only watch helplessly. But do you know what, Chrysteffor? He was beautiful. As I watched him, it seemed as if time had slowed to a crawl. His last few moments seemed to pass like hours. Yes, he was beautiful.

Not yet a man but more than a boy, he fought with passion. And in contrast to the ugly violence all around him, he moved with flowing grace as if in a dance. He was so pale and slender compared to the monsters around him, but he gave it his all. His face glistened with sweat and his hair whipped in the air as he turned this way and that attacking the beasts every way he could. I wish I could have frozen him in that moment. Inevitably, one of the creatures struck him cleanly on the back of his head and he folded over like a piece of fabric. He fell to the ground in a heap and I screamed with all the rage and sorrow in my heart, but my cry was drowned out by the overwhelming sounds of the battle. I wanted to run to him, to take him up in my arms, but there was no way that I could. I knew all too well that my own moment was drawing near. I knew that the battle was about to end for me, just as it had for him."

For a few moments her words gave way to open sobbing.

"He would have been a marvelous man, Chrysteffor. He would have been the best of us. Of all the things Leannain robbed from us, that is the most unforgivable. He stole from us that beautiful boy and the beautiful man he would have become."

Chrysteffor did not know what to say. No words of his would ever be adequate. So he said nothing, as he continued to hold her in his arms. They remained silent for a good long time.

Eventually, Feidhlim returned to the room. He smiled to see that his sister had awakened.

"Eilís," he said, "it is over at last. The long night has ended. And we have this prince of Alinvayl to thank."

"Many people fought to end the nightmare," said Chrysteffor solemnly. "And sadly, not all of them are here to celebrate the victory with us. I will not let you leave again, Feidhlim, without hearing about the end of the battle and the fate of the Black Sorcerer."

"Yes, yes, I keep forgetting that you did not see those final moments, Chrysteffor. Of course, you must be bursting to know how it all ended. Forgive me. If only these blasted nobles would give me some peace."

Feidhlim sat on the edge of Eilís's bed.

"The truth is that I came late to the battle. While the two of you were leading the charge against the unholy invaders, I was gathering the nobles and their warriors as they arrived in dribs and drabs from the neighboring castles. In the midst of the panic over the battle raging beyond, it was all I could do to organize them into some sort of coherent force that could defend the castle. Before we were properly ready, the Eidola were already at the gates. I had no idea what had happened to you, Chrysteffor, or to poor Ruaraidh or most of the others. Eilís, you were still fighting the enemy, battling them as fiercely here inside the castle as you had on the field beyond. I only knew that the hordes were at the point of ramming themselves down our throats. I knew in my heart that there was no hope, but I did my best not to betray my despair to those mounting the final defense. I exhorted them to give their all and, in fairness to them, they did.

"Every man and woman who answered the call fought with all the courage that anyone could have asked. The battle raged inside the castle for a good long time, though it was clearly only a matter of time until we would be inevitably overwhelmed. In the midst of the fighting two of our best men came to me. They were carrying you, Eilís. They had seen you fall, and they abandoned the battle to bring you to me. Chrysteffor's strange sword was with you. I presumed that meant he had fallen as well. My heart sank. I was certain that both of you were dead. They asked me what they should do with the princess, and I told them to bring you as quickly as possible to your chamber and then to rejoin the fight.

"As the battle continued, I expected the end at any moment. All of our struggles against the Black Sorcerer for so many years were coming to naught. And then unexpectedly, in the space of a single moment, the fighting simply ceased. At the sound of a booming command, the Eidola stopped in their tracks. That is when I saw him. Our despised uncle Leannain. He was not as you saw him, Chrysteffor, in his lair. He was not some benign old man. He seemed to have grown two times in size and to be half his age. He exuded strength and power atop his black stallion. He wore a metal breastplate the color of ebony and a black flowing cape. His hair was now darker than before, the color of coal. He raised his staff and called for his hordes to wait while he entered and took control of the castle. I did not know what to do. I was all too aware that, if I raised a hand against him, any one of his slaves could easily strike me dead where I stood. He dismounted and strode quickly toward the interior of the castle. I ran after him and followed him to my father's chamber. I do not know what his precise intention was. Was he going to slay his brother once and for all? Or merely taunt the old man with his victory? In any event, he was disappointed.

"You see, after the two of you had left to meet the invasion, I went to see my father and to let him know that I was alive. Ruaraidh followed me to his chamber. The king lay on his bed with Aigneis faithfully attending him. Once I saw him, it was all too apparent that he was dying and that precious little time remained for him. I feared that the shock of seeing me would be overwhelming for him but, strangely, he did not seem all that surprised to see me. I hoped that knowing his son was alive would lift his spirits and give him the will to fight harder for life. My return had a different effect, however. He grasped my hand as tightly as he could and weakly raised his head to speak to me. 'At last!' he whispered. 'I place my kingdom in your hands. At long last I can die in peace.' This was not the reunion I had been hoping for. As much as I longed to spend more time with him and tell him everything I had done and everything that had happened to me while I was away, I knew that I had to get back to the defense of the castle. I told Ruaraidh to stay with him and Aigneis, but the lad refused. He insisted on staying by my side and I did not have the time to argue with him. If only I had…"

The weight of regret could be seen plainly on Feidhlim's face, as he paused for a moment.

"As the situation grew more dire, Ruaraidh grew impatient. He said that he could no longer stay in the castle while the two of ye were fighting for your lives in defense of Afranor. He picked up his sword and headed for the battle. I yelled at him to stop, but he did not listen. If only I had gone after him, but there were too many demands for my attention and too much to be done. I will regret that boy's death for the rest of my days. I only hope that the end of this war means that no more young men like him will have to die so needlessly."

"And the Black Sorcerer…" prodded Chrysteffor delicately. He was still waiting anxiously to hear the fate of the villain.

"Yes, sorry. I urgently followed the triumphant Leannain to the king's chamber, fully expecting to see my father terrorized by the sudden appearance of his hated brother. The sorcerer must have been as disappointed as I was, although for different reasons. My father had died only moments before and, to my surprise, had a look of complete peace on his face. Aigneis, always at his side, was sobbing quietly. Leannain scowled at first, but then he began to laugh loud and long.

"'After all these years,' he cried, 'at my moment of victory I now inherit the crown in the way that your laws always said that I should. You and Lúcás and Néall are all dead. I am the next in line! Are you happy now, Reicheart?'

"I knew I had but one chance to take advantage of the moment. As he cackled like a madman, he seemed to have forgotten me. Grasping my sword with both hands, I raised it with the aim of plunging it into his back. It was not an honorable way to attack, but with his formidable powers there was no other hope of stopping him. In any event his breastplate would have shielded him from a frontal attack, but it did not matter. As if he had eyes in the back of his head, he swung around and, with a single gesture, he froze my body. My sword dropped from my hands and I was lifted slightly into the air. Suspended and helpless in front of him, I felt an invisible hand around my throat and I could not catch my breath. He stepped closer to me and looked into my eyes with an intensity that unnerved me. His face was so close to mine that I could feel the heat of his breath and smell its vile odor.

" 'Do not fear, dear Feidhlim,' he said. 'I would never dream of harming you. You have always been my favorite. I have always felt a connection to you. I suspect that, underneath it all, we are not really all that different you and I. With enough time I think that we could become truly close.'

"And then he stroked my cheek with the back of his hand. I tried with all my strength to turn away from him, but movement was impossible. In all my life I have never felt so helpless or so completely at the mercy of someone else. Then he drew closer still and kissed me gently, in fact tenderly, on the cheek. I am still shuddering at the memory and the horror of it. I turned my eyes in every direction, trying to think of some way to get out of the horrific trap I was in. Aigneis was watching in revulsion and regarding me with pity. I then noticed something on the floor near her. It was Chrysteffor's sword. At some point she must have left her brother long enough to look in on Eilís and noticed the weapon in my sister's room and brought it with her. It occurred to me that the sword with its unusual powers might be the only weapon that could actually kill the sorcerer. In my state at that moment, though, it would have been useless to me.

"I kept staring at it, hoping against hope that I could somehow will it into my hand. Aigneis noticed my eyes continually darting in the weapon's direction and understood my thought. I watched her pick up the sword. Its strange glow grew brighter. I wanted her to bring the sword to me. I knew how foolish this was. While under the sorcerer's power, I would not have been able to hold it. Instead, she did something I did not expect. She approached the sorcerer from behind, raised the sword in her own hands and shouted, 'You forgot something, Leannain! You are not next in line! I am!' This truly surprised the sorcerer. He quickly turned around and raised his hand to her, freezing her in her tracks. Like myself, she was now suspended in the air and totally under his control. That released his hold on me and I dropped to the ground. I struggled to stand, but my breath had been cut off for so long that my strength was completely drained. I knelt helplessly on the floor. All I could do was watch to see what he would do to his sister. He stepped toward her, looking as though he meant to kill her where she stood, but then the most amazing thing of all happened. Suddenly Aigneis was lowered to the ground and he no longer had control of her. He gestured as he had before, attempting to regain control of her, but he had no effect on her. He stared at his own hand in bewilderment and then stared upwards, as if he could train his sight on something outside of the castle and miles away. 'My power!' he cried. 'The towers!' He stood dumbfounded, not knowing what to do. He turned and looked down at me, as if for some reason I might actually help him.

"I was still helpless on the ground, but Aigneis was free. She raised the sword once again and this time, with all her strength, plunged the sword in his back. I was staring directly into the villain's face, and I could see his look of shock and dismay perfectly. He turned back around to face her and roared as he struck the old woman with the full force of his arm, and she fell to the ground with a sickening sound. I could see a trail of blood from where her head had struck the floor, and I would say that the poor woman was dead before she landed on the stone. I struggled to stand, not knowing how badly the villain had been injured or what he might do next, but at that point I was still little more than useless. I needed more time for my strength to return. I watched as he twisted and writhed in pain. All the while the sword in his back glowed brighter and brighter. It grew so bright that the light enveloped his whole body. It burned so white that I had to shut my eyes to avoid them being burned. After I dared to open them, I was blinded for a good while. Gradually, though, my sight did return. It took longer still, however, for me to believe what my eyes saw. The sword was lying on the floor, tangled in the sorcerer's cape. Its glow was now faint. Between the breastplate and the cape was a bloody skeleton.

"By the time my strength returned, I could hear cheering. Before going anywhere else, however, I picked up the sword and brought it to a safe place where it now waits for you, Chrysteffor. I then made my way back to the castle entrance and saw our men and women rejoicing that every last one of the Eidola had fallen where they had stood. And every man and woman was looking in amazement at the sky. The jaws of the younger ones hung low in awe. They had never seen the sun before in their lives. Some of the older ones were weeping with joy. The long nightmare was over at last, but I myself had no heart for celebration. I brought two men with me to the king's chamber where we placed Aigneis's body on the bed next to the king. We then gathered up the skeleton and all of the sorcerer's things and brought them outside where we dumped them in a pile. To those gathered around I said, 'This is all that remains of the villain who kept our land in darkness for so many years. The Black Sorcerer is no more. We burn what is left of him so that he may never return.' As the flames consumed the skeleton, the cheers rose once again."

"I should have been there," said Chrysteffor ruefully. "I would have so dearly loved to see that monster's demise. I wish I had been the one to drive the sword through him."

"No, it should have been me," said Eilís. "For years I lived for that day. No one hated him more than I."

Feidhlim laughed with more than a little bitterness.

"The important thing is that he is dead, once and for all. Let us take satisfaction that we all played our part—and none more than Aigneis, who was queen of Afranor for one brief shining moment—when it mattered most."

"And now you are the king, my brother. You are the one who will lead this land back to its former glory."

The black-haired prince looked downward.

"I… I do not know if I am up to the role. Honestly, Eilís, you would be a better monarch. Let me step aside and give you the crown in my place."

"What mad talk is this?" she countered. "You are the elder of us. Tradition dictates that you wear the crown. You have earned it. Are you not after recounting how our father went to his rest in the comfort of knowing you would replace him?"

"I… I do not know if I am worthy. I am haunted by the things that Leannain said to me. He said that he and I were alike. He saw something dark in me. There are things that happened during those years in the wilderness that changed me. After the life I have led, I do not know if I can sit in this castle and fulfill the role of monarch for the rest of my days."

"This is nonsense," said Chrysteffor. "I will confess that, when I first met you, I did not like you one bit. You were rough and violent and, frankly, I did not like the fact that you defeated me so easily and soundly. I thought you were one of the brigands that had murdered my brother. The more I have come to know you, however, the more I have come to know what a good man you are. I have come to love you like one of my own brothers."

"Enough, both of you," said Feidhlim. "There will be more than enough time to talk about this later."

In the days that followed there were many hours spent tending the wounded, disposing of the repugnant remains of the Eidola, and generally cleaning up after the destruction. There were also many funerals.

Although this was not the sort of work that suited Valloniah's crew, they gamely helped out with the labors wherever they could. While never completely comfortable with them, the people of Afranor came to have a grudging respect for the pirates.

Finally, one morning the Pirate Queen came to the blond prince.

"I tell you honestly, Prince Chrysteffor, this has been too much time on land for me. My crew is restless, and that is never a good thing. I have decided that I shall be setting sail in the morning. I advise you to come with me. You owe it to King Allard to return home and tell him face to face about all that has happened and what befell his two eldest sons."

"You are right, of course, Valloniah. With your kind permission, I will indeed be sailing with you. There is just one thing I need to do first."

He found Lady Eilís, who had been making a rapid recovery from her injuries, and asked her to go for a walk with him along the cliff's edge with its now breathtaking views of the azure sea.

"How beautiful these days are," she said. "I can still scarcely believe that we have the sun again."

"The sea and the land are nothing compared to your beauty, my beloved Eilís."

"Do not be witless, Chrysteffor. There is a word in our language for such talk, and it is not a pretty word. I am what I am and I have the scars to show it."

"On the contrary, my love, I think the eyepatch suits you. It makes you even more beautiful—at least in my eyes."

"There you go again with your daft talk. Let us speak of something else. Tell me, what do you think of the old prophecy now—after all that has happened?"

"The truth is I do not know what to think. On one hand, it is difficult to see it as anything other than an old wives' tale. On the other, it is true that, had I not undertaken the quest, I would have never learned the secret of the Black Sorcerer's power and found the means for us to defeat him. Was that mere coincidence or some foreordained destiny? Who can say? But I do know this. It is at our own mortal peril that we cast aside the tales, the lore, the lessons and the admonitions of those who went before us."

"Yes," said Eilís. "You are right. If only I had paid more attention to my aunt Aigneis. In the end she was the wisest of us all. Not only did she send you on your quest, but in the end it was her hand that did slay the villain."

The princess's mood turned somber.

"I cannot believe she is gone. I cannot believe all of them are gone. What a strange world it is, Chrysteffor. For well over a year I mourned my brother. Now, miraculously, he is back, but the rest of my family is dead. My father, my aunt, my cousin. All dead. We defeated the sorcerer and lifted the curse, but at such a cost. I thought I was well accustomed to death, but now I find it weighing all too heavily on my soul."

With a sigh Eilís laid her head against Chrysteffor's breast. He was surprised because this was not at all the sort of thing she was given to doing, but it pleased him that she had come to rely on him for support. In general, her form had improved greatly as she recovered from her injuries, and he enjoyed conversing with her during their moments alone. He did not want these conversations to end, but he knew that he now needed to have the most serious conversation of all.

"Eilís, my love, in the morning I leave for Alinvayl. After all this time I am returning to my own land. I so dread having to tell my father how his two sons died and how I was unable to do anything about it. There was a time not that long ago when the prospect of facing him would have paralyzed me with fear. Now, after all I have been through in Afranor, I have learned what real fear is. Now I know clearly what things are worth fearing and what things are not."

She looked at him with deep affection.

"I wish you did not have to go. I will truly miss you."

"That is the thing, Eilís. I do have to go. And when I do, my life will be irrevocably changed. I will no longer be merely the youngest of the king's three sons. I will be his only son. I will be the crown prince. My destiny is now to one day be king of Alinvayl."

"And you will be a good king."

"That I do not know. What I do know, though, with all my heart is that, when that day comes, I want you to be my queen. I want you to be my wife. Now. As soon as possible. I have loved you with all my heart from the first moment I saw you. That first day in the woods when you saved us from the Eidola. I want you to come with me tomorrow when Valloniah sets sail for Alinvayl."

The princess was genuinely distressed.

"Chrysteffor, how can I leave now? There is so much work to be done. So much rebuilding. So many tasks for making life normal again. It all falls on Feidhlim's shoulders as the new king. You have seen how unsure he is, how difficult this is for him. How could I possibly leave him on his own now?"

The prince felt stung by her words. Did she not appreciate all that he was offering her? How could she refuse his heartfelt proposal after all he had endured on behalf of her and her country? He nearly said something harsh to her but then thought better of it. As he calmed down, he admitted to himself that her keen sense of loyalty was one of the many reasons that he so deeply loved her. Would he not be doing the same if he were in her place? Still, although the thought of leaving her broke his heart, he knew that he had to go home—with or without her. He embraced her tightly and wished that he did not ever have to let her go.

"I have no choice but to accept your answer," he said, "but here and now I am swearing an oath. One day I shall return. And one day I shall marry you. And one day you will indeed be the queen of Alinvayl."

"My dearest Chrysteffor, I truly do appreciate your proposal. Really I do. And if things were different I would gladly go with you. As it is, I will not hold you to your promise. In this uncertain world it is probably wiser not to try planning so far in the future. With the passing of time, you may be glad of your freedom."

"There are indeed many things that I am unsure of, but not this. I will love you forever, Eilís. Forever."

They stood there a long while, watching the sun set and making the most of their last evening together.

In the morning he gathered his things. He had brought little with him to Afranor, and he would take little with him back home—except for the sword. He unsheathed it to have another look at the marvelous weapon. He marveled that the blade still had its faint glow. Despite the fall of the three towers and the death of the Black Sorcerer, it had not vanished into nothingness as Chrysteffor had thought it might. More wondrously, it gave every appearance of still having its enchanted properties. If he could not have Princess Eilís with him on his return journey, the sword was certainly a good consolation prize. It would give him a handy advantage in any future adventures he might have.

Ready now for his journey, Chrysteffor went to say his farewells to King Feidhlim. He found the new monarch with Princess Eilís.

"My dear friend, may you have a long and glorious reign. And make the most of your sister's help—while you may. One day—and I hope it is soon—I mean to come back and take her away from you."

"I can think of no better man for her," replied the king, "but I selfishly hope that day will not come *too* soon. I would miss her dearly. She is all I have left."

"My friend, you are the best man I know. And though you may now be the king of Afranor, you are young and in the prime of life. There is no doubt that you will have no trouble finding a queen of your own. Is there no one that you have had your eye on?"

The king's mood turned wistful.

"There was someone. A long time ago. And it is not a happy story, but that is all in the past now. I honestly do not know if I am cut out for love or a family of my own."

Chrysteffor was curious to know more, but before he could speak again, the conversation was interrupted.

"This is all very moving, but we must catch the tide. We have to go now, Prince Chrysteffor."

It was Valloniah. As always, she was lacking in patience.

"You are right, of course. Just give me one more moment."

The prince made his last kiss with the princess last as long as he could, but it was over all too soon. The Pirate Queen grabbed his bag and slapped him on the shoulder.

"Do not worry, Prince Chrysteffor. I will do my best to console you during the voyage. I am looking forward to getting to know you better. You are so different from the boy I knew before. You are reminding me more and more of my poor dead Adryan. As I promised you before, during the voyage we shall do much drinking to his memory and to Benet's. And perhaps we shall make a few new memories while we are at it."

She gave him a wink and laughed heartily as she led the way down to the rowboat. The prince followed reluctantly.

Lady Eilís watched in silence until they were well out of earshot.

"I do not like that woman," she said.

Her words surprised her brother.

"You do realize, my dear Eilís, that woman saved your life."

"Yes, exactly."

It dawned on Feidhlim that he was seeing something in his sister that he had never seen in her before—jealousy.

"You do not need to worry, sister," said the king. "It is clear that Prince Chrysteffor has eyes for no one but you."

"I wonder," she said, with more than a trace of melancholy.

The princess walked to the highest point of the cliff and, standing alone, watched Chrysteffor, Valloniah and the others row to the ship and board it. With her one good eye, she continued to watch as the ship made its way slowly out to sea. She remained well after it had disappeared from view completely.

About the Author

Scott R. Larson grew up in California's San Joaquin Valley. He has also lived in France, Chile and for many years in and around Seattle, Washington. He currently finds himself in the West of Ireland where he writes one of the internet's longest running film blogs. His first novel was the coming-of-age story *Maximilian and Carlotta Are Dead*, for which he is currently writing a sequel. His favorite television shows, at various times in his life, have been *Dark Shadows*, *Babylon 5*, and *Doctor Who*.